"Why don't you stop being so stubborn, Joseph? It's all right to let someone help, you know," Katie urged.

"Easy for you to say." Joseph ground out the words, his frustrated gaze set down the road.

Katie took a step closer, then gently grasped his hand, inwardly cringing when he jerked at her touch. "Please," she whispered. "Let me help you."

When Joseph didn't pull away, she placed his hand at her elbow and led him home, acutely aware of the stiffness in his touch. And when they reached his porch, she turned to find his unseeing gaze fixed on her, his eyes the most beautiful golden-brown she'd ever seen.

For a moment neither one of them moved. Delicious, comforting warmth spread through her when he swept his thumb over her hand in a light caress. Her heartbeat quickened at his comforting presence. Stirred at his soothing voice, she found herself longing for his nearness to lend her hope and confidence. And longing for his touch…

PAMELA NISSEN

loves creating. Whether it's characters, cooking, scrapbooking or other artistic endeavors, she takes pleasure in putting things together for others to enjoy. She started writing her first book in 2000 and since then hasn't looked back. Pamela lives in the woods in Iowa with her husband, daughter, two sons, Newfoundland dog and cats. She loves watching her children pursue their dreams, and is known to yell on the sidelines at her boys' football games, or cry as she watches her daughter perform. She relishes scrapbooking weekends with her sister, coffee with friends and running in the rain. Having glimpsed the dark and light of life, she is passionate about writing "real" people with "real" issues and "real" responses.

PAMELA NISSEN

Rocky Mountain Match

Steeple
Hill®

Published by Steeple Hill Books™

STEEPLE HILL BOOKS

Steeple
Hill®

PLEASE RECYCLE

THIS PRODUCT IS RECYCLABLE

Recycling programs
for this product may
not exist in your area.

ISBN-13: 978-0-373-82838-8

ROCKY MOUNTAIN MATCH

Copyright © 2010 by Pamela Nissen

www.SteepleHill.com

Printed in U.S.A.

Having the eyes of your hearts enlightened,
that you may know what is the hope to which he
has called you, what are the riches of his glorious
inheritance in the saints.

—Ephesians 3:18

For my lovely daughter, MaryAnna, whose strength and perseverance inspires. You are a heroine in the very truest sense of the word.

Acknowledgments

Thank you to my friends and family: your encouragement has carried me through seasons of doubt. And to Melissa and the Steeple Hill family, thank you for believing in me and loving my characters as much as I do. Sincere gratitude goes to my amazing critique partners: Diane, your words and friendship are life-giving; Jacque, your tenacious loyalty is comforting; and Roxanne, your gentle expertise coaxes me out of my comfort zone. To my wonderful children, MaryAnna, Noel and Elias: thank you for being so supportive, and for tolerating more than one "cold cereal dinner" on this journey. And special thanks go to my husband, Bill, who (when I couldn't get these characters and story line out of my head) said, "Why don't you write a book?"

Chapter One

Boulder, Colorado—1890

Inky darkness crowded Joseph Drake from every side. It shrouded him like a thick coat, with power so substantial that it was almost suffocating. Its bleakness mocked his vulnerable state, sending humiliation barreling through him with avalanche force.

He hated this. Every bit of it. He could barely stomach the thought of asking for help or being pitied. And he loathed the idea that those helping him would be monitoring his each and every pathetic move.

Drawing in a steadying breath, he braced himself against the pitch blackness as he sat on the edge of the feather mattress, clutching the thin sheet in his hand. He was so dizzy. His head swam and his ears rang incessantly, deepening his bad mood. He couldn't have imagined how unsettled he'd still feel after being on bed rest for three weeks. Raising his hands to his head, he slid his fingers over the fresh bandages shrouding his eyes. How he wished he'd just wake up and find that his accident in the woodshop had been a horrible nightmare.

"God, please," he pleaded, his throat thick with emotion. "I need my sight back."

When Ben, his older brother by two years and a doctor in Boulder, had removed the wraps yesterday, Joseph had been confident that he'd be able to see again. But that confidence had vanished like some taunting wraith as he'd frantically grabbed for any image through the thick, dark cloud.

He'd tried to stay calm, but deep down he'd felt a crumbling begin at the very base of who he was. All along he'd minimized his injury. After all, it could be too soon to tell any permanent outcome—and Ben was new to doctoring. The thought had crossed Joseph's mind more than once that maybe Ben was a little green around the edges and lacked experience.

He'd reasoned it all, but the prospect of being permanently blind staked out his soul like a dank, stony grave marker. And the huge furniture order he'd taken on just days before his accident lay like dead flowers crushed into the fresh turned dirt. He'd cushioned the deadline when he'd signed the contract, but with his brother, Aaron, being the only one working in the woodshop for the past three weeks, the padding had been jerked away hard and fast.

Fighting to remain hopeful, he pushed himself off the bed, his cracked ribs protesting with the movement. He inhaled sharply, digging his toes into the rag rug's nubby texture.

His jaw ticked with instant irritation as a distant chorus of giggles wafted through his open window. It didn't take much to conjure up the origin of the twittering noise. He could see it now…a cluster of bonneted women standing in front of the hotel. Lined up like flowers for the picking, just another batch of mail-order brides brought in to help populate the west.

It was downright demeaning, in his book, the way they'd set themselves on display like that.

When a knock sounded on his front door, he startled. Clad in just underclothes, he lurched forward, struggling for balance as he probed for the wall where his clothes were hung.

Ben's strong urging that Joseph gradually ease back into life on his own whipped through his mind like a warning knell. But bandages over his eyes or not, Joseph was a twenty-seven-year-old man, and like a caged animal, he craved independence and freedom. Privacy.

"I'll be right out," he yelled after another knock sounded.

His fingertips brushed against sturdy cotton fabric and he sighed with relief. He pulled on his britches and boots, then shrugged into his shirtsleeves, although a new level of frustration assaulted him as he intently focused on lining up the five wooden buttons with buttonholes.

Eight years ago he'd built his own home, but now he could barely dress himself. He shuffled out of the bedroom, galled at having to give such simple routines a second thought. Groping along the wall, his breathing grew shallow as each awkward step echoed over the hardwood floor—a mocking reminder of his vulnerable state.

When his leg knocked hard into something, Joseph flinched, reaching down to steady the imposing piece of furniture. His hands careened into the small table and tipped it over, sending a loud bang reverberating throughout the quiet house.

"Joseph? Are you all right?" Ben rapped at his door again.

He stooped to right the piece. "I'll be right there," he shot back through tightly clenched teeth.

Hands quivering, he felt the satin-smooth finish. He'd always prided himself in this well-known trademark, but now he wondered if he'd ever be able to resume his profession.

And his plans to marry and have a family... None of that was certain now. If his vision didn't return, there was no way he'd saddle any young woman to life with a blind man.

Humiliation cloaked him soundly and offending images of himself stumbling through life alone and without sight intensified his bad mood.

When Joseph finally reached the front door, he fumbled for the handle, then eased it open. A gust of fresh air hit him square in the face, reminding him just how long he'd been down.

"Mornin', Joseph!" Ben clapped him on the arm. "Sorry. I didn't mean to hurry you, but you said you didn't want me barging in anymore, but then when I heard..." Ben's voice trailed off. "I see you made it up and about."

"Were you expecting something else?" Joseph retorted.

"Not exactly, I guess."

Joseph tried to push aside his sour mood as he caught the rumble of a buckboard rolling slowly by in front of his house. "What brings you over? I thought you gave me a clean bill of health yesterday." Sliding a hand up the front of his shirt, he checked for misaligned buttons.

"How are the ribs? Are they giving you much trouble?"

"I feel fine," he lied, ignoring the constant dull ache and

the comment he could swear he overheard from inside the wagon, regarding his bandages. His accident had probably been the talk of the town for the past three weeks.

"Well, your color is better. Not bad for a man who's been through what you have. Are you sure you're feeling strong enough to tackle things today?"

"I said I'm fine." Joseph furrowed his brow. "But if I didn't know you better, I'd think you were expecting me to trek up the Flatirons with you. That's not likely to happen."

"Believe me, a quiet day in the mountains sounds great after visiting with ol' Donovan Grimes. The fellow's hearing must be just about gone, the way he shouts. My ears are still ringing." Ben shifted his booted feet on the porch floor. "By the way, Aaron said that Ellie had planned to bring dinner tonight, but she's not feeling well. I'm going to check in on her after this."

Joseph grew immediately concerned for his sister-in-law. She was having a difficult time of this first pregnancy and he knew it weighed on his younger brother Aaron. Especially now that he was carrying double the load in the woodshop with Joseph being laid up.

"Tell you what, I'll just have the hotel diner make you up a plate and deliver it to you. How's that sound?"

Joseph balled his fists. "I said yesterday that I'd take it from here."

"I'd accept the help if I were you," Ben urged. "Soon enough you'll be begging us to have a little pity on you and bring over some good, home-cooked meals again."

"What's that supposed to mean?" Stepping outside, he closed the door behind him so Ben wouldn't get any ideas of staying for a visit.

Ben cleared his throat, a trait Joseph had begun to recognize over the past three weeks as a nervous gesture. "Remember when we talked, shortly after your fall, about getting you training in case you don't—"

"Whoa. Whoa." He swiped beads of perspiration forming on his brow. "*We* talked? I think you mean *you* talked. I didn't agree to anything."

"I know how adamant you are about being independent—I want that for you, too. But you'll get there quicker with training," Ben finished as though racing to get it out.

Gritting his teeth, Joseph plastered himself against the door. He'd prove to his older brother that he could make it on his own, but he couldn't even seem to move his feet enough to turn and stalk back inside. Truth be told, he was scared to death to take a step forward into the darkness.

And he'd never been afraid of anything.

"What are you getting at, Ben?" A bout of lightheadedness assaulted him and he struggled to keep his balance as he stood to his full six foot, three inches. "What's going on?"

Ben sighed. "Promise me you'll hear me out before you go jumping down my throat, all right?"

"I'm not promising you anything." Joseph tightened his fists. "Just tell me what you did. Now!"

"I—I arranged for a teacher to come out from Iowa."

"You did what?"

"I arranged for a teacher to help you," Ben declared with a little more firmness. "I know you don't want to do this, but you need to give it a chance."

"It's a waste of time. My vision is *going* to return."

"I hope you're right. You know that I've read everything I can get my hands on. But like I told you yesterday, the more time that passes with no change, the less chance there is for restoration," Ben said, his voice tight. "I know this has to be hard, but if your vision doesn't return, what then?"

That question had staked out territory in Joseph's mind for the past three weeks. That his entire life could be permanently altered infringed on his well-planned life like some dark omen.

In a softer tone, Ben continued. "Will you refuse help even when it could make things easier for you?"

Every muscle shuddered with anger. "I—don't—need—help!"

Even as the declaration crossed his lips he knew he might be deceiving himself. But the thought of being trained in the simple aspects of life rankled like nothing else. He'd always been self-sufficient. Always.

Joseph forced himself to stop shaking. "Wire the man and let him know he doesn't need to waste a long trip like that."

Awkward silence draped heavily between them, making Joseph's skin prickle and a foreboding creep down his spine.

Ben sighed, slow and heavy. "I—I can't do that."

"You can't send a telegraph wire?" His pulse pounded in his ears. "Why not? It's not that hard."

When his brother stepped back, Joseph loosened his fists, unfurling them one finger at a time. Ben could be stubborn, but so could Joseph—and he had a long history of winning arguments.

"Miss Ellickson," Ben called out toward the street. "Why don't you come on up."

Joseph froze. "Tell me what's going on," he demanded, his heart slamming against his chest. "I mean it, Ben."

Ben came to stand directly in front of him now, so close that Joseph could smell his brother's subtle, clean scent. "Your teacher arrived by stage two days ago."

Hearing the faint clicking of boots across the boardwalk, a trembling shook Joseph to the core. Unbidden, he pictured an old schoolmarm clad in a dowdy brown dress, a severe knot of mousy-brown hair clinging to the back of her head and rimmed glasses perched on her long nose.

His jaw muscle ticked. "Why wasn't I informed? This is *my* life we're talking about here."

"You'll probably never forgive me for this. And I knew that you'd refuse, no matter what sense I tried to talk into you. You're stubborn, Joseph, too stubborn for your own good. As your brother and doctor, I made the decision for you."

"That's just great! I get to have my life planned by you now." Joseph gave a mock laugh. "I may have lost my vision for a while, but I haven't lost my mind. Send the woman back!"

Just shy of Joseph's height, Ben leaned closer, his voice dropping to a stern whisper. "I also knew that as a perfect gentleman, you wouldn't give this dedicated *young* woman a hard time."

The distinct sound of the front gate clicking shut and the woman's slow, light steps coming from the walkway sent Joseph's heart racing inside his chest. His breathing grew ragged.

"Listen, Joseph, she comes highly recommended, with a glowing letter sent by the school she's been working at for the past five years. She's Sven and Marta Olsson's niece," Ben added as though that tidbit of information would make him agree.

Well, he was anything but agreeable. The last thing he wanted was some teacher coming in and watching him stumble around his own house.

He tensed, only faintly aware of his sore ribs. "It's a waste of her time," he said in a harsh whisper.

Ben firmly gripped Joseph's shoulder. "Whether you gain back partial vision or no vision, she can help you right now. She's used to this."

"Used to what? Seeing someone make a fool of himself?"

The soft treading of the woman's shoes up the stairs sent a quaking through Joseph's entire being. Beads of sweat trailed down his forehead, soaking into the bandage.

"I wouldn't be so quick to make a judgment," Ben urged. "You never know, she might just be the answer to your prayers."

The answer to his prayers? Katie mused silently.

Clutching her instruction books tight against her chest, she stepped up to the porch and stared at Mr. Drake who stood legs braced wide, fists clenched at his sides and his chin set in stubborn defiance. She slid her gaze up, noticing that even though bandages shrouded his eyes, they couldn't hide the fact that he looked none too happy. An unmistakable, aggravated scowl creased his forehead.

The answer to his prayers… I'm probably more like his worst nightmare, she admitted, swallowing hard.

Hope had bloomed on the long journey from Iowa to Colorado, but now uncertainty choked out eager anticipation like a dense thicket of weeds invading tender spring flowers. Never had she questioned her ability to teach and certainly she'd never shied from taking on a challenging student, so why should she now?

"Miss Ellickson, I'd like to introduce my brother, Joseph Drake." The twinkle in the doctor's gray-blue eyes belied his simple brown attire and had put her at ease when she'd met him yesterday, but now he appeared anything but confident.

Slipping her fingers over each fine pearl button trailing down her powder-blue waistcoat, she grappled for confidence. "Good morning, Mr. Drake. I'm pleased to meet you."

When she reached for his tight-fisted hand, he drew back as though she'd seared him with a hot iron. His mouth was set firm and hard. He shifted his weight from one foot to another, his leg muscles bunching beneath camel-colored britches. And as he drew his shoulders back, his chest stretched wide, revealing a well-defined muscular build beneath a white cotton shirt.

Embarrassment flushed her cheeks and she quickly averted her gaze to the fresh coat of dark gray paint that gleamed like icing on the porch floor.

"You may not feel ready for it, Joseph, but Miss Ellickson is prepared for a full day's work." The doctor gave her a lame look of encouragement, then shifted a wary gaze to his brother. "I know you're probably mad enough to spit nails, but give it two weeks. At least until you see the doctor in Denver."

While he continued with a halfhearted pep talk, Mr. Drake remained grim. His commanding presence filled the small porch, sending a quiver of unease down her spine. And a brief, unwanted flash of fear through her mind.

Nervously she smoothed back wispy strands of blond

waves, wondering when the unbidden memories from the past year would stop haunting her. When would she be free of her attacker's vile grasp? Even months later, she could still feel his hands pinning her down to a dire moment in time that would never end.

Her chest pulled tight, the same painful questions swirling through her mind…. Where was God then? Why hadn't He helped her? Why hadn't He protected her?

She wanted to trust God, wanted to rest knowing that He was watching out for her. But it seemed a mountain of anguish stood in her way of finding the childlike innocence she'd once had.

Squeezing her eyes tight, she refused to let her past get in the way of this new job assignment. When Uncle Sven had wired her about this opportunity, it was like a thousand Christmases all wrapped into one. This was a chance to start fresh, far away from the continuous reminders. A chance to distance herself from the constant threat she felt back home.

Squaring her shoulders, she studied the man before her.

Stubborn. She'd seen it more than once while working at the Braille and Sight-Saving School, but she'd never encountered someone so dead set on refusing help. His imposing stance spoke far louder than the words of protest she'd overheard as she'd waited on the boardwalk for the doctor to summon her.

"I won't keep you two any longer." Dr. Drake's voice broke into her thoughts. "If you need anything, Miss Ellickson, please don't hesitate to let me know."

Nodding, she smoothed a hand down her full damask skirt, pasting on a tranquil smile in spite of feeling as if he was leaving her to one mean, hungry wolf. "We'll be just fine."

She watched the doctor's long strides take him down the walk and almost wished she could follow. Scanning the tidy yard surrounded by a white picket fence, she experienced a measure of safety. But as she slid her gaze to the rugged Rocky Mountains, she felt a tangible unease at the untamed land.

While she turned to face her new student, she braced herself before she spoke. "I can understand your discomfort, Mr. Drake, if my presence here doesn't sit well with you. If it eases your mind at all, I can assure you that you will get neither pity nor charity from me," she stated simply, hoping to allay such fears.

"Quite honestly, you'll get as much out of this as you're willing to put in," she added, unsuccessfully trying to gauge his response. "And if you readily embrace a challenge as your brother says you do, I think that you'll be pleasantly surprised at the outcome."

From the stoic stance he'd demonstrated so far, she'd obviously underestimated the doctor's claims that he was stubborn. Had Uncle Sven not vouched for Mr. Drake's stellar character and assured her safety with him, she might just turn and leave for good. Which was exactly what he wanted right now.

And precisely what he didn't need.

Firming up her wilting strength, she made a desperate grasp for boldness as she stood directly in front of him. "Mr. Drake, you need me. And I'm prepared to give you my all to help you gain independence. So perhaps we should begin our first..."

The words died on her lips as a low, deep growling sound came from the porch's dark shadows. Her breath caught in her throat. Hair prickled on the back of her neck. She flicked her gaze to where a mound of black fur lumbered into the sunlight.

"Bear!" Stifling a scream, her books dropped to the porch floor. "Quick! Get inside! He's coming!"

She lunged for Mr. Drake and wedged between his large frame and the clapboard house. Fear gripped like a vice, clamping down with brutal force as she wrapped her arms around his broad chest and tried to tug him toward the front door.

"Mr. Drake, please. We must—get to safety!" she grunted, struggling in vain to move him.

Peeking around him, she could see the hulking black bear closing in on her, its wide boxy head hung low, thick shoulders bearing its lumbering mass, and its long fluffy tail…

She froze. Grasped his chest tighter as waves of prickly heat spread through her. *Bears didn't have tails. Did they?*

Narrowing her gaze, she braved another glance around Mr. Drake's chest, all firm and muscular beneath her tight hold, to see a huge dog with a head the size of a barrel staring at her with big brown, expressive eyes. The dog dropped to the edge of the porch with a weighted thud and bored sigh, looking up at her as if to say it had been mortally wounded by her accusation.

"Miss Ellickson, that is a dog, not a bear," he said, prying her hands loose from his chest.

Katie let out an unladylike whoosh of air. Utter embarrassment at her impropriety overwhelmed her as it dawned on her how close she was to Mr. Drake. Her cheeks flamed hot and she wiped a quivering hand over her lips.

She slipped out from behind him. "I—I apologize."

Tugging at her waistcoat, she smoothed back her hair,

grateful he couldn't see her crimson cheeks. He could probably hear her heart pounding in her chest, though. "How foolish of me. It's just that with the shadows I thought—"

"Perhaps it's not me who has less-than-perfect sight," he cut in without even the hint of a smile. "Colorado is no place for the faint of heart."

Flames of anger nipped at her composure, but she quickly snuffed them out. "I'm sure it's not—and I regret my outburst. I suppose I'm just leery of the wilds of Colorado," she admitted on a shaky sigh. Even though she was a little more than leery of him right now, she was determined to remain professional. "Is this your dog?"

"Boone's a Newfoundland, and he wouldn't hurt you for anything," he said as Katie stooped to pet the dog. "Unless he senses that I don't like you."

She pulled her hand back and passed a wary glance from the dog to him. "Well, then, I guess you'd better change your mind about me—or your dog will be having me for lunch."

Chapter Two

Was she friend or foe?

That question reverberated through Joseph's mind as he sank deeper into the chair across from where Miss Ellickson sat on the sofa. The faintest scent of lilies, pleasing and natural, drifted from her direction and he took a long, measured breath.

Since meeting her this morning, he'd been cross. He didn't want her here, but felt trapped because his brother had set things up in such a clever way that Joseph wouldn't have a choice but to slap his jaws shut and suffer through.

He'd entertained illusions of the woman taking off like a scared rabbit. Instead, she'd seemingly marked her territory and called him to climb this uphill battle—and he never backed down from a challenge.

He could hardly blame her if she'd chosen to leave because he wasn't exactly Boulder's idea of a welcoming committee. He was sour, indifferent and unfriendly, and he knew it.

Reaching down next to his chair, he found Boone's head, soft and furry beneath his touch. He gently stroked the dog's thick coat, acutely aware of Miss Ellickson's presence.

Rivers of wounded pride coursed through his veins at his predicament. This woman may have come highly recommended and be competent, but she couldn't give him what he wanted most… His vision.

Slumping deeper into the cushioned chair, he pressed the pads of his fingers over his bandaged eyes, something he often did hoping the pressure would somehow produce a change. He'd do most anything if it meant regaining his sight, but nothing seemed to make a difference. Strong will and hard work had always been his friends, but now it was as if they were bound on the sidelines while he stood alone in the midst of a raging battle.

Joseph held out hope that in two weeks, when he'd travel to see the doctor in Denver, he'd find more encouraging news. If so, he'd never take another day of blessed sight for granted.

Raking his fingers through his thick hair, he shifted uncomfortably in the chair, knowing that until then, this woman would witness each humiliating attempt to do things right.

Would she laugh? Turn away in embarrassment? Pity him?

He loathed not seeing! And was determined not to be a burden. But remembering how meager tasks such as dressing or walking through his own house took every bit of concentration he could amass, he wondered if things would ever come easy.

"Yoo-hoo…Joseph?" Julia Cranston's high-pitched

voice jerked him from his thoughts as the front door creaked open. "Are you home?"

Joseph briefly recalled the day of his accident when Aaron had found another love note from Julia at the door. She'd sealed it with red wax.

"Kinda bold, don't ya think?" Aaron had jibed.

Joseph had glanced warily at the heart-shaped seal. He'd gone on a few innocent outings with Julia, but had no plans to go running down the aisle yet.

"Whatcha' waitin' for?" Aaron had asked. "If you're holdin' off till all your ducks are lined up, you'd better get movin' fast or they're gonna go line up in somebody else's pond."

At the time he'd thought little of Aaron's prodding, figuring he had plenty of time to set in place that part of his life. But just minutes later his whole life had changed. A single moment, a careless movement on a ladder, had altered his entire life. Now he could only hope that God would answer the barrage of petitions he'd made for healing.

Hearing the door rattle again, he realized that Julia hadn't visited for a week. Now that he was up from bed rest, he felt acutely aware of his inadequacy because a woman like Julia, delicately beautiful and refined, was used to being pampered. She'd sat by his bedside a few days since his accident, spending most of her time relating the latest news of Boulder's upper crust, rarely inquiring about his injury.

"Come on in." He stood and struggled for balance.

"Oh, there you are! I'm so glad to see you up," Julia crooned as she beelined toward him, her skirts swishing and heels clicking across the wood floor.

The overwhelming powdery perfume she wore preceded her in a thick cloud, triggering the sudden need to sneeze. He raised a hand to his nose and warded it off as her light footsteps came to an abrupt stop in front of him.

"I—I thought you were going to be through with those silly old bandages," she bleated, her excitement suddenly deflated.

He could almost feel her piercing hazel gaze bearing down on him. "Ben put new ones on to give my eyes more time."

"More time? Whatever for? You said that you were going to be as good as new when those awful wraps came off."

He swallowed hard. "My eyes need more time to heal."

Julia gave an exaggerated whimper. "Well, that ruins positively everything! I had a very special surprise for you today, but now you won't even be able to see it."

"What was the surprise?" he asked, his jaw clenched tight.

"My dress, of course." Stiff fabric rustled at her touch. "I just came from the dressmaker's and I was going to surprise you. Daddy *insisted* I have a new dress made for the Glory Days celebration in a few weeks. It's simply the most beautiful cobalt-blue taffeta you've ever seen," she announced. After another long whimper she added, "Now you can't even see it to tell me how stunning I look."

Miss Ellickson cleared her throat from the sofa.

"Why, Joseph!" Julia perched a hand on his forearm. "I didn't realize you had company."

"Julia Cranston, this is Miss Ellickson." He felt Julia stiffen, as though some invisible rod just shot up her back.

"Good morning, Miss Cranston," his teacher said.

Julia threaded an arm through his. "Miss Ellickson, you say? I don't recall the name from around here."

He could only imagine the confused look on her face. Even though her family had arrived just months ago from Boston, she was already familiar with everyone within twenty square miles.

"You must be new to the area," Julia finally conceded.

"I arrived just Saturday," Miss Ellickson answered stiffly.

"Miss Ellickson is here from Iowa. Ben sent for her to—to carry out some training I may need." The admission needled him.

"Whatever would you need training for, Joseph?" Julia sidled closer, her voice rising in pitch. "Uncle Edward says you're the finest craftsman this side of the Rockies."

He sighed. "Not training in carpentry. Training in case my sight doesn't return—right away." *Or at all,* he thought, the very prospect making his stomach churn.

"This certainly is a shock!" She hesitated, then patted his hand. "Well, you poor thing, Joseph, looking pitiful in those wraps the way you do. Maybe you should be back in bed?"

He winced at her choice of words. He didn't want to be pitied. "I'm fine. Really. What brings you here, anyway?"

"I stopped by the shop thinking, of course, that you'd be there working your little heart out after being in bed for so long." Her voice was loud enough to call in cattle. "You can imagine my surprise when Aaron said you were still at home."

"My eyes are bandaged, not my ears." He dug his fingers into the chair's thick stuffing. "I can hear you just fine."

"Of course. As I was saying," she continued, the pitch of her voice showing no noticeable change. "I brought you a most wonderful meal. I'm quite certain you'll be very pleased."

A tantalizing aroma wafted to his senses, penetrating the cloud of perfume. He tried not to show his surprise at her sudden display of domestic prowess. "Did you make this yourself?"

"Well, I…not exactly. But I gave Cook *very* specific instructions. She absolutely puts me to shame, Joseph," she simpered, then whisked out of the front room toward the kitchen. "I am simply dreadful in the kitchen."

"Don't be so hard on yourself. You probably do a fine job," he called after her, but remembering the sawdust taste of the cookies she'd made last week, he was pretty sure that wasn't true.

"You're a dear to say so. But I dare say that I won't be winning any first-place ribbons in the pie-baking contest at the town celebration." Julia's high-pitched laughter shot through his house like bolts of lightning. "Come and eat, Joseph."

Vile fear wrapped around him when the almost twenty feet he had to go suddenly felt more like a mile. Perspiration beaded his forehead and a slow trembling coursed through his body like deadly venom. His pulse pounded in his head, throwing off his concentration. He gritted his teeth. Drew in a shuddering breath. Just as he started forward with his hands outstretched, he felt a light touch on his arm.

"Mr. Drake," Miss Ellickson whispered beside him as she gently guided his hand to her elbow. "Would you be so kind as to escort me to the table?"

He jerked his head down to her, ready to refuse. But the overwhelming relief he felt as she led him with steady measured steps to the kitchen brought his protest up short.

"You must be positively famished," Julia gushed.

When Miss Ellickson placed his hand on the back of a dining chair, he whispered, "Thanks."

Bracing his hands on the chair, he willed the trembling to stop. "So, what do we have here?"

Over a deep sigh, he could hear Boone's lumbering gait coming toward him. Joseph could just see the dog throwing his tail lazily from side to side as he swaggered across the room.

"Oh no, Joseph! Are you going to let that horrid animal sit here while you eat? God only knows where she's been." No doubt Julia's pink lips were pursed tight, her small nose wrinkled in disgust. She never did like Boone and wasn't shy about saying so. "I don't see how you can stand having Bongo in your house like you do."

"Boone," he corrected, irritated that she could never seem to get his dog's name right. "And 'she's' a 'he.'"

"Boone, Bongo, he, she…it matters not to me. The beast is just so uncouth. Mother would surely faint if she could see it in your house. Why, that creature is nearly a horse."

"He's a dog, and he's fine. *He* minds his manners."

Lowering himself to the long trestle table, he trailed his fingers along the sturdy walnut's smooth finish, remembering when he'd crafted the piece. He'd built it, eager for the day when his wife and children would be seated here with him.

Julia clanged silverware against a plate, jerking him out of his reverie and invoking a fast-building sense of dread. That anxiety multiplied by ten as he realized that this would be the first time since his accident that he'd sat down for a meal.

"Everything is all set for you, Joseph. You can eat now."

He swallowed hard. Clenching his fists in his lap, he wondered what *everything* was…pork and beans, soup, chicken? He had no idea what she'd laid out or where it was located on the table. Beads of perspiration formed on his brow, his pulse pounded a deafening rhythm in his head.

"I wasn't planning on joining you, but maybe—"

"No, that's not necessary," he quickly cut in.

"Honestly, I did have plans to have tea with Colleen Teller, the *senator's* daughter," she twittered. "Of course, I'd have to go home and change. It would simply be unacceptable if she were to see me wearing my new dress today and then again for the celebration. Don't you think?"

He offered a hearty nod, thankful she had other plans.

"Well, then, by all means let me see you out, Miss Cranston. You won't want to be late," Miss Ellickson clipped off.

"That's completely unnecessary. I can see myself out." Julia clutched his hand and leaned closer, her perfume nearly choking him. "Maybe I should stay. What do you think, Joseph?" A whine of regret laced her whispered words. "I suppose I could reschedule with Colleen. Her agenda is busy, but I'm sure—"

"Please, go. Have your lunch with Colleen. I'd rather eat alone." He braced his elbows on the table and steepled his fingers under his chin. "Miss Ellickson, you can take a dinner break, too. There's a good diner just down the road—have them put your bill on my tab."

"I'll be joining you here. Thank you all the same," she responded quietly.

Julia's sharp intake of breath wasn't lost on Joseph. She grasped his shoulder. "Miss…Miss Ellington—"

"Ellickson." Joseph shook his head.

Her nails bit into his flesh. "Miss Ellickson, perhaps you didn't hear Joseph. He said he'd rather dine alone. If you—"

"Julia, I can handle this," he ground out, disgusted at her steely tone. Although he'd taken her on a few outings in the past two months, he didn't fancy being treated like some possession of hers. "Miss Ellickson, you're probably in need of a break. I'm sure I can handle it on my own."

"I can understand your hesitance, Mr. Drake. Believe me, I do." Her voice trembled.

Tension chorded his body as he wondered why everyone couldn't just let him make his own decisions. If he wanted to eat alone, shouldn't he be afforded that one small courtesy?

"I'm sorry." Miss Ellickson's voice was soft and even, coming from the chair to his left. "But I'm here to—to teach you. Not to coddle you."

Julia withdrew her hand from his shoulder, mumbling as her booted heels clicked loudly across the floor. When she slammed a plate down on the table, he nearly jumped out of his skin.

He swallowed hard, trying to control his mounting frustration. "I didn't ask you to coddle me, Miss Ellickson."

With a harrumph, Julia plopped down in a chair across the table from him. "Oh for goodness's—"

"You've made that quite clear," Miss Ellickson continued as if oblivious to Julia's presence. "But as with all my students, I'm here to instruct you in how to get along on your own, and that's what I'm going to do—starting with dinner."

"Joseph has been eating dinner for twenty-seven years, Miss Eberhard," Julia informed on a nervous laugh. He could hear her dishing something onto her plate. "He can get along just fine. Can't you, Joseph?"

"Just drop the subject." He grasped at his fading calm.

"Fine, I see the way of things." Julia gave her napkin

a swift snap and a puff of air fluffed over to him. "You have never had a problem doing things on your own," she reminded him, the shrill sound of her voice contrasting sharply with the delicate chorus of birds outside. "I realize that when you were laid up flat on your back you needed assistance. But now—"

"But now, with these bandages on, I still can't see." Raising his focus to where she sat directly across from him, he wished he could see, but he couldn't even open his eyes through the thick bandages. "And there's a slim chance that my vision might not be what it was."

He swallowed against the admission. If his sight didn't fully return, he'd have to find independence as soon as possible or he'd never be able to stomach himself.

"Oh, Joseph, don't be silly. You're going to be fine," Julia dismissed, then took a bite of something that crunched.

Awkwardness flooded his resolve. He could hear Miss Ellickson arranging things on the table, even dishing items onto his plate while he sat rigid as a board, every muscle in his body stiff and unyielding to the internal cry to relax. All he wanted was to be left alone, but Julia was being unusually possessive and Miss Ellickson was intent on doing her job.

A job he didn't even hire her to do!

"Your plate is in front of you," Miss Ellickson began, her voice low and measured. "Now, like numbers on a clock face, there's a thick wheat roll at nine o'clock, mashed potatoes at twelve o'clock, cooked carrots at three o'clock and roast at six o'clock. If you'll raise your hands to feel for your plate," she directed, pausing as if waiting for him to follow her lead, but he couldn't seem to move his hands from where they were tightly fisted in his lap. "You'll find your fork to the left of your plate, spoon and knife on your napkin to the right. And your glass of grape juice is about three inches to the right of your plate, at two o'clock."

From across the table, Julia's sharp scrutiny bore down on him like a locomotive. He tried to ignore it. The aroma rising from the food normally would've made his mouth water, but instead his stomach churned. His discomfort could reach a swift end if he insisted they leave, but at this point he was too stubborn to give in.

"Shall we give thanks?" Miss Ellickson asked.

The distinct air of vulnerability in her voice pricked Joseph's heart, but he quickly brushed it aside as though it were a pesky bug. In spite of his surging anger, he bowed his head as Julia's utensils clanked to silence against her plate. Truth be told, over the past weeks he'd spent more time telling God what to do than talking with Him or thanking Him. Had God heard his plea for healing? Or had He passed him by for good?

On a long sigh, he began to pray. "Lord, thank You for this meal. Bless the hands that prepared it." Remembering his sister-in-law's tenuous health and the certain stress Aaron had to be under, he added, "And be with Ellie and the baby. Keep them safe."

"Amen," Miss Ellickson whispered after a long pause.

With a curt nod, he sat in the offending darkness, trying to ignore the daunting insecurity as he struggled for self-control. Pulling his sagging shoulders back, he braced himself, unwilling to look like a helpless excuse for a man—especially in front of Julia.

Crisp, metallic sounds from her silverware sounded against her plate. She hadn't uttered one word in the past moments, but he knew she must be closely monitoring his every move. Her sharp inspection pierced like tiny shards of glass.

Could he do this? With his head bowed, Joseph tried to picture the things set before him. He slowly slid his hands up to the table, probing for his knife and fork. Once he'd located his utensils, he raised them to the plate.

"Now, when you've located your fork and knife—"

"I've eaten without help in the past, Miss Ellickson," he cut in, knowing even as the words formed on his lips that he should just swallow his pride. "And I can do it now."

Joseph fought to still his trembling hands. As he made a stab for the meat to cut it, the supple chunk seemed to dodge his effort, sliding away from him. His fork fell from his grasp, clanking loudly against his plate.

He couldn't miss the small gasp Julia gave. "Oh, no, Joseph, you dropped your fork," she announced loudly.

"Really?" Fumbling for his fork, he put it to the plate again while inside tremors of fury thundered. When he couldn't locate the piece of meat with his utensils, his agitation increased.

"Here you are, Mr. Drake. The roast is back on your plate," his teacher spoke evenly.

The roast had flown off his plate?

Steeling himself, he struggled to gather his composure as he repositioned his fork toward the carrots. With intense focus, he tried to recall where she'd said they were—three o'clock or ten o'clock? Framing one side of the plate with a hand, he set his fork to the plate, succinctly stabbing one long spear and cutting it in two. A small sigh of relief passed his lips as he opened wide and directed the carrot in. It brushed his lips, tumbled down his shirt, then fell to the floor with a moist thud.

He gritted his teeth as Boone immediately shifted across the floor and sniffed at the vegetable. Joseph's breathing came heavy, labored. The loud rushing in his ears grew almost deafening.

"It's all right." Miss Ellickson's tone was low and even.

He slammed his fist on the table to ward her off. He would do this alone or drown in a pool of humiliation.

"If you'll put your fork to the plate," she offered, forced patience lacing her words, "and first gauge where the food—"

"*I* will do it!" Joseph interrupted angrily, acutely aware that not one morsel of food had made it to his mouth yet.

Humiliation ricocheted in his mind like a shotgun blast in an underground cavern. Groping for his knife, his hand careened into his glass of grape juice. It tipped, the glass clinking on the solid wood.

"Oh, my new dress!" Julia yowled, her chair scraping away from the table. "My beautiful new dress! It's ruined!"

Joseph sucked in a shaky breath. He stood, knocking his chair over with the back of his legs and sending Boone scurrying away, toenails scratching across the floor as the loud crash reverberated throughout the house.

Hearing the frantic sound of Julia wiping at her garment, Joseph brought his hands to his head, threading trembling fingers through his hair. "I'm sorry," he forced on a broken breath.

"Please don't worry, Mr. Drake. Accidents happen," Miss Ellickson responded quietly as she rose and crossed to the sink. "I'll get it cleaned up."

He drew quivering fingertips over the bandages covering his eyes, failure's evil taunt screaming through his thoughts. He was sickened at his stubborn pride. Balling his fists firmly at his sides, he clenched his teeth tight. Even if he couldn't see, he should be able to make it through a meal.

Simple things were now difficult. Difficult things, seemingly impossible. When he'd been released from bed rest, he thought he'd feel more comfortable, more capable. Instead, he felt more like a prisoner than a free man.

He jerked suddenly at Miss Ellickson's light touch on his arm. "I didn't mean to startle you. I just wondered what you'd like for me to do?"

Julia huffed. "Isn't it *obvious* that you've already done quite enough? Just look at the mess he's made," she hissed. "Poor Joseph obviously isn't ready for this. I'm certain that you can't be doing him a bit of good by pushing—"

"Stop!" he growled. "Just leave, now."

A moment of crushing silence was followed by the whoosh of Julia's skirts as she walked toward the front door. "I can tell when I'm not wanted," she spat, her voice laden with unveiled disgust as she stormed out, slamming the front door behind her.

"Mr. Drake? I'm terribly sorry about all of that." Miss Ellickson slid her hand off his arm. "I'll understand if you want to call it a day."

Tilting his head down toward her, he wished he could see her. He just wanted one glimpse. From the moment they'd met this morning, she'd seen him at his worst, with behavior he didn't know he was capable of. She'd taken his rude, unyielding responses with a stiff upper lip. Why? Who was this woman who would sacrifice her own comfort and willingly endure the ugliest part of him?

Chapter Three

Unadulterated fear had shown like gaping holes in Mr. Drake's stony wall of composure. From five years of experience working with the blind, Katie had learned to recognize the sure signs. And she'd never seen such desperation. All morning she'd witnessed it in his tensing jaw, tight fists and grim expression. She was worn out just watching him work so hard to fortify himself against the fear.

She stood for several moments on his porch, her legs weak as she clutched her books to her chest. He'd said that he'd lost his appetite. That he needed some time to think. And she knew when to let up a little. After all, this was all so very new and painful for him.

Breathing deep, she welcomed the soothing west wind filtering through her skirts, cooling her skin. For over three hours she'd remained stalwart in spite of his un-yielding behavior, though she'd nearly bit her tongue in two when Miss Julia Cranston had shown up. It wasn't Katie's business who that woman was to Mr. Drake, but whatever her relationship, Miss Cranston wasn't taking into account his vulnerable state. And for that Katie felt fiercely protective.

Compassion for him tugged at her heart. It was clear that this man of strength and self-sufficiency had been dealt a very difficult hand in life. Things were horribly unfamiliar to him. Maybe for now, anyway, he felt like a shell of what he had been.

Still, Katie could see an iron will there—and a fortitude that perhaps he didn't even realize existed. He was unlike anyone she'd worked with. Decidedly stoic, yet beneath that stony exterior, a vulnerable man, scared to death. And she wanted to do everything she could to give him back his life.

Squaring her shoulders, she struggled to gather her wits before walking the distance back to Uncle Sven and Aunt Marta's. She'd never hidden her feelings well. No doubt they'd worry if she showed up looking as distraught as she felt.

Brushing wisps of hair from her face, she started down the three steps, but came to an abrupt halt when Mr. Drake's voice penetrated the solid walnut barrier.

"Why? Why me?" he choked out, his halting footsteps shuffling from the area of the kitchen where she'd left him, toward the front room. "How could you do this to me? What did I do to deserve this?" Mr. Drake's voice rose in volume, twisting her heart with its mournful, almost terrorized sound. "Why, God? Why me? You have to let me see again!"

His deep, raw cry sent shivers down her spine and a piercing sword to her heart. When she heard him knock something over, her breath caught in her chest.

"Oh, God! You—*promised!*" Heaving sobs broke his words.

A heavy object slammed against the door.

Swallowing hard, she blinked back hot tears stinging her eyes. She could try to comfort him right now, but he'd reject it. She could do everything she knew to aid him in gaining physical freedom, but only God could heal his wounded heart.

Lifting a trembling finger to her face, she swiped a tear sliding down her cheek as she remembered his awkwardness this noon when he'd prayed. She didn't need eyes to see that his relationship with God was being sorely tested. How well she knew that reality— her own trust in God had been pulled up painfully short in the past year.

"God, please help him," she whispered. "Help me."

From behind the door, Mr. Drake's breathing came in audible gasps. "God, You pr-promised you wouldn't forsake Your own!"

"Go ahead, Joe-boy. Hit me as hard as you can," Aaron provoked, his words sounding more like he was offering to loan Joseph his boots, rather than his face.

"Hit all three of us till you can't pull another punch if it makes you feel better," Ben added in complete earnestness. "You need to do *something*. You're about ready to explode."

Joseph balled his fists and sucked in a slow breath, trying to hold his mounting frustration at bay. Since yesterday he'd felt like a tightly coiled spring begging for release. The reality of his inadequacy had hit him full force, and since then he'd been fighting just to stay clear of the bitter rage that nipped at his heels. In the past if he were angry, he might've laid a well-aimed ax to logs, splitting wood till he dropped, but now he couldn't even seem to make it around his house without knocking something over or bumping into a wall.

Last night he'd successfully warded off his brothers when they'd shown up on his doorstep. But this morning they wouldn't be put off. For the past thirty minutes Ben, Aaron and Zach had been trying to get him to talk about yesterday. They'd said that Miss Ellickson wouldn't divulge a thing, but that Julia had given away plenty. She'd been loose-lipped all over town.

If he needed a reason to be mad, that definitely could've been it, but for some reason he didn't really give a coyote's hide. Whatever she'd said was probably true. He could hardly blame her for spouting off. Had he insisted that he be left alone to eat his meal, then she wouldn't have had a thing to talk about.

Julia's stories were to his benefit anyway. His blessed privacy would be ensured this way. No one would brave visiting if they knew how uncomfortable they'd be.

"Come on, Joe-boy, swing at one of us," Aaron urged. "We're standing right in front of you."

"This is your chance, big brother," came Zach's low voice. At twenty, he was the youngest of the Drake brothers and had been striving to sow something other than wild oats. "I reckon you've probably been wantin' to do this to me more than a time or two."

"Ha! Are you giving us the opportunity, too?" Aaron guffawed. "Line on up, boys! Maybe we could knock some sense into Zach—keep him from making any more dirt-poor choices."

Joseph could hear a scuffle in front of him and figured that Aaron was probably ruffling Zach's hair or faking a punch. Like a couple of playful bear cubs, they were always messing around, but he knew it wouldn't amount to much. Zach had made some bad decisions—decisions that had almost landed him in jail. They were just glad he was finally holding down a job as a ranch hand, and hadn't gone the way of the third brother, Max, who'd taken off eight years ago with his inheritance and then some, and was living on the run.

"You two yahoos cut the bantering! We're not here about Zach, we're here about Joseph," came Ben's firm warning. "Come on, Joseph. We're not kidding. Let loose—it'll do you good."

Joseph gave a low growl. "Would you three knock it off?"

Shaking his head, he pushed between them and with hands outstretched and clumsy, shuffling steps made his way to the dining table. He grasped the top rung of a chair, leaning heavily into it. "You might as well stop this charade. I'm not going to hit any of you. Never have, never will."

Aaron came to stand beside him. "Maybe you *need* to haul out and hit us. We know you enough to see that you're about ready to blow. I've never seen you so dog-gone angry."

"I'm not allowed to be angry?" His jaw muscles tensed.

"No. It's not that," Aaron answered. "We can't blame you at all for being angry. Can we, Ben?"

"Absolutely not." Ben's long strides brought him to flank Joseph's other side, followed by Zach. "You've been calm and collected since your accident—handling things better than most people would. Believe me, I've seen folks go through far less, only with a mountain of ill-tempered attitude. I'm just glad to see you finally showing some kind of emotion."

Pushing up to his full height, Joseph raked his fingers through his hair. "Well, then, what is it? Would you do me a favor and clue me in on what you're getting at here, because so far you're not making a lick of sense."

After a long moment of silence Aaron spoke up. "Flat out, Joseph…we're worried."

"Worried? About what?" Shoving his hands on his hips, he shook his head. "If anyone should be worried here, it's me. The three of you are acting like you just got kicked in the head by a horse." Waving his hand in the air, he yelled, "Quick! Get a doctor!" Then he knocked the side of his head with his hand. "Oh wait! You *are* the doctor."

"Don't try to dodge the attention like you always do," Ben retorted, clearing his throat. "Now listen, we're here, in part, because we're worried about Miss Ellickson."

He jammed his hands on his hips and furrowed his brow. "Miss Ellickson?"

Just thinking about the mess he'd made of dinner yesterday sent shame, thick as mud, coursing through his veins. But then like a flag of warning, concern for Miss Ellickson rose inside him. "What about Miss Ellickson? Has something happened?"

"She'll be here any minute now. And Ben, Zach and I—we're here to make sure you plan on being civil to her."

He gave a short harrumph. "You don't think I will?"

"I don't know. You tell me," Ben answered in a no-nonsense tone. "Like I said yesterday, you've always been a gentleman in the past, but as angry as you are, we don't want you scaring her off. She's come a long way to work with you."

Another day with her definitely didn't sit well with him. Not at all. Last night he'd barely gotten a wink of sleep thinking about her. He'd been bracing himself for her return and now here his brothers were, showing more concern for her than loyalty to him.

He felt trapped. Trapped in his home. Trapped in his body. Trapped in a fear so unfamiliar.

Taunting disorientation blanketed him and he struggled to steady himself against the unnerving effects. "What would make you think that I'm going to scare her off, anyway?"

Ben slid a chair over the hardwood floor and sat down with a weighted thud, Zach and Aaron following his move. "Oh, you wouldn't intentionally do that—I don't think, anyway. But believe me, you can be intimidating even when you're not angry."

"Yeah. It's like the Red Sea parting every time you walk through a crowd," Aaron quipped with a chuckle. "Wish I had that effect."

Joseph tightened his grip on the chair. "I'm not the one who invited her here. When you mentioned the idea in the first place, I made it clear how I felt. But then you showed up with her in tow, pushing me into this whole thing. I went through with it yesterday and I'll do the same again today, but I'm telling you, I'm just going through the motions."

When Aaron reached over and grabbed Joseph's arm, Joseph flinched at the unexpected touch. His brothers meant well—Ben had gone above and beyond in his care of Joseph. Aaron had been carrying twice his usual load in the shop, and Zach had risked losing his tenuous position as a ranch hand to help out. They were doing so much, but nothing they could do right now would make him feel better. True, he could batter them bloody, but somehow he knew it wouldn't touch the strange bitterness and pain that had settled deep in his heart.

Ben squeezed Joseph's forearm. "You don't have to like the training and you don't even have to like Miss Ellickson. All we're asking is that you be *civil* to her and give her a chance."

Oh, he'd give her a chance all right. He'd suffer through two more weeks of this. She might even show him something that could make the time bearable. But if he had his way, she'd be gone after he returned from Denver to see the doctor. It didn't matter where she went—she could even stay in Boulder for all he cared— he just didn't want to need her.

Joseph lowered himself to a chair, set on hiding his raw emotions from his brothers. "All I can say is that I hope she's not disappointed when I don't need her after all. Seems like an awful long way to travel to work for only a couple of weeks."

When he heard Ben clear his throat, his pulse began a rapid beat in his ears. He could imagine what Ben would say next, so he quickly added, "And you can breathe easy. You have my word...I'll be on my best behavior. I'll be a veritable welcome wagon from here on out."

Mr. Drake stood in front of Katie, his tall, tightly muscled frame filling the doorway. "Come in."

Come in? Katie silently mouthed as she peered up at him to see one of his hands hooked over the top of the door, the other gesturing for her to enter. Since yesterday she'd prepared for a goodbye fare-thee-well, sure that he would refuse further training, but now he'd invited her to—to come in?

She'd prayed all night long that he wouldn't give up, and if he did, she'd try to persuade him otherwise. Terrified of going home, she needed a reason to stay here in Colorado. But also, after meeting Mr. Drake yesterday, she wanted desperately to help him find freedom again.

"Thank you," she said, her voice steadier than she felt.

With an armload of books, she squeezed by him, acutely aware of his solid form so near hers. When she removed her pale straw bonnet and hung it on a coat hook, her attention was drawn to the floor where a Bible lay sprawled open. Her breath caught as she remembered hearing something crash against the door yesterday. She tenderly scooped up the Bible, its cover worn with the passage of time and its pages yellowed and frayed from use. Carefully cradling it against her chest with the other books, Katie steadied her wavering emotions. "Your Bible. You must have dropped it."

Without a word, he quietly latched the door.

"I'll just put it over here on the mantel for you." After she'd laid it on the beautifully crafted mantel, she turned and noticed Boone lying beside one of the wingback chairs. "Well, good morning, Boone. How are you this fine morning?" Kneeling beside his massive head, she held out her hand to him.

Katie smiled as he pressed his big, wet nose into her palm and stared up at her with expressive brown eyes. After giving her a wet kiss, he flopped his head down on the wood floor with a dull thud. She smoothed the unruly hair on top of his head. "I certainly hope this means we're on friendly terms."

Still smiling, she rose and returned to where she'd left Mr. Drake standing. She nervously fingered the row of silver buttons trailing down her high-necked white blouse. "And how are you today, Mr. Drake? Are we on friendly terms, too?"

He pushed away from the door, a smirk lifting the corner of his mouth. "I suppose you were wondering if I'd call it off?"

"To be perfectly candid, the thought had crossed my mind." Threading her fingers together in front of her, she added, "I was very much hoping you would continue with the training."

He jammed his hands into his pockets, his jaw muscle ticking. "I don't quit things that easily, but even if I did, I have three brothers holding my feet to the fire."

"They must care a great deal."

When he just nodded, she walked to the kitchen where the bold scent of fresh coffee met her squarely. Setting her books on the table, she smoothed her pale yellow cotton skirt. "Smells like you made coffee. Do you mind if I help myself?"

"Go right ahead." He shuffled to the table, his hands splayed in front of him. "My brothers were over earlier this morning and Ben made a pot." Reaching for a chair, he added, "I'm warning you, he makes it strong enough to wake the dead."

"Perfect. I didn't get much sleep last night. I must not be used to my new surroundings yet," she half lied. In truth she'd lain awake thinking of how she could best help him.

And how she could keep this job.

She couldn't bear the thought of going home already— too many dark clouds threatened on the horizon there. Here, she had hope that the sun's warmth would shine on her face again. With or without a job her aunt and uncle would welcome her to stay, but Katie would never think to impose on their goodness overly long, especially if she wasn't earning her keep.

"Mr. Drake, could I get you a cup, too?"

He shifted nervously, then reached out to his adorable dog who sauntered up beside him, his big, furry feet sweeping across the wood floor as though he wore heavy boots. "Sure. Thanks."

As she scanned the cupboard shelves for two mugs, she wondered what had come over Mr. Drake. The contempt he'd readily shown yesterday was barely visible today—in fact, she might even go so far as to say that he was congenial.

Spotting a row of mugs on the third shelf, she said, "They're a little out of reach."

He stood, quirking one brow. "What?"

"The mugs… I'm not tall enough to reach them."

Lifting his head in silent recognition, he moved toward her, his movements jerky and uncertain. When he'd pulled them from the shelf, he turned, almost knocking into her.

"Here you are," he said, holding the mugs out to her.

Katie squeezed back against the counter as he towered over her. An eerie chill crept up her spine as she struggled to block out the haunting memories that assaulted her. But the way Mr. Drake stood over her, trapping her and closing her in like he was, she wanted to scream and escape from the suffocating confinement.

Gulping back the bile that rose in her throat, she snatched the mugs from him with trembling hands. "Thank you."

She slipped around him and crossed to the stove. As she steadied her hands enough to pour the steaming liquid, she willed her heart to stop pounding. Setting the pot back on the burner, her brow beaded with a cold sweat and her vision narrowed. She fought to even out her short gasping breaths, clutching the stove handle as though it were some lifeline.

Katie reminded herself over and over that he was not Frank Fowler, the man who'd set into motion a year of turmoil that she could share with no one. She'd had to carry the burden alone and at times it threatened to shatter her under its weight.

Frantically grasping for some thread of hope, she struggled to drag herself away from the edge of despair. Like a faint, saving call, she could hear a comforting voice, reminding herself that she was safe now. Hundreds of miles away from Fowler and from the wicked sneer that would stretch across his face each time he'd see her.

Squeezing her eyes shut against the images, she felt her stomach tense. She'd thought that putting distance between herself and home would eliminate moments like this, but the miles had done nothing. The memories were stronger than ever. The fear, consuming. The images had struck with the force of a landslide, unearthing every raw emotion she'd attempted to bury.

"Miss Ellickson?" Mr. Drake's tentative voice broke through her swirling thoughts.

Rising above the fray of images barraging her mind, Katie slowly spun back around. "Here you are." Her voice was thin and strained. Her hands still quivered as she set down the cups of coffee. "Here's your coffee— be careful, it's hot."

She lightly grasped his hands and directed them to the stone mug. His hands, large and work-worn in hers, felt strong enough to ward off any enemy, yet gentle enough to soothe a baby.

And brought an immediate, tangible calm to Katie.

The fear that had mounted so quickly, rocking her off kilter, dispelled just as fast. A shaky sigh escaped her lips.

"Miss Ellickson?" His brow furrowed. "Are you all right?"

Sinking into a seat across from him, she took a slow sip of coffee. "Yes, I'm fine."

"Are you sure? I'd get you something to eat," he said, gesturing toward the cupboards, "but I'm not sure of what's here anymore. If you can find something…"

"Thank you, but Aunt Marta made sure I ate this morning," she managed, cupping her hands around the warm mug and staring at him from over the rim. She noticed, for the first time, how his deep chestnut hair hung in playful waves across the white bandages on his forehead, and the way a stubborn cowlick kicked a thick clutch of hair to the side, giving him an innocent look.

Something about him was so captivating, intriguing, almost demanding of her attention. Was it the confidence he exuded in spite of his fear? Was it the way he filled the room with his strong, quiet presence? Or was it his undeniable good looks?

Eager to distract her thoughts, she looked away, noticing a long cane leaning in the corner. She hadn't seen it there yesterday, but then with all of the commotion she easily could have missed it. "I see you have a cane?"

When he paused, she couldn't miss the way he turned his head away from the object as though it were an offending image in his home. "Ben brought it by this morning."

Her heart pulled tight. "Well, if you're up to it, maybe

the best use of our time today would be to help you get more comfortable around your home. We'll count out steps between rooms and furniture—that sort of thing."

Bowing his head, he fingered the edge of the mug. "So the walls and furniture don't find me first?"

"Exactly."

He raised his chin. "We might as well get it over with."

Although resignation hung heavy in his voice, Katie could hardly believe he'd so readily agreed. She stared for a long moment, not quite sure how to take his cooperative agreement.

"You're awfully quiet. Are you still there?" He traced his fingertips slowly over the table's smooth surface.

Katie shook off her surprise, then pushed up from the table. "I'm sorry. I apologize if my mind is elsewhere this morning."

Nodding, he rose from the table.

"We'll begin at your front door, counting steps from there first. You can use the cane for—"

"For *firewood,* maybe." He threw a scowl her way, then shuffled toward the door.

"Well, now, that's not a very agreeable thing to say," she threw back at him.

"That's because I'm not feeling overly compliant, Miss Ellickson." He leaned a shoulder against the door. "At least not as far as that thing goes."

"Using that *thing* might prevent you from a mishap." She perched her hands on her hips, surprised and strangely relieved at his show of stubbornness. "Back at the school we liken a cane to eyes. It will help you see where you're going."

He gave a sarcastic laugh. "Well, we're not at the

school and I don't plan on being this way forever, thank you."

Crossing her arms at her chest, she eyed him. "Stubborn, aren't you?"

Her heart squeezed at his insistence that things were going to change for him. She hoped, for his sake, they would.

He raised his chin the slightest bit. "So I've been told."

"Then you can take my elbow, like we did yesterday. It's the preferred way to navigate as opposed to holding one's hand or being pushed along. But if you use the cane, as well," she added, hoping to appeal to his greater sense of reason, "you'll be able to tell what might be lying in your path."

"No, thanks." His curt response and the way his jaw tensed left her void of any argument.

"Why don't you tell me about the layout of your home? Don't be vague about where your furniture is located, so that you'll have a clear picture in your mind."

With a slow exhale, he made a detailed description, his tone reminiscent at times as he described his home to a T.

"Perfect. Now, try to relax and walk at a normal pace and I'll match your stride." When she gently guided his hand to her arm, a tingling warmed her skin. She fought to ignore the sensation, resolute in her desire to remain professional. "I'll do the counting and make sure you don't run into anything."

He tensed beside her, his grip tightening slightly. "All right. But I'll warn you that I'm a little shaky on this."

"You'll do fine. Trust your instincts. If you're aware, you should be able to sense when something is in your way."

Cautiously he took a step while she began counting.

Then with each step following, his grip tightened as though she alone kept him from falling off a steep precipice. His hand trembled. His breathing grew shallow.

At eighteen steps and just inches from the back door, she stopped. "Now, use your hand that is outstretched to see how close you are."

Perspiration beaded above his full lips. With one hand he clutched her arm, with the other he tentatively reached out, groping for the unseen. When his trembling fingers brushed against the wall, he exhaled a broken sigh.

Covering his hand at her elbow, her heart squeezed at seeing how much this had cost him. She peered up at Mr. Drake, taking in the stark change in his demeanor from just moments ago, when stubbornness waved like a proud battalion flag, to now, when raw fear weighed his shoulders and head down low.

She swallowed past the lump in her throat. "Very well done. Your pace was just fine."

He slid quivering fingers over his lips, then raised a fist to his bandaged eyes. "You'd think I could make it across the room without breaking a sweat," he ground out. "I may as well have been scaling a mountain."

"Don't be discouraged." She squeezed his hand. "It takes time getting used to all of this."

"It's my own home. I should be able to walk across the room without trembling in my boots."

"You're doing just fine—especially since you've only been up for a couple of days." She turned to face him. "Taking everything into account, you're doing very well."

His face softened some, the corner of his lips lifting slightly. "You're Little Miss Sunshine, aren't you?"

A warm blush crept up her cheeks. She smiled at his

comment, surprised once again by his congeniality. "Better that than gloomy."

"Far as I can tell, you could never be accused of that," he replied, his hands still trembling some.

"There's a bright side to everything."

"What could be positive about this?" He gestured to his bandaged eyes.

Hugging her arms to her chest, she stared at him, the way he wore frustration like an unwanted old coat, and desperation like an acquaintance of ill repute. "You're right, Mr. Drake. Your injury is not something easily reckoned with. Not having your sight is certainly nothing short of difficult, and I'm sure you wouldn't wish it on anyone. Even an enemy." Katie tried to steady the quiver in her voice. "But even as uncertain as things are right now, you can focus on where you've been or on where you're going."

His lips formed a tight, distressed line. "I wish I could. But taking a step forward when I can't see where I'm going…it scares me to death."

At his admission, sadness rose within Katie. She was shocked at the tiniest crack he'd allowed into himself, an opening that gave a glimpse into his silent battle.

Threading her fingers together in front of her, she searched for the right words. "I know this isn't easy. In fact, I'm not sure how I could face such a thing. If you don't regain your sight, there'll be challenges. It won't be easy, but I promise you it will be rewarding." Katie gathered a bit more boldness, then added, "And if you'll allow me, I'll be here beside you to help you find your way to the other side."

Chapter Four

Embarrassed once again, Joseph's face flamed hot. He was sure he'd suffered more humiliation in the past five days than he had his entire life.

He bit back a groan, trying to ignore his frustration. Having worked with Miss Ellickson for almost a week, why was he having such a hard time doing a simple task like pouring water from a pitcher? If he didn't fully regain his vision, how would he ever be able to work in the shop again, handling sharp tools?

"Here, let me help you," Miss Ellickson offered, the quiet calm in her voice beckoning him like a peaceful stream. "Sometimes trying too hard makes things more difficult. Now, lightly grasp the glass like this." She gently positioned his fingers around the glass, her touch soft and soothing. As she slipped his forefinger at the last knuckle over the rim, she said, "Don't hold too tight. Keep a light touch. Remember how that feels and now find the pitcher."

Deeply concentrating, he was determined not to spill

again as he slid a hand along the counter to find the pitcher. When his fingers connected with the stone pitcher, he noticed how it was beaded with perspiration from the hot August day.

"Got it," he confirmed.

Once he'd painstakingly set the lip of the pitcher over the rim of the glass, he poured the water. And when the cool liquid reached his finger, he pulled the pitcher back and sighed.

"There you go, that was perfect! Not one drop spilled." The reassurance in her voice brightened his gruff mood enough that he even relaxed a little. "See? You can do it."

He angled his head down to Katie. "Thanks, Sunshine." Joseph smiled at her, hoping that she noticed, because so far this week it seemed as if all he'd done was scowl. In turn, she'd never once gotten impatient or cross with him. "Always the encourager, aren't you?"

"You deserve it. You're working very hard."

When she gave his hand a light squeeze, he couldn't help but wonder what she looked like. "You know, I figure that if I was a cat, I'd be dead."

"What?" she asked on a laugh.

"I'd be dead from curiosity." Raising his brows, he took one step closer to her. "You see, Miss Ellickson, you're the only new person I've met since my accident. And your appearance—I mean the way you look—is still a mystery to me."

The air seemed to grow warm and thick between them. His entire being hummed in full awareness of her presence beside him.

"Good thing you're not a cat, then," she finally responded, her voice sounding tight, strained.

Joseph gave an almost imperceptible nod, wishing that his brothers would indulge him with a few words about her physical appearance. They'd sure been vocal about him treating her well, and being a man of his word, he'd been on his best behavior. Although at this point he didn't really need encouragement to do that—Miss Ellickson was easy to like.

He decided that when he returned from Denver with his vision intact, she was the first person he wanted to lay eyes on. If her appearance mirrored at all what he'd grown to understand of her character, he was sure she'd be beautiful.

Wouldn't that be the irony of it all…a beautiful woman watching him stumble through simple things.

Leaning back against the counter, he momentarily cringed. "So, what next, Sunshine?"

When she stifled a laugh, his lips curved into a smile again. For some reason, the sound of her light laughter warmed his heart and made him want to make her smile again.

"Is this your name for me? Sunshine?"

"If the shoe fits." He recalled different moments throughout the week when her encouragement had been the balm he'd needed to keep going. To keep moving forward toward normalcy, however meager it was compared to independence.

"You're very kind, but I hardly think I warrant anything quite so grand." He could hear her gathering some papers on the table.

Four steps and Joseph had crossed to the table, noticing for the first time how much less halting his footsteps sounded compared to just a few days ago. "Why don't you let me be the judge of that?"

Unbidden, a deep fondness for her rose within him, and that unnerved him. Because somewhere along the line he'd missed how attached he was becoming to her. Was it because she'd given him hope at a time when things were bleak? Was it because she was so selfless in her work with him? It was just a job for her, wasn't it? Maybe she had this effect on other students, too.

Or was it something more?

If so, he'd have to guard himself. She didn't deserve his strained indifference, but he couldn't let himself grow any fonder of her. If he didn't regain his sight, his future as a single man would be irrevocably sealed because he wasn't about to burden anyone with his blindness.

Her voice finally broke through the raw, unsettling revelation. "Well, Mr. Drake, why don't we—"

"If it's all right with you, would you mind calling me Joseph?" Guarding himself or not, he couldn't stand another day of being addressed as Mr. Drake. He jammed his hands into his pockets and stood tall. "Mr. Drake is, well, it's just too formal for my liking."

She paused for a brief moment. "All right, then. Joseph it is—if you'll call me Katie."

Or Sunshine, he thought, helpless to keep his emotions from running away.

If Joseph had been planted on the pulpit with flowers growing out of his Sunday clothes, he wouldn't have felt more conspicuous than he did right now.

He shifted uncomfortably in the wooden pew, wishing he'd just ignored Ben's challenge for him to attend church. Each step away from his cocooned world and nearer the church building had brought him closer to people's stares, even if he couldn't see them. Having arrived a few minutes before the service started, he couldn't avoid being a sideshow for curious onlookers or a conversation piece walking in with a bandage wrapped around his head.

He sat stock straight in the second row of pews, the back of the bench hitting well below his shoulder blades. Even though Ben's tall frame was close to him and he'd kept a steady flow of whispered small talk going since they'd sat down, Joseph might as well have been alone. Inky darkness seemed to enfold him, isolating him in a room crowded with friends and acquaintances.

He shrugged off his uncertainty as faint comments regarding his attendance wafted to his ears. Joseph gritted his teeth. There was certainly nothing wrong with his hearing.

As much as he wanted to remain inconspicuous, he'd always seemed to attract attention in a room, especially that of women. It sure wasn't something he set out to do. Julia had been no different. She'd sidled up to him like moss on a log as soon as she'd met him. But since his accident, certain little things, like her high-pitched voice, grated on his nerves.

Thoughts of seeing her again settled on him like cold rain. She'd not stopped by since that first day he'd worked with Katie, and Joseph wasn't surprised. He hadn't needed to see Julia that day to know that she was madder than a hornet. He could hear it in her sharp tone, the swish of her skirts and the brisk clip of her heels.

A few times when he lay awake listening to all the sounds of the night, he'd think about his relationship with her. Would she want to see him again if he didn't gain back total sight? And sight or no, did he even want to pursue anything other than friendship with her? He just couldn't ignore how ill at ease he'd felt with Julia in the last three weeks.

When he'd first met her, he'd been intrigued by her vivacious, flamboyant ways. Maybe it was an eastern air about her, or maybe it was just Julia. Whatever the case, it was as though he could see what she was really like, now that he couldn't see her. And he wasn't sure that he liked what he saw.

Shrugging off his glum musings, he focused on the sun's warmth pouring through the row of tall windows to his left. Thoughts of Katie filtered into his mind, spreading calm through him like warm honey. He couldn't deny that he missed her presence by his side today. She'd given him a tangible confidence in moving about his home, eating without incident and even doing some cooking.

Was it her expertise she'd been so eager to give him that made him feel alive again? Or was it something more?

Katie's heart clenched tight inside her chest when the pastor spoke in his sermon about trusting God. Like a broken-down wagon ransacked along a trail, she was almost empty of trust. Could she ever get beyond feeling like she alone must protect herself? It seemed as though God hadn't protected her, but instead had allowed the vilest of things to happen to her—and by a man who claimed to serve God!

She'd trusted and been betrayed. Offered goodwill and been preyed upon. She'd been wounded to her core and endured it alone in shame for all of these months.

When Uncle Sven had wired her about coming out

here, she'd jumped at the chance to leave Iowa—leave her past behind. And after meeting Joseph, she knew she'd made the right decision.

As the service concluded with a familiar hymn, Katie rose from the pew and stood beside Ellie and Aaron. She felt a pull at her heart, thankful for the quick friendship that had developed with Ellie. From the moment she'd met the young woman a week ago, they'd bonded like blood sisters.

Although Katie joined in the hymn, her focus was constantly drawn to Joseph. He stood taller than those around him, his chestnut waves stirring in the warm breeze that blew through the tall windows. His shoulders impressed her with their broad and sturdy strength. On occasion she even glimpsed the resolute set of his jawline.

The pastor's voice finally broke her reverie. "I want to remind everyone of the Glory Days celebration in three weeks. Mrs. Duncan is in charge of it again this year," he announced, gesturing to the round-faced woman who stood waving to the congregation as though she were on parade. "So, if you'd like to volunteer, talk with her after the service."

Katie sensed an excitement stirring in the room as the parishioners began filing out of the white clapboard church.

Edging her way out to the narrow aisle, she glanced at Joseph one last time and her stomach dropped. Miss Julia Cranston stood gazing up at him, her silky dark tresses and striking smile punctuating the room with icy elegance.

A stab of protectiveness shot through Katie's heart. Was Miss Cranston saying thoughtless things yet again? Katie couldn't imagine that the woman set out to be hurtful, but some people just had a knack for saying the wrong things.

Watching the interaction, she wanted to shove her way between the young beauty and Joseph, but she restrained herself. Clutching the pew in front of her, she felt almost giddy when the woman gave up with a shrug after just a few moments.

Inordinately relieved, Katie exited the church with Ellie.

"Did you see how Ethan Hofmann looked at you, Katie?" Ellie inquired, her cheeks flushed pink, matching the tiny rosebuds dotting her simple white cotton dress.

Katie stopped at the bottom of the steps, waiting for Ellie to catch her breath. "I'm not sure what you're talking about. Who's Ethan…Hofmann?"

Ellie's hands went to her stomach and gently held the swell. "Ethan Hofmann. The blacksmith's son. He was sitting to your right, several rows up, and he spent the entire service staring back at you." Her crystal blue eyes grew wide. "His neck will be giving him fits tomorrow— and it serves him right!"

An icy quiver traveled down Katie's spine. Over the past year, she'd received bone-chilling stares in her church back home. It was almost as though Frank Fowler, a well-respected deacon, innately knew when no one was looking, when his leering gaze and snapping black eyes wouldn't set gossipy lips flapping.

She pushed aside the unwelcome memories and gave a weak laugh. "I don't even know the man, Ellie."

"That young man didn't even have the decency to hide his infatuation. He was way too bold, if you ask me," Ellie insisted as she steadily beelined for a towering pine tree, its tall, weighted branches stretching wide. Cautiously sidestepping exposed roots, she turned and leaned heavily against the trunk, her cheeks flushed as though she'd just walked miles.

"Miss Ellickson, is my wife fussing over you like an old mother hen?" Aaron teased from behind her.

She turned to see an amused, boyish grin plastered across Aaron's face. Bowing her head, she took in the invigorating scent of fresh pine needles beneath her feet. "She's just keeping a watchful eye on things."

"I'm not the only one keeping an eye on things." Ellie hooked an arm through her husband's, snuggling up next to him. "Darling, you're going to have to speak with Ethan Hofmann. He's acting like a foolish schoolboy. He could hardly take his eyes off Katie during church." When she hooked Katie's arm also, Katie couldn't help but smile.

Aaron winked at her as he patted his wife's hand. "I'm sure Katie can take care of herself."

Katie swallowed hard and schooled her expression. Had Aaron known how brutally untrue those words really were he never would've said them. She'd tried to fight Frank Fowler off, but her meager five feet four inches was no match to Frank's size and his evil determination.

"But if you ever do need help or have any concerns, Katie, just let Ben, Zach or me know. Joseph, too. He may not be able to see right now, but he's always had a way of bringing order to things without bruising a single knuckle. People around these parts think twice about crossing him."

Ellie sighed, slumping her shoulders. "Well, I still think you should talk with Ethan about this. After all, Katie's a young, beautiful *unmarried* woman. The single men around here seem to lose all common sense when it comes to someone like her."

Giving Ellie's hand a warm squeeze, Katie pulled away. "It's fine. I didn't notice the man."

That was true. She hadn't noticed him because she couldn't seem to take her eyes off Joseph.

Glancing momentarily back at the church, she spotted him standing alone, and her heartbeat quickened inside her chest.

"Ellie-girl, I think you've about worn yourself out for one day," Aaron cautioned in a most gentle and loving way. "I'm gonna get you back home where you can rest. And don't you go arguing with me either." Katie turned to see Aaron wrap an arm around his wife's slight shoulders, then gently settled her back against the tree. "Stay here while I check on Joseph, then we'll be on our way."

"I'd be glad to do that," Katie offered, noticing, too, how Ellie appeared nearly spent. Her face was flushed and her brow beaded with perspiration. "Really. It's no trouble at all."

"Are you sure? I just want to make sure he's all right." Aaron glanced around the churchyard. "I thought Ben would be out here by now."

Katie gave Ellie a quick hug, then turned to Aaron. "Just get Ellie home. I'll check in with Joseph."

"Good enough." Aaron nodded.

"We'll have you out for supper some night this week," Ellie offered as her husband swept her up in his arms. She hooked her arms around her Aaron's neck, her laughter resounding like a bird's joyous spring song as he carried her toward their wagon.

Smiling, Katie waved. "I'll look forward to that."

Walking toward Joseph, she stared through a shimmer of tears, wishing that she, too, could know that kind of love.

But who would ever want her the way she was…used?

That horrifying reality never seemed to lose its sharp sting. Her heart clenched with overwhelming sadness, but she couldn't give in to it.

Ignoring the old familiar dirge, she glanced up to see Joseph sitting on the steps, his hands clasped in a tight ball between his knees. He was probably trying not to be noticed, but there was nothing inconspicuous about him. Like honey to a bee, he drew every bit of her attention with his commanding, masculine build encased in a stark white shirt and dark bronze britches, and his chestnut hair hanging loosely about his head. She barely took notice of the air of discontent tainting his features.

"Good morning, Joseph." She slowed to a stop in front of him. "It's a splendid morning, isn't it?"

"Miss Ellickson?" He stood and clung to the railing.

"Thought you could get rid of me for the weekend, did you?"

His face relaxed ever so slightly as he slid his hands off the rail and tucked them in his pockets. "Well, not exactly. I just didn't know you were here this morning, that's all."

"I was sitting in the back with Ellie, Aaron and my aunt and uncle."

"Oh." Was that a tinge of disappointment she heard in his voice? "I—I was sitting with Ben."

"Yes. I noticed. Are you still waiting for him?" She briefly scanned the yard for Ben.

"Actually I was hoping to find Aaron. Ben's inside meeting with Mrs. Duncan about the upcoming celebration. He said it might be a while, so I told him I'd get Aaron to walk me home. Or Zach if I can round him up."

Katie hugged her arms to her chest. "Ellie wasn't feeling well, so Aaron took her home. But if you don't mind, I could walk with you."

He shook his head. "No, that's all right. You don't need to do that on your day off."

"It's no problem at all. I'd be glad to walk with you. Besides, it's such a beautiful day." Holding her elbow out in front of him, she offered, "Here's my arm. You just set the pace." When he reached out and found her arm, his touch sent stirring warmth through her.

He started forward at a leisurely pace. "It galls me how tired I am from just this one outing."

"Don't be so hard on yourself. It takes a great deal of mental energy to do what you've done today."

"Well, I can tell you one thing, Tuesday of next week can't come fast enough. When I get these bandages off and can see again, I doubt I'll close my eyes for a week straight."

She hoped that he was right. That he would see again.

Noticing the curious stares of a few of the church folks who still lingered on the grounds, she asked, "You don't think people will talk, do you?" She stepped around a bed of fragrant lavender. "I mean, with me walking you home?"

He came to a stop and tilted his head down at her. "I'm sure that by now they're aware that you're my instructor. Word gets around fast here. But if it's uncomfortable for you, I could just wait for Ben."

"Oh, no," she said, a little too eagerly. "I mean, of course it's not uncomfortable."

With a smile tipping the corners of his mouth, he nodded, then continued an even stroll toward his home.

"Joseph. Katie, wait up!" a voice called from behind them.

Katie turned to see Ben jogging toward them.

"Sorry about leaving you stranded." Ben clapped Joseph on the arm and pulled in a long breath. "I got tied up with Mrs. Duncan and you know how that can go. Pastor Winters almost paid a hefty ransom to free me. At the rate she's going, you'd think she was planning a presidential inauguration."

"Mrs. Duncan isn't a woman to miss details," Joseph said, leaning slightly toward Katie.

"That's very diplomatic of you, Joseph. Personally, I'd rather strain at gnats all day than iron out details with that woman." Ben gave a wide-eyed look. "I hope you're in for a fast walk, Joseph, because I've got to hightail it out to the Randalls' place. Jeb laid an ill-aimed ax to his leg yesterday and I just got word that it's not looking too good."

Katie winced. "That sounds bad."

"When I left him late last night I said I'd be back later this afternoon, but I'd feel better if I got out there as soon as I can. Besides that, I've just acquired a couple of stray kittens that showed up in my barn yesterday."

"Your newest four-legged patients?" Joseph asked.

"Yep. And they're in need of round-the-clock attention right now. I have them bedded down in a crate beside my bed."

Joseph smiled and focused down at her. "Ben's always taking in strays and doctoring them back to health."

"Aww…"

"I can't help it. They just show up."

"That's so sweet of you," Katie said, her throat going tight with instant emotion. She loved animals.

"Yeah, well, what else is a fella to do?" Ben remarked as if he were trying to step out of the focus.

"Go on ahead. Katie said she'd walk with me." The sideways grin Joseph gave her set her pulse skittering. "That is, if you still don't mind?"

She shook her head. "Not at all."

"Good, it's settled." Ben clapped his hands, then came forward and gave Joseph's arm a quick squeeze. "Thanks again for coming with me today."

Joseph nodded. "By the way, you sent the wire for my appointment in Denver Tuesday, right?"

Ben passed a wary glance to Katie and her heart instantly squeezed with compassion for Joseph.

"Nine o'clock Tuesday morning," Ben confirmed.

A tightness strained Joseph's features. Over the course of the week, she'd discovered from the few times he'd spoken of the appointment or his vision, he'd become instantly irritable.

Ben glanced at his pocket watch and snapped it shut again. "By the way, Katie, you've made quite an impression on Aaron and Ellie. She can't say enough good things about you." On a wink, he turned and jogged away from them.

Katie felt a warm blush color her cheeks as they walked in silence for several moments.

"He's right, you know…"

"Right about what?"

"Ellie has really taken to you." His voice was as low and soothing as a cool breeze on a hot day. "Last night when the two of them stopped by, she couldn't stop talking about you. Said you were beautiful, inside and out."

Embarrassment flamed hot now. Her knees went weak and her mouth grew dry. She couldn't seem to be around him without noticing every little thing about him and being affected in ways she'd never experienced.

But she was Joseph's teacher. Nothing else. She had to keep telling herself that.

"Sorry if I embarrassed you." His deep, mellow voice had countless other effects on her besides soothing her. His voice incited a warm quiver in her stomach and a slow, steady tremble up her spine. "When Ellie said that, it blew the very first image I had of you when Ben called you up from the street."

She slowed to a stop. "There's a step here. Gauge its height with your foot, then move ahead." When he continued without incident, she went on to ask, "What image did you have?"

He puffed out his cheeks on a big sigh. "Oh, just that you were a prune-faced old woman with a sharp nose and even sharper tongue. Good thing I didn't ride away into the sunset with that impression all week."

She smiled at his description, recalling how sour and gruff he'd been when she'd first met him. "Likewise, it's a good thing I didn't hold you to my first impression, either."

Wincing, he pulled at his collar as though it was suddenly too tight for comfort.

"For a while there, I thought my uncle's high opinion of you was overrated." She came to a stop and stared up at him. "But now, I think that it might just be underrated."

Chapter Five

"If there's one thing I cannot abide, it is an overbearing woman!" Julia proclaimed with a flourish. "Mrs. Duncan...why, the way that woman prattles on, you'd think she owned half the town. The woman is overbearing, I tell you. Overbearing!"

Joseph slid a hand across his mouth, masking his grin. He figured it took an overbearing person to know one, and Julia was close to an expert in the ways of overbearing women.

"Mrs. Duncan does—"

"She was nothing if not imperious," she interrupted with a terse huff. "Out of the goodness of my heart, I offered my valuable expertise in helping to organize the box social and barn dance for the Glory Days celebration. And she refused! Flat-out refused, I tell you."

"Maybe she already has things arranged," he offered in a lame attempt to console her.

He couldn't imagine why she'd come looking for consolation from him. Between the meal catastrophe when she'd stormed off mad and the indifference he'd shown her at church yesterday, he sure didn't expect her to try and cozy up to him again. But from the minute she'd barged into his solitude some fifteen minutes ago, she'd been as much as crawling into him, mining for sympathy.

He'd been sitting on his porch awaiting Katie's arrival to start a second week of training when Julia's taut, brisk steps brought her up the walk. Funny, the second he realized the footsteps weren't Katie's, disappointment crept over him like a dark cloud blocking out the sun's warmth.

Training his ear to the street, he listened for Katie's approach, feeling a strange sense of regret knowing he wouldn't really need her after his appointment next week. When his vision returned, Katie wouldn't have to. He had to admit, having her around every day had been nice. She'd gotten under his skin with her sweet but confident disposition, her sunny encouragement and the way she made him feel so at ease. So much like himself again.

"I just do not understand that woman!" Julia wailed, jerking him out of his thoughts. "Apparently she just doesn't want the celebration to be a success. Here I was only trying to help, and I—" A loud sob broke her lamentation.

The sound of her sniffling gave the indifference in Joseph's heart pause. Honestly, he felt sorry for Julia. She was an oddity out here in the west, away from her eastern friends and high-class ways. She was cultured. A large brilliant diamond in the midst of an earthy environment, and the startling radiance, which had caught his eye once, seemed almost offensive to him now. Like a shocking blast of light piercing a protective cocoon.

Unable to ignore her loud cries, he took a couple steps forward, reaching out to her. If there was one thing he couldn't bear, it was a woman upset and crying. His compassion always got the best of him.

"Aww, come here." He found her shoulder and gently pulled her to his side, her stiff skirt bristling like crisp rice paper against his britches. "I'm sure Mrs. Duncan doesn't really mean anything by it. She's just been the one in charge of organizing this shindig every year. Don't take it personally."

Julia sniffed daintily, and he could almost feel her big, emerald-eyed gaze upon him. "Do you think? I mean, I only wanted to help and then she—" Her voice broke on another sob.

For several moments he held her, feeling as awkward and stiff as a gruff old hermit embracing the Queen of England. But the way her sobs were subsiding, he was glad that at least his pathetic try at sympathy was helping.

"Good morning," came Katie's voice from his walkway.

Joseph turned, slipping his arm off Julia's shoulders.

"I—I'm sorry if I interrupted something." Her voice seemed to lack the warmth he'd grown accustomed to. "I thought we were beginning at eight-thirty this morning."

"It's fine. No need to apologize," he quickly responded, shoving his hands inside his pockets. "I was sitting out here waiting for you when Julia stopped by. We were just talking."

Sensing Julia's wilting spine stiffen, he silently groaned. He shifted his feet on the hard-packed earth, noting that the sizzling sparks she emitted could've started a wildfire.

"Come on up," he offered, in an attempt to ease the awkwardness Katie must have felt.

"Miss Cranston, good morning." Even though she'd

stopped mere feet from him, Katie sounded strangely distant.

He wished he could see her face, to gauge what kind of reaction registered there. Was she given to hiding her emotions? It dawned on him how little he knew of her, of what made her tick, what made her shudder in fear and of what made her heart leap.

And he determined to rectify that as soon as possible. If they were going to work side by side, even if it was for just another week, he wanted to know more about Katie Ellickson. Something about her drew him, compelling him to ignore common sense and step beyond a professional relationship to friendship.

"Miss Ellington." Julia's icy response could have frozen a flower on the spot.

"Ellickson," Joseph corrected with a shake of his head. Sliding a hand down his shirt, he checked for misaligned buttons. "I'm ready to start if you are, Katie."

Katie lightly cleared her throat.

Then Julia's parasol snapped open next to Joseph's head, and he sidestepped, startled and irritated.

"I certainly thought you would be done after an entire week of working with him, Miss *Ellickson*." Although Julia's voice was as smooth as honey, it lacked any sweetness. He could almost see her red lips clipping off each word with sharp precision. "All day long even? Why, goodness, surely there can't be *that* much information to cover. You must be new to this."

He raked his fingers through his hair. "Actually, she's not new to this at all."

Ben had ticked off her qualifications on that first morning, and at the time Joseph hadn't given a horse's behind about any of it. But he cared now. "Far as I can tell, the glowing recommendations accompanying her are too conservative."

"Whatever could you possibly learn from her? I mean, you're a grown man, fully capable—except for those silly bandages obstructing your vision. You're used to life on your own. I cannot see what more you could need to learn."

Joseph gave a frustrated sigh. "You'd be surprised."

"All right, so perhaps you needed help eating at first. How well I remember *that* disaster. My dress…" she began with a whine. "Well, never mind that. But if you were to ask me, she's just confusing things, complicating simple matters with all of her five o'clock, three o'clock, six o'clock, ten o'clock gibberish. In my humble opinion—"

"I don't remember asking for your humble opinion," Joseph ground out. If he hadn't heard the brazenness of her sentiments for himself, he might not have believed she could be so thoughtless.

"I was just trying to help." Syrupy innocence dripped like putrid tonic from her words. She sidled up next to him and perched a hand on his bicep, trailing her fingers down his forearm. "Of course you know that I just want the best for you. Our relationship means a great deal to me."

Struggling to keep his composure, he picked up her hand from his arm as though it were a dead fish, dropping it back down to her side. "Julia, *I* need to get to work. And you—*you* need to leave."

"Very well." She took a couple steps away from him when he heard her pivot firmly. "Oh my, how could I be so remiss," she breathed, coming to stand in front of him again. "I came to give you a message from Daddy. That large furniture order he entrusted you with…well he hopes you understand how *very* important it is that it be completed—on time."

Joseph clenched his fists, trying to remain calm. When her father had placed the order over four weeks ago, Joseph had agreed on the completion date, exactly three months from the time of the order. He'd agreed to front all expenses with the understanding that he'd find hearty compensation in the end. Normally he wouldn't have put so much on the line, but the money he'd make from this one job would more than cover wages; it would pay for an extensive addition onto his shop, as well as some new tools.

Three months gave ample time to finish each piece to the standard he was known for. After all, he didn't want to jeopardize his reputation, not to mention this job. Aaron had been at it alone now for four weeks and even though he hadn't alluded to any problems, Joseph had a horrible feeling that they were losing precious time.

Thinking about everything that hinged on the return of his sight, a thick knot balled his stomach.

"It'll be done," he finally said. If it didn't get completed, he wouldn't have a livelihood left to resume.

"Wonderful! I'll let Daddy know." Without another word, Julia clattered back toward the heart of town.

When the sound of her brisk footsteps faded into the distance, he sighed and rested the pads of his fingers over his bandaged eyes. Frustration and irritation weighed heavy on him. But mostly he felt sick that Julia had been so unkind to Katie.

"Listen, Katie, I'm sorry about that." He shook his head, shoving his hands on his hips. "I don't know what came over her. I mean, I haven't ever seen this side of her and I—"

"You don't have to explain." The understanding in her voice pierced his heart all the more.

"No, she shouldn't have—"

"It's fine. I don't need an explanation."

He stepped toward Katie, wanting to reach out to her, to encourage her the way she'd encouraged him so many times with words or with a simple touch. For a week she'd poured herself out for him, a stranger really. Enduring, encouraging and lending faith when his was flagging.

"I just want you to know—"

"Please. Not another word." He could hear the light brush of her hand against her dress. "Now, then, if you're ready, why don't we begin for the day?" The suggestion she made was bolstered by levity that seemed forced. And he'd spent enough time with her to hear the difference.

"No," he stated simply.

"No?" Her voice was almost a whisper.

"That's right. No." He offered her a sidewise grin. "I have another idea. A surprise."

She gave an audible sigh. "What might your surprise be?"

"Well, it'll still require your assistance—that is if that's all right with you?"

"Of course. What can I do?"

Tucking his hands in his pockets, he felt a wave of sudden shyness. "I thought a picnic might be just the right thing today. What do you think?"

"A picnic? That would be lovely." The smile in her voice gave Joseph all the encouragement he needed.

After he and Katie packed a picnic lunch of cold meat, cheese and bread, they set out with Boone at their side for a day by the stream, a place Joseph had loved for years.

"Boone knows his way better than any hound dog, but just in case he's having an off day, let me know when you spot a big cottonwood edging the stream." Joseph gently grasped Katie's arm as they walked. "If my guess is right, we should be about there."

"I think it's right in front of us, about an acre ahead."

He caught the faint gurgling sound of the mountain stream. "Is it the biggest tree out here?"

After a short pause, she answered, "Yes. There's an old rope hanging from one of the branches. Is that the tree you're looking for?"

Childhood memories with his brothers came rushing back. They'd scale the rope, hand over fist to sit on the thick branches that spread like sturdy arms from the tree's broad trunk. "That's the one." Breathing a sigh of relief, he quickened his pace. "It's been a while since I've been here. I didn't know how much I missed this place."

"I can see why. It's beautiful."

"It is, isn't it?" Tilting his head back, he breathed deep, invigorated by the clear mountain air. Although he wished he could see it for himself, he could conjure up a clear mental picture of the landscape. Tall pines infusing the area with rich, dark green patches of color. Slate gray rocks positioned here and there in an order all their own. The quaint little valley nestled in between the mountains.

"It must be a beautiful day," he said. "The sun's already bearing down and it can't be past ten o'clock. How 'bout if we find some shade so you don't get too hot?"

"I don't mind the sunshine if you don't."

Slowing his pace, he came to a stop, turning her toward him. Tenderly slipping his fingers down her slender arm, lightly covered in soft cotton fabric, he grasped her hand—so petite in his, so smooth, so perfect. When he held her hand, his nerve endings hummed to an altogether different awareness. He could hear her breath catch in her throat, could almost feel her pulse pounding a rapid beat at her wrist. Threading his fingers through hers, he gave her hand a gentle squeeze, thankful for her presence today.

"No…I don't mind sunshine at all." Joseph's throat had gone thick and suddenly raw. "Sunshine."

Every moment spent together made him desire her brightness in his life all the more. As much as he wanted to rein in his heart, he felt helpless to hold it back. He may as well have been trying to lasso the wind. Like warm embers glowing to life by a gentle breath, his feelings for Katie sparked brighter.

Was he playing with fire? What if he'd never see anything more than dim shadows for the rest of his life? He wouldn't strap a woman with that—especially not Katie. Even though she was used to being around blind people, he wouldn't think to saddle her with that until death do them part. She deserved a whole man, not half a man. No matter how seemingly normal she said his life could be without sight, he'd never be a whole man, able to see trouble before it came, able to protect the ones he loved, able to provide an adequate living.

No. He'd have to bat down his heart until he knew what his future held. If his vision was restored, there'd be nothing stopping him from pursuing Katie. But if his vision didn't change, he'd have to settle for simple friendship with her.

Shrugging off the pain searing his heart at the thought,

he released her hand and reached down to ruffle the fur on Boone's boxy head. "Come on, boy. I intend to enjoy the sunshine while I can."

Katie's hand still tingled from his touch. It felt as though his long, work-worn fingers lingered there, entwined in hers still, even though she and Joseph had been settled beneath the majestic tree for nearly an hour already. She brushed her fingertips across her lips. However gentle and tentative his grasp, the contact had affected her far more than she could've imagined.

And far more than she could allow to happen again.

She had to remain professional. She couldn't allow her emotions to wander about, unchecked. It just wasn't safe. Not when everything within her felt a strange pull to this man.

She stared down at the colorful scrap quilt where Joseph had stretched out on his back, hands stacked beneath his head. Her gaze roamed to his lips. The smile she'd glimpsed there the past few days had warmed her from the inside out. Her gaze lingered on his defined chest muscles stretching taut his cotton shirt. What would it be like to rest in the strong protection of his embrace? He was beautiful and honorable. So masculine and so… so taken!

She slammed her gaze down to where she'd clasped her hands in her lap. He obviously had an attachment to Miss Cranston that Katie would never be able to figure out. Why a humble man like Joseph would be attracted to a woman like Julia Cranston—so full of herself and thoughtless—was beyond Katie. She'd dismissed the possibility in the past couple of days, thinking perhaps the relationship was just one-sided, but after seeing the way he'd embraced Julia this morning, Katie's certainty crumbled like a day-old biscuit.

She was so confused. Had she read more into Joseph's touch and his sentiments than he'd intended? She must have.

But she hadn't missed the way he'd caressed her hand not more than an hour ago. Something had happened in that moment that had made them both struggle to breathe evenly. For some reason, his touch hadn't evoked the fear she'd battled since the attack a year ago, but instead filled her with comfort. And for the first time, she felt as if there might be hope for freedom.

Did she innately trust Joseph? She was beginning to think so. But as much as she felt a compelling draw toward him, she had to maintain her professionalism. Even if he did echo her feelings, he'd dismiss them if he discovered what had happened to her. There were just certain stains that could never be removed—no matter how hard you tried.

Katie drew her knees up to her chest, shutting out the shame that pricked her once again.

"So, Sunshine..." Joseph's soothing voice lifted her attention as though he'd gently crooked a finger beneath her chin. He rose on an elbow, facing her. "When you're not teaching, what do you enjoy doing?"

She peered at him. "We're not here about me, Joseph."

"That's where you're wrong," he responded with a shake of his finger. "What sort of things do you enjoy? Reading? Needlework? Big dogs that resemble bears?" A smile spread across his face as he reached to where Boone had dropped his hulking, dripping-wet form just off the blanket.

Katie laughed at the memory. "That was definitely not one of my better moments." She reached to stroke Boone's massive paws, noticing the fur that grew between his toes. "I'm sorry, boy. I hope you've forgiven me."

Joseph pushed himself up to sit and leaned back on his hands. "I'm sure he has. He doesn't hold grudges."

"Good. I'd hate to be on his bad side."

"Boone doesn't have a bad side."

"That's good to know. But you have to admit, it'd be unnerving to have a run-in with a dog like him. I thought I was a goner that first day on your porch."

She peered over at Boone, whose big brown eyes eased shut as though he was pretending not to eavesdrop on their conversation. In one deliberate, weighted movement, he rolled onto his back, his paws poking up in the air.

Katie laughed. "Not that you'd think he meant harm the way he looks now. You should see him, Joseph."

"Oh yeah?" he asked, smiling. "What's he doing?"

She leaned over to run her hand up and down the dog's long form. "He either wants his tummy scratched or he's sunning himself. He rolled over and has his feet stuck up in the air like wild flowers."

"He's done that since he was a young pup. He was one of Ben's strays, you know. Just a bag of bones with the most forlorn look in his eyes when we first found him. But Ben gave him lots of love and good care. I couldn't help myself from pitching in."

"The poor thing. That must've been horrible to see him like that."

"It was. But he's well-cared for now. Aren't you, boy?" Joseph ruffled the dog's fur. "Go on, Boone, play to your heart's content. It may be a while before we get back here."

When the dog lumbered off toward the stream, breaking out into an awkward lope, Katie turned back to Joseph. "Do you think he'd sense danger?"

Joseph nodded. "Boone's smart. He may look dead to the world the way he lazes about all day, but believe me, he has a keen awareness of people and what goes on around him. Far as I know, he's never bared his teeth at anyone, but I'm sure he'd sense it if someone meant harm. And I wouldn't be surprised if he did something about it, too."

Katie watched as Joseph leaned his head back for several moments. The sun splayed over his face in a golden glow, and a look of utter contentment spread across his features, his mouth curving slightly in a look of pure pleasure. The radiance diffused through the tree's silvery leaves enhanced his chestnut waves, turning them into strands of rich burnished bronze.

She couldn't deny the way she felt so safe and protected out here with Joseph. Ever since the attack, she'd avoided remote areas like this, determined to keep herself far from harm. But this place, this haven tucked away from the world, was so peaceful. Katie could easily see why Joseph had so many good memories here. She already felt refreshed.

"This was a good suggestion, coming out here today."

He snapped his attention toward her, his brows raised over the white bandage. "You didn't answer my question. What do you enjoy doing?"

Nervously, she picked at imaginary pieces of lint on her robin's-egg-blue print dress, then smoothed her hands down her skirt to her brown laced boots. She didn't like being the center of attention—especially after the attack. For the past year her job had been a good hiding place for her. She'd poured herself and every waking moment into her students. It was a small consolation that they weren't able to see her—that way she'd not have to worry about unwanted attention.

"Katie," he urged. "My question?"

The sideways grin Joseph sent her way did something uncommonly wonderful to her insides. Her stomach fluttered with the inexperience of a butterfly with new wings. Warmth crept through her like liquid sunshine.

"What makes Katie smile? What do you enjoy doing?"

"Hmm…what makes me smile?" she echoed, unable to keep her gaze from taking him in once again. "I'm glad to see you so relaxed."

"That I am, thanks to you. But we're not talking about me." He shifted to face her. "What about your family? Do you enjoy spending time with them? You must miss them."

Sliding her hands over her boots, she fingered each hook with great deliberation. "Oh, believe me, I do. But Uncle Sven and Aunt Marta are wonderful."

Joseph drew a knee up and draped his arm over it. "If things go well next week at my appointment like I think they will, do you think you'll go back home right away? I'd hate to see you take off so soon."

Katie sent up yet another silent prayer that he'd see again. But already she dreaded the emptiness she'd feel not being with him every day.

"I won't go home if I can help it." Unbidden, images of Frank Fowler, his eyes full of all manner of evil, played through her mind. "I have no desire to go back—" She cut her words off, her cheeks flushing hot beneath her hands.

"Can I ask why?"

"Why what?" Pulling her legs securely against her

chest, she tried to block out the shadowy images that had instantly and without mercy assaulted her thoughts.

"Why are you avoiding going home? Is there a problem?"

"Oh, it's nothing," Katie dismissed, brushing at her skirt, wishing she could just as easily brush away the memories. "I'm just enjoying my time in Boulder. That's all."

"Enjoying your time, huh? I've been a real pleasure to be around, haven't I?" He smirked. "Is there more to it?"

"Nothing more." She winced at the quaver in her voice.

"Katie, I may not be able to see you, but I can hear a difference in your voice. And I've never heard you sound like this before. Want to talk about it?"

When a loud crack sounded from the tree line, she jumped, unable to stop a small scream from piercing the air.

"What? What's wrong?"

Her heart lurched to her throat as she scrambled over to Joseph and clung to his arm. "Did you hear that?"

"Hear what?" He set a hand on hers.

She craned her neck, searching the dense grove of trees, sure she would find Frank there. "That—that loud crack?"

Squeezing her eyes tight, she fought in vain to ignore the memories that came now in crashing waves. Frank Fowler's leering gaze. His long, tapered fingers clamping down around her arms, her neck, her breasts. His cigar-tainted breath hovering over her like a poisonous cloud.

She bit back a cry and swallowed against the sickening lump in her throat. Tightened her grip around Joseph's arm as though her very life depended upon it.

When she opened her eyes, she saw Joseph's forehead creased in concern. "It's all right, Katie," he soothed, wrapping his arm around her shoulders. "I think what you heard was Boone. He probably stepped on a branch and snapped it in two."

She shot her gaze back toward the stream to see Boone emerge from the trees, his four sturdy legs braced and head hung low. As though building up momentum, he finally broke out into a full-body shake, sending tiny, sun-glinted droplets of water spraying from his glistening black fur.

"I—I'm sorry," she breathed, retreating to the other side of the blanket again.

"Please, don't apologize. Whatever has you so shaken, I want to help. I'm a good listener."

Katie fought for control over her emotions. She bent her head to her shoulder and swiped at the perspiration beading her brow. Rocking back and forth, she silently reminded herself that she was safe now, hundreds of miles away from Frank Fowler.

"I appreciate your concern," she finally squeezed out. "But it's something I'd rather not talk about."

"Sometimes it helps to talk." He slid his fingers slowly across the blanket toward her, as if searching for her hand. "Can you give me your hand, Katie?"

Katie stared at his outstretched hand, already missing the safe protection of his arm around her. Her heartbeat sped up inside her chest. She wanted to trust him, wanted to believe he could help her. Seeing the way his hands bore all the marks of hard work and sacrifice, she nearly groaned with the need to feel his strength, his support, his care.

"Listen. I realize you haven't known me long, but I mean it when I say I want to help." His words were offered like some lifeline.

Although she'd vowed that no one would ever know

what had happened over the past year, a desperate part of
her yearned to tell someone her secret. Someone she could
trust. Someone she could lean on. Someone she could run
to when the haunting memories nipped at her heels.

Like now.

She gulped back the all-too-familiar bile burning in her
throat, slid trembling hands to her face and covered her
mouth. Blinking hard, she fought to focus on Joseph's
strong, capable hand. But the images, the haunting memories clouded her vision, turning the bright day upside
down.

Frank Fowler's sharp, aristocratic features, his tall,
foreboding frame, loomed like a sinister demon. A highly
respected citizen, part-owner of the railroad and a deacon
in the church—some thought he was fit to be a genteel
lady's winning catch.

But Katie knew better. He was an awful, hurtful man,
who'd done the unthinkable, not once, but twice. He'd
stolen her—all of her—the first time in a dark copse of
trees. Leaving her dress torn and dirty, her simple trust in
others wounded and her purity sullied forever. He'd said
that she'd always be his. Left her with a pointed threat that
if she ever told a soul, someone she loved would die. He'd
said that no one would believe her anyway, not when her
father had lost a long and bitter court battle with him over
a land dispute. Frank had promised that she'd be the
shame of the community, a pawn in her father's hands,
lying in a bid to discredit Fowler.

Katie had been desperate to tell someone, but what if
Frank was right? She'd never forgive herself if something happened to a loved one because she couldn't keep
her mouth shut. She'd lived with the secret for twelve

months now. And she'd have to take it with her to her grave. No one could know.

She couldn't—wouldn't break her silence, now or ever.

"Katie? Are you all right?" Joseph's voice, his calming, rich voice, broke through her pain.

With quavering hands, she rubbed her eyes, wiped her perspiration-beaded brow and willed her body to stop quaking so. "Yes. I'm fine."

"Are you sure? Because you don't act like you're fine."

"Boone just startled me, that's all," she responded, her voice sounding almost normal again.

On a long pause, Joseph slowly braced his hand behind him again. "If you say so. But if ever you do feel like talking, I'm here."

She tried to shake off remnants of the haunting memories, but they were like tiny, stinging shards of glass. How she wished she could feel Joseph's hand around hers right now, assuring her everything would turn out fine. But she couldn't risk losing her job, and she definitely couldn't risk losing her heart. And she would, because no man—no matter how kind, how considerate, how upstanding—would want her once he knew she was soiled.

Inhaling slowly, she struggled to gather her composure as she rose to her feet. "We really should head back and get something accomplished today."

He gave his head a shake. "Far as I'm concerned, we're accomplishing plenty. I'm getting to know you a little better."

"That's what I mean," she countered, adjusting the pleats draping her skirt. "We shouldn't be wasting our time talking about me."

Joseph stood in one slow movement, every bit of his

tall, muscled form exuding strength and fluidity. He took one step her way and set his hands on her shoulders. "Katie…I want you to listen to me. You're not a waste of time. You're *far* from a waste of time."

ed, chuckled afterwards, and placed another log on the fire, stepped over and put his hands on her shoulders. Katie, I want you with us today...

Chapter Six

Joseph knew he should be relieved to have his brothers here, but for some reason he sensed this was more than just a shoot-the-breeze kind of visit.

He shifted uncomfortably in the wingback chair, feeling like a worm caught in the baking sun. Unable to stand the tension permeating the room, he finally broke the silence. "So, what's going on? I don't need eyes to see that you came here for a reason. I can't imagine what I've done this time. I've been on my best behavior with Katie." Which hadn't taken any effort since she was so easy to like. "We even spent the morning with a picnic down by the stream."

He couldn't miss the creaking of the sofa or the boots scuffing on the floor.

"So...who's going to talk?" he queried.

Ben cleared his throat from the winged-back chair opposite Joseph. "I guess what we're wanting to know is...how important is it that the furniture order be done on time?"

Foreboding crawled down his spine. "What do you mean, how important is it? It's important."

"*How* important?" Ben's reply was unnervingly measured.

"If the job doesn't get done, what'll that mean?" Zach's no-nonsense tone of voice grated on Joseph's nerves.

Joseph braced his elbows on his legs, steepling his fingers beneath his chin. "Aaron, I thought you said things were coming along. I believe those were the words you used. So are they?"

Aaron sucked in a deep breath. "Well, when we first st—"

"Just answer my question," Joseph ground out.

Zach huffed. "He will if you'll snap your jaw shut and let him."

"Quiet, Zach!" Joseph fired off, then shoved himself out of the chair and stood firm. "Is the job coming along or not?"

"Well, no," Aaron answered hesitantly.

He balled his fists, an unbelievably helpless feeling taunting him. "I thought you had everything under control."

"Take it easy," Ben urged. "He's been at it from early morning to late at night for almost five weeks straight."

Guilt for his quick temper pricked. He struggled to tamp down his irritation. "I know you've been working day and night, Aaron, but we've got to get this done."

"Remember, it's a very large order." Ben cleared his throat. "An entire restaurant worth of furniture."

Jamming his fists on his hips, Joseph felt every muscle in his body jerk taut. "So, what's the problem? Tell me."

"Ease up, Joe," Zach spoke from the sofa. "Aaron's been doing the best he can."

"The best he can?" he repeated. Raking his fingers

through his hair, he grasped at what little calm he had left. If it wasn't for his injury, he wouldn't be in this mess. "Aaron, tell me, what is the status with Mr. Cranston's order? Because so far every time I've asked you how things are going, you've said that things were fine. Have you been giving me the straight story or not?"

"Both." Drumming his fingers on the arm of the sofa, Aaron made a loud hissing exhale, then continued. "I don't see how the job's going to get done at the rate things are going. There's no way, Joseph, even with Ben and Zach helping out."

"What about when I'm able to work again after I get home from Denver?" He crossed his arms at his chest.

"You're forgetting one small thing," came Ben's voice, low and sobering. "What if you don't get your sight back?"

"That's *not* an option, Ben," Joseph shot over his shoulder.

The wingback chair scraped against the wood floor as Ben shifted. "We all want you to see again. But the fact remains that you might not distinguish more than the dark gray shadows you saw the first time I took off the patches. And the doctor in Denver may not have any alternatives for treatment."

His skin prickled. "I hate this!"

Balling his fists in front of his face, he wished he could just pound his eyes and bring back his vision.

Frustrated, he hastily stalked toward the entryway, coming to a sudden, humiliating stop when he collided with the wall. Gritting his teeth, he braced trembling hands up along the wall. Leaned his forehead against the cool plaster.

"Right now I can't make it down the street without

help and I may not have a business left, all because of this." Pressing hard against the wall, he added, "I *have* to see again."

"I hope you do, Joe-boy. Believe me, I do," came Aaron's voice just behind him. "I'm sorry. I should've said something sooner, but I didn't want to make things worse for you than they already are. Even if you do get your vision back, though, I'm afraid we still might be too far behind."

"Too far behind?" He pushed his fists against the wall, wanting to just shove them all the way through.

"I'll talk to Mr. Cranston." Aaron's voice was swathed with forced optimism. "I'm sure he'll understand if I have a chance to explain everything."

Joseph spun around and pulled his shoulders back. He wanted to lash out, take his anger and deep-seated desperation out on something or someone. Instead, he slowly headed back to the chair, inwardly gauging his steps as Katie had taught him.

"You're not going to go making excuses for me. Even if you did, I already know the answer." Turning, he sank down into the tall, padded chair. "Mr. Cranston is a shrewd businessman. We made a deal. Signed a contract. His hands are probably tied just like mine."

Joseph braced his elbow on the arm of the chair and leaned into his hand, attempting to massage away the pain in his head that suddenly bore down upon him without mercy. "You know as well as I do that I fronted all the money for materials and labor. I stand to lose the shop if we don't deliver on time."

"So, what do we do?" Aaron moved to stand next to Joseph.

"Right now I can't do much," he said, trying for a more contrite tone. "I know I've heaped a lot on you, Aaron—especially with Ellie not feeling well. And I know that you, Ben and Zach have been over there helping when you can. If you can just hang on a little longer till these bandages come off, I'll make it up to you. I promise."

"What about the finish work?" Aaron asked, dropping down to squat beside the chair.

Joseph pressed his fingers to his bandaged eyes. "When I return from Denver next week, I'll work night and day if I have to, to catch us up so we won't be late."

"But what if—" Aaron began.

"My vision doesn't return? It will. God *will* give me back my sight. He has to."

Joseph bit back a curse. He slapped the knife down on the counter, resisting the urge to shake off the throbbing pain assailing his finger. He'd been cutting vegetables—Katie's latest lesson—and had cut more than just the carrot.

"What's wrong?" Katie approached his side, her arm lightly brushing against his.

He covered one hand with the other, trying to snuff out the anger that had sparked so quickly. "Nothing."

He was learning the hard way that he couldn't afford to let his focus drift or he was vulnerable to mishaps. Every task he did seemed to require double the effort, double the energy, double the focus. And double the patience.

He'd been agitated *all* day. Couldn't seem to keep his mind on any task—not after his brothers had paid him a visit last evening. He'd lain awake through the night wracking his brain, searching for a way to complete the job on time.

Katie lifted his hand, her touch light, sure and warm. "It's not *nothing*. You're bleeding, Joseph." Cradling his hand in hers, she drew him over to the washbasin and began pumping the squeaky handle. "We'll get this cleaned up."

"I can do it." He pulled his hand from her grasp.

"If you insist," she stated, stepping away from him and leaving him instantly wishing for her closeness again. "Can you tell me where to find something to put on that?"

"On my cut?"

"No, your wounded pride," she shot back.

He winced. "So I'm irritated. You would be too if you cut yourself like a youngster."

He directed her to where he kept medicinal supplies while he ran his forefinger under the stream of water, feeling it trickle into the wound. If he could see, he'd be able to handle the situation easily. Knowing he couldn't see past the bandages covering his eyes firmly established his irritation like a stubborn weed with tentaclelike roots that crept into his dignity.

After she'd returned, she gently wrapped his hand in a cloth and led him over to the table. "You seem to forget that other people cut themselves, too. It doesn't matter whether you can see or not, it's bound to happen."

"Other people can see whether they're bleeding all over the floor," he retorted, feeling justified in his response.

She pulled out two chairs. "Here, sit down while I bandage your finger."

He sat down directly in front of her and fought the urge to ask her to leave. Fought even harder the sensations provoked by the way she cradled his hand in hers.

"The cut's pretty deep," she breathed, gently turning

his hand as though to get a better look. "Maybe we should have Ben take a peek at it. You might need a few stitches."

"No." Every muscle in his body pulled taut. "I don't need Ben to take a look at it."

"Are you sure?" She gently dabbed at his finger with a cloth. "I could go and find—"

"No! I said I'm fine. I don't need him."

"Joseph Drake, you are as grumpy as a wounded bear."

He couldn't argue with that. Why was it so hard to submit to the soothing ministrations of this one who cared, who didn't see his weakness as something to exploit? For several moments he sat there, torn between wanting to distance himself from her and wanting to trust her in his vulnerability.

Refusing to center on the upheaval he felt, he decided to focus on her hands, so smooth and tender on his skin. With the faintest of strokes from the pads of her thumbs, she began to calm the tension that commanded his body.

"Here," she said, handing him a cloth. "Apply pressure to stop the bleeding while I get a wrap prepared."

He did as she'd directed, acutely aware of the slightest brush of her legs against his.

"What's wrong, Joseph?" Her words were guarded.

"It's just a cut. Like I said, I'm fine."

"That's not what I mean." She cradled his hand in hers again and carefully lifted the cloth from his finger. "Good. It looks like the bleeding's stopped. We'll get this fixed in no time." She began applying an ointment to his cut, her touch so gentle. "You seem on edge. You have been since I showed up this morning. Did something happen?"

On a long exhale, he felt his tight neck muscles relax a little. "I'm sorry. I just have a lot on my mind."

"Anything I can help you with?"

"No." With a wry grin he added, "Not unless you're as good at building furniture as you are teaching."

When she stopped her ministrations, he could feel her gaze on him. "Is there a problem out at the shop?"

"Yes. You could say that," he admitted, then related the circumstances he faced.

"What are you going to do? I mean is there any way Mr. Cranston could postpone the date a few weeks?"

As she began to wind a bandage around his finger, he was sure she was unaware of the way her warm, comforting touch sent sensations through him.

Straight to his heart.

It seemed there was no way to keep from being affected by Katie. He'd have to send her away to accomplish that, and he wasn't sure he was willing to go to that extent. In just two short weeks she'd become a part of his life. A bright, promising part of his present and hopefully his future.

"There's no way he'll postpone," he answered, distracted by the tightening in the pit of his stomach. "Either we deliver on the date, or lose it all."

"Could Zach or Ben help Aaron out?"

"They're already pitching in where they can. But there's only so much they can do. Ben's a great doctor and Zach's a natural with horses, but of their own admission, they're not cut of the same cloth as Aaron and me."

"Oh, I see." She secured the bandage with a knot.

When she finished, he set his elbow on the table, holding his hand up to ward off the throbbing. Her touch had been so comforting that he wished she hadn't been so efficient.

"What about you, Joseph?" Katie rose and crossed to the sink where she pumped water. "I'm sure you could do things in the shop."

Shifting uncomfortably in his chair, Joseph figured she might as well have kicked him in the shin. "I never thought I'd say this but you're starting to sound like Julia."

"I'm sorry." She set a hand on his shoulder. "I didn't mean for the suggestion to sound unfeeling." Katie grasped his good hand. "Here's some water."

He felt the cold stoneware and gripped the cup as she sat down in front of him again. "Thanks."

"What I'm trying to say is…why *couldn't* you try some of the work out there? From what I hear and the proof I've seen, you're a master at the craft. Couldn't you—"

"Don't be ridiculous." Gulping down the water, he swiped the moisture from his lips with his shirtsleeve and set the cup on the table. "If you've forgotten already, I sliced my finger cutting vegetables." He held the bandaged finger in front of him. "With a saw or chisel in my hand, I'd be a bloody mess."

"No, you wouldn't," she shot back.

Joseph shook his head. "You're not being realistic."

"No, Joseph. I'm being completely realistic. You're just being stubborn. I told you on our first day together that I wouldn't coddle you, but help you to find independence." She rose and pushed in her chair. "And that's what I'm here to do."

He drew his lips into a grim line, not sure whether to be angry or relieved. She could be so compassionate and then turn right around and goad him without shame.

"Why couldn't Aaron spend his time putting the furniture together, while you focus on the finish work and sanding? Don't you depend a lot on touch to do that kind of thing?"

With a grunt, he slouched in the chair, sliding his long legs out in front of him. "Nice thought," he said, draping one boot over the other. "But it'd never work."

"Why wouldn't it work?" He could hear her gathering the medical supplies on the table. "I see you often, smoothing your hands over things as though searching for imperfections. It's in you, Joseph. You can't get away from it."

"Well, I'll be a dad-burned donkey if it ain't Sam Garnett!" Mr. Heath, the mercantile owner proclaimed. "How have you been?"

The shopkeeper's jubilant greeting perked Katie's curiosity. She cocked an ear toward the door without turning away from the elegant hair combs she'd been inspecting. She was trying to decide which one to buy with some of the pay she'd received yesterday, at the end of her second week of work.

Honestly, she hadn't wanted to take one dime from Joseph, feeling more than ever that her time with him was not a job at all, rather a privilege, a pleasure. He'd gotten visibly irritated when she'd balked at taking the envelope. Said he wasn't interested in charity. Insisted she take the money.

"Mr. Heath, you're a sight for sore eyes. It's good to see you," the stranger called, his deep voice echoing in the room.

"You, too, Sam. You, too. It's not often we get a city-slick lawyer in these parts."

From the corner of her eye, she saw the two men

shaking hands across the long glass-front counter. Even from her vantage point she noticed that the man wore a crisp three-piece suit, professionally tailored.

"What brings you to these parts?" Mr. Heath inquired.

"I need to tie up some loose ends on my folks' land since they passed away."

"We sure are sorry about their passing. They were good people." Mr. Heath's voice went unusually quiet.

"Thank you." After a short pause, Sam added, "That wave of influenza hit hard last winter, didn't it?"

"Yes, sirree. But thank goodness it didn't last long. Since Ben Drake came back from his schoolin' and started practicin' his medicine here it seems like we've been fairin' better through things like this."

"Ben's a good doctor. I've no doubt about that." Sam took his rounded top hat from his head, tapping it into perfect form.

"So, will you be headin' back to the big city right away? Or can you stay a spell?"

Katie held up a comb as though examining it, but her attention kept getting pulled to the man named Sam. She didn't feel the same unnerving wariness she normally had around strange men, and that surprised her. Maybe it was because he was a native to the area. Or maybe it was the way he'd been received by Mr. Heath like a richly decorated hero come home from war.

"I thought it'd do me good to take in some fresh mountain air to clear my head." His voice swelled with satisfaction. "I decided to take a month's leave from the law firm and mix a little business with pleasure."

"If that ain't a fine how-do-you-do!" Mr. Heath slapped Sam on the shoulder. "Me and the missus—why we'll be lookin' forward to havin' you over to our place for supper. Bet you don' get cookin' like the wife's back in the big city."

"Probably not. I'm looking forward to that already. Thank you for the invitation." Sam reached into his pocket and pulled out a slip of paper. "Here I came in to say hello and get these few things, and I end up with a dinner invitation. I believe I'm getting the better end of the deal."

"Ya say ya need a few things, do you? Well, what can I do you for?"

Katie briefly glanced toward the exchange and listened to the conversation, all the while peering at the same comb she'd held for the past several moments. She didn't mean to eavesdrop but couldn't help it. The wood floors and high ceilings only aided in carrying the sound of their voices.

The tall stranger, whose dark hair accentuated his almost Romanesque features, handed the list to Mr. Heath. "I'll be staying at Mrs. Royer's boarding house, so I won't need much."

"Don't think there's a selfish bone in that woman's body. She'll take good care of you. Mother you till you wish you were eight again." Mr. Heath quickly perused the list. "I'll get these things. You just make yourself at home." He turned to start filling the order and called over his shoulder, "You might notice some changes we've made since you were last here."

When Sam turned and leaned against the counter, his arms folded across his chest, Katie snapped her attention back to the combs. She stared down at them, wondering why she was so curious about this man.

"It's good being back in your store," Sam called out.

"I can't count how many times Joseph and I would stop by and try to finagle you out of a licorice whip or a peppermint stick in return for a good hour's labor."

Katie's pulse skittered. Was he talking about Joseph Drake? Were the two of them friends?

"You were good help, too," came Mr. Heath's response from the far side of the room. "That is, when you weren't tryin' to impress some lil' lady. Couldn't get an honest *minute* of labor outta ya then."

She bit back a smile at the thought of Joseph and this man, vying for some girl's attention. And as she easily recalled the feelings she'd had when she'd held Joseph's hand while doctoring his cut, she couldn't imagine him ever having to work too hard for any girl's affection.

After several more moments Sam said, "You *have* made some additions to the mercantile. Business must be good."

"Had to add those two new rows of shelving to house the extra goods. Our customers expect an ample selection, you know." Mr. Heath poked his head out from the back room. "And speaking of Joseph, take a look at that new counter he made. She's a beauty. Ain't another one like it."

Katie glanced at the beautiful counter in front of her. Another tribute to Joseph's expert craftsmanship. Another reason why she had to help him get his life back again.

When she spotted Sam approaching from out of the corner of her eye, she tried her best to appear fully transfixed on the items before her.

"Good afternoon, ma'am. I don't believe I've had the pleasure of making your acquaintance." He stopped next to her and held out his hand. "My name is Samuel Garnett. And yours?"

She stared stupidly up at him, and with minimal grace shoved her hand toward him. "I'm Katie Ellickson."

When he gently grasped her hand in his, her cheeks grew warm. Much to her chagrin, her embarrassment had never been easily hidden, not when her fair skin told an undisguised story.

She abruptly pulled her hand from his. "It's nice to meet you, Mr. Garnett."

"You must be new to town. I don't believe I remember seeing you here the past few times I've made it back. I would *never* forget a face like yours." He studied her face, his liquid brown gaze intent.

"New?" She gulped. "Yes, I moved here from Iowa a little over two weeks ago."

"What brought you here?" When he glanced down at her finger as though looking for a ring, her hands trembled.

"I—I came to start a new life." She immediately cringed at her ridiculous choice of words, no matter how true they were.

"The old life not so good, eh?" His eyebrows arched over his dark, penetrating eyes.

"Oh, no—I mean—it was fine. Well…more than fine." She shook her head and laughed nervously. "I'm terribly sorry. I don't know what has come over me."

"Forgive me," he said, offering an apologetic grin. "I didn't mean to make you uncomfortable nor did I mean to pry. I guess it's just the lawyer coming out in me. You know, always wanting to know every little fact. Let me try again."

Backing up a few paces, he started toward her. "Good afternoon. I don't believe I've ever met you. My name is Samuel Garnett. And yours?" His eyes twinkled with delight.

She hesitated for a moment, unsure whether she should run from this very bold man, or stay put. That he was a longtime friend of Joseph made her relax a little. When she peered up at him, noticing the kindness in his strong features, she held her hand out to him and smiled. "I'm Katie Ellickson."

"Well, Miss Ellickson, I hope we'll be seeing each other again. Perhaps at church tomorrow?" Brows raised, he tilted his head toward her, as if waiting for a response.

"Yes, Mr. Garnett. I'll see you at church."

"I have your order together, Sam," Mr. Heath called out.

Mr. Garnett slid his gaze to the counter and pointed to one of the combs. "My vote is this one," he whispered, giving her a warm smile. "A sure compliment to your beauty."

Katie felt her cheeks flush. Again. He was a charmer—that was for sure. But she didn't know why in the world she was responding like some smitten schoolgirl.

"What do you keep yourself busy with besides lawyering?" Mr. Heath's booming voice filled the room. "Is there a missus yet? Young 'uns?"

He started back over to Mr. Heath. "I've been so busy at the law office with all the movement west, I haven't had time for much else."

Katie felt his gaze directed her way and angled a glance to see him leaning casually against the counter on one elbow. Staring at her as though there was nothing else in the room.

"I actually might start thinking about settling down," he continued with the hint of a smile. "Especially if I happen to find the right lady."

Chapter Seven

"Why is it so unbelievable to think that Joseph has feelings for you?" Ellie prodded. She graced Katie with one of those cat-that-ate-the-canary kind of smiles, and rubbed a hand lightly across her protruding belly.

Exasperated, Katie gave her friend a wide-eyed look. "I'm his teacher. I seriously doubt he's thinking beyond that."

"Just because you're his teacher doesn't mean he couldn't develop feelings for you."

Raising the dainty flowered teacup to her mouth, Katie breathed in the warm cinnamon scent, then took a sip. She remembered how agitated Joseph had been yesterday after he'd cut himself. And then when she'd suggested he could work in the shop without sight, he'd gotten downright belligerent.

No. She doubted very much that he felt anything but irritated by her.

"I'm sure he feels nothing of the sort," Katie dismissed. "I'm more like a thorn in his flesh than a rose in his garden."

But then she replayed, as she had countless times, the

softness with which Joseph had touched her, the gentleness and respect with which he'd treated her on their picnic. His words had been like warm caresses and his momentary touch had set her off-kilter. Even the memory incited the same skittering feeling all the way down her spine to her toes.

Surely she must be reading into all of that. How could he possibly have feelings for her when he had so much to deal with as it was? His lack of sight. His work. A general upheaval in his life. And there was always Julia, with her thoughtless, manipulative, even abrupt, ways. Julia, with her striking dark tresses, porcelain-white complexion and piercing emerald gaze. She was a beauty, probably pure as the wind-driven snow. Probably flawless in every way.

Except in the way she treated Joseph.

Vindictiveness rose within Katie like a sword unsheathed. She'd never felt so hostile toward another person, so hungry to dish back the same thoughtless handling.

She tried to rein in the errant emotion, chiding herself for being so hard on Julia. Maybe there was an understanding side of Miss Cranston that had drawn Joseph in the first place.

If so, Katie just couldn't seem to look past the obvious manipulation she saw happening. The woman had conveniently been walking in the direction of Joseph's home on more than one occasion this week and had stopped once, keeping his attention for a good hour with some drivel about getting nominated to cochair the Boulder Ladies' Committee. Katie had gladly made herself scarce at the time, although she couldn't help stealing glances of the two out on the porch, noticing how clingy Julia was with Joseph, like a barnacle hugging tight to a ship's hull.

Shaking off the disturbing image, she folded her hands in her lap. "Joseph has so much to think about right now. I'm sure he has no thoughts of me other than as a teacher."

"Whatever you say." Ellie shrugged, tucking strands of strawberry blond hair into her loose braid. "But Aaron and I—even Ben—agree that he's a different man since you've come. You've been good for him, Katie." The mischievous smile she sent Katie faded fast when she stood from the table. She winced and set hands to the small of her back.

"Is something wrong?" Katie asked.

"No, no. I'm fine." Ellie fixed a smile on her face. "You definitely have a way with Joseph. We *all* think so."

"I'm sure you're just noticing that Joseph is feeling more comfortable with himself and his surroundings. He's been getting to know his world through touch," she said, unable to ignore the ready memory of just that. The way his fingertips irrevocably branded her flesh with absolute tenderness.

Bowing her head, she blinked hard and glanced down at the handkerchief she twisted in her hands. "I do think he's beginning to trust me, though. I'm glad of that."

"Well, that's something." Setting a fist to her waistline, Ellie dabbed at the perspiration beading her upper lip with her white apron. "You've gotten a lot farther with him than the rest of us would've been able to."

A sudden flush worked its way up Ellie's cheeks, inciting another swell of concern in Katie. "Do you need to sit down?"

Ellie trailed her hands down her dress, plucking at the wide stretched pleats. "It seems like these days, with less than a month to go, and the baby being so low, I'm more comfortable on my feet."

Standing, she moved over to grasp Ellie's hand, unable to shake the concern she felt. "Can I do something for you?"

"Really, don't worry." Ellie smiled and squeezed Katie's hand. "I hope you don't mind me saying so, but I'd be elated if Joseph did have feelings for you. You'd be the perfect sister-in-law."

"Ellie! How can you say that?"

"Because you'd be wonderful. Besides, I'm tired of being the only woman among the Drake brothers," she added, swiping her brow and taking a deep breath as though she'd just run a mile. "Those brothers need to each find themselves a bride. And I've decided that you'd be the perfect start."

Crossing her arms at her chest, Katie shook her head. "You're picking the wrong flower in the field here."

"You can't stop me from hoping."

Ellie was right. Katie couldn't stop her from hoping. At times she could barely stop herself from hoping. Too often for her own comfort, she'd catch herself daydreaming about Joseph, fancying herself as his bride. Sharing a full, beautiful life with him.

But it seemed as if the more she dreamed of that, the more her shame overshadowed her like a threatening storm cloud.

Swallowing past the lump in her throat, she tried to remain levelheaded. "You're right. I can't stop you from hoping. But let me assure you that nothing like that could ever happen."

"You two are perfect for one another. Besides…" Ellie added, resting her arms on her belly. The scrupulous perusal she gave had Katie squirming. "I've seen that *look* in your eyes when you speak of him—or when you spotted him at church."

Katie pinned her gaze to the rag rug. "What *look* is that?"

Out of the corner of her eye, she saw Ellie slowly twirl around like a belle at a ball. "That starry-eyed, soft look that happens when a woman…feels something for a man."

Katie unsuccessfully bit back a smile. At times like this, she wished she was better at schooling her expressions. "I won't dispute your observation," she said simply.

"Ah ha! I knew it!" Ellie clasped her hands beneath her chin. "Just last night I was telling Aaron that—"

"But—" she interrupted, holding out her hand, "—that's the extent of it."

Katie crossed to the window. For several moments she stared out through clear glass at the protected valley, bathed in a late-afternoon August glow. Would there ever be beauty like that, all warm and promising in her life? Maybe she was selling Joseph short. Maybe he wouldn't allow her past to define their future. Maybe he could look beyond her shame.

What was she thinking? She knew how upright men wanted their brides unstained. Fowler had told her as much. He'd hissed the reality in her ear, his words striking her like buckshot, piercing her in so many ways that she didn't know how to begin putting herself back together.

Turning away from the window, she passed a wary glance to her friend. "There are things from my past that—" Katie stopped midsentence when Ellie grabbed her abdomen and bent over, drawing in a sharp breath.

"Ellie, what's wrong?" She scurried over and set a hand of support at Ellie's back. "What's going on?"

A muffled cry came through clenched teeth. After several moments Ellie straightened, her hands clamped to her abdomen.

"Have you had pain like this before?"

"Not sh-sharp cramping like this." She gasped for air. "But I'm sure it's nothing."

"That wasn't nothing," Katie argued. She helped Ellie to a chair, noticing how her friend's whole body trembled. "I'm going to go get Ben and Aaron."

Ellie snapped out her arm and grabbed for Katie. "No, I'll be fine. Please don't bother them."

"Sorry," Katie responded, patting her friend's hand. "But I'm certain they'll want to know."

"Katie, really, Aaron can't afford to be gone from the shop right now," Ellie pleaded, her brow beaded with perspiration, her cheeks flushed. "There's too much to do. I don't want him worrying about me."

Dipping a washcloth in cool water from the basin, she laid it on Ellie's forehead. "I understand how urgent things are in the shop. But I know he'll agree that you take precedence over anything there. Now, I'm going to help you to bed and then, if you'll be all right for a short while—"

"I'll be fine—I'm fine now. You don't need to go." Her hands drifted to her protruding stomach where she carefully caressed the life inside. "Please, I'm feeling better already."

"I'm not taking any chances. This baby could be on the way and I'll feel much better knowing that you're well-cared for."

After she got Ellie situated in bed, she ran the one-and-a-half-mile distance to Boulder, all the while praying that God would help Ellie and the little baby yet unborn.

Bounding up the boarded walk to Ben's office, she flung the door open. "Ben, are you here?" she called between panting breaths. She peeked into the back room, then ran out of the office and to the mercantile. "Mr. Heath, do you have any idea where Ben Drake is?"

"Well, yes, as a matter of fact, he was just here. Said he was gonna be stoppin' by to pay Joseph a visit."

She called her thanks on the way out the door and hurried over to Joseph's home. Picking up her skirts, she leaped up the three steps to his porch and rapped on the door.

"Ben, are you here?" Katie called out.

The door swung open. "Katie, what's wrong?" Ben's face was etched with obvious concern.

"It's Ellie. She needs you. Something's wrong."

"What happened?" He stepped out onto the porch.

"I—I'm not really sure. I just know she didn't look good. She's in pain. Cramping. I'm very worried about her."

"Joseph, is Aaron still in the shop?" Ben called.

"Yes, he should be." Joseph emerged from the front room. "You go ahead and get what you need at the office, Ben. We'll have Aaron meet you down there."

Ben called his agreement as he ran down the walk. After Katie rushed behind Joseph's house to the shop and alerted Aaron, she jogged back to find Joseph waiting for her.

"I do hope Ellie will be all right," Katie choked out, winded. Her strength bolstered just being in Joseph's presence.

"She's in good hands," he assured her. "Ben will take good care of her—Aaron, too."

Pulling in a deep breath, she walked alongside him to the front porch, grateful for his company. In a very unladylike fashion, she collapsed next to Joseph on the steps, resting her head in her hands in an effort to calm herself.

When she felt his gentle touch at the small of her back, her heart skipped a beat. A tingling sensation, thick as honey, spread through her entire body and her heart threatened to beat right out of her chest at the reassuring warmth of his touch.

When she hauled herself to sit up straight, his hand remained settled, a warm claim at her back. A shiver worked down her spine, and she was certain he could feel her heart beating right through her rib cage. Her head swam with emotions, sensations that made her light-headed.

"It's good you were there, Katie." His caring tone made her all the more weak-kneed. "Ellie needed you."

"Yes, but I should've been more attentive to her." A wave of guilt assaulted her. "At first when I asked, she said she was fine. And then I was so busy telling her why it wasn't possible that you and I—"

She clapped a hand over her mouth, downright mortified at her careless choice of words. Shoving herself up to standing, she established some much-needed space between herself and Joseph. His touch was way too disarming and threatened to break down her protective walls.

He stood, edging slightly closer. "Why it wasn't possible that you and I what?" His voice was low and smooth.

Her knees began to tremble beneath her soft yellow day dress. The air grew stiflingly thick as she peered up at him, her stomach pulling taut at his all-consuming focus. Sliding her gaze over his form, her focus riveted on his shoulders. They were firm, thick with muscle and broad enough to support the biggest burden. In the short time she'd known him she'd seen him bear trials a lesser man would've buckled under.

Oh, that she could trust him with her troubles.

Moving her gaze down to his muscle-roped arms, she quivered. Katie could almost feel his sinewy arms, placed protectively around her shoulders, shutting out her fears. She closed her eyes, indulging herself in the notion.

Emotions that rocked her deep inside, intensified.

She squeezed her eyes tight, willing the feelings not to surface. Not now. If she couldn't control her emotions, she'd have to quit working with him. And he'd made so much progress. He'd been giving a grand effort in his training, and if his vision didn't return, there was still so much more she could show him, so much more she could open up for him.

Besides, she was only making it harder on herself. There was sure to come a time when the sparks that arced between them would fade from brilliance, snuffed out by her past.

"Katie, are you there? You're awfully quiet," he breathed, easing her back to reality.

Her entire body trembled now, an uncontrollable shaking that stemmed from deep within. For months she'd run ragged, fighting to keep the walls she'd erected firmly in place. If someone breached that barrier, the secret she'd diligently hidden would be exposed.

But right here…right now, she ached to have a shoulder to lean on. An arm to support her.

She startled as Joseph settled his hands on her shoulders, then lightly slid them down her arms.

"You're trembling," he said, his voice husky.

She swallowed hard, staring up at him. Hugging her arms tight to her chest, she fought against her unruly emotions.

Every nerve ending sprang to life as he trailed his fingers, whisper-soft, to the nape of her neck. Cradling her head in his hand, he inched closer and drew her to his chest.

Katie stiffened, feeling his hard upper body beneath her cheek. Curling her arms snuggly at her chest, she warred against the innate need to feel protected, cared for. She teetered on the edge. But as he lightly stroked her hair, trailing his fingers to her back, calm settled over her like a thick blanket.

His warm breath filtered through her thick tresses and she melted against his chest. Drawing in a quivering breath, she took in the woodsy male scent that was Joseph. She uncurled one fist, placing her fingertips reverently against the rigid muscular wall in front of her, feeling his untapped power beneath her touch.

He rested his chin on top of her head, and a rush of warmth poured over her as though she'd just stepped into glorious, welcoming sunshine.

"I know that you probably regret coming out here to work with me." His voice grew rough with emotion. "Even on my good days, I've taken out a lot of frustration on you."

She wanted to stop him, realizing that he'd misunderstood her, but she couldn't find her voice. She was completely overcome by the sensations he stirred inside her.

"Don't let my gruff exterior scare you, Katie. I'd never—never hurt you." Like a hearth fire's soothing glow, his husky voice penetrated the swirl of emotion. "I care too much about you."

Joseph could kick himself for how he'd responded to Katie yesterday—embracing her like he did and saying what he had. But she'd been so upset about Ellie—and rightly so. Ellie was not doing well and Ben had put her on strict bed rest until the baby arrived.

Joseph's heart had squeezed at the compassion and care he'd seen in Katie, and he'd relished the few moments when he'd held her close. It had felt so right. *She* had felt so right in his arms. It had taken every bit of strength he had to finally release her.

Now, as he stood outside the church waiting for Ben, he still didn't feel as though he had control over his traitorous heart. He'd done his best to rein in his runaway emotions around Katie, but his heart beat sure and strong, the ancient rhythm pervading every breath, thought and moment. Even knowing she was most likely there in church this morning set his pulse to pounding.

Everything about her tugged at Joseph's heart, making him want to comfort her, encourage her, protect her. And for some reason, he couldn't help but wonder if maybe breaking through the barriers she'd set up around herself might be the biggest challenge he'd ever faced.

But considering his uncertain future, he couldn't allow himself to get too close. He'd spent far too much time thinking of Katie. The way her gentleness soothed his deep-seated fear and the way her patience had given him needed confidence. She'd made him feel like a man again.

Turning his face to the cool breeze, he marveled at how he'd become captivated so quickly. But from what he'd heard, she'd had the same effect on others, too, winning hearts like some long-lost heroine.

"Hey, there, Joseph!" a voice called out, startling him from his musings. "I've been looking all over for you."

Joseph turned toward the familiar voice. "Sam?"

"It's me, all right!" Dry grass crunched beneath Sam's feet as he approached Joseph. "Am I ever glad to see you."

Joseph stretched out his hand to give Sam a firm handshake and wasn't surprised to find himself pulled into a manly embrace. When Sam released his hold, Joseph noted how his friend seemed more filled out than the last time he'd seen him. His shoulders felt broader and his chest fuller.

"Good to have you back in town, Sam," he said, resisting the awkwardness that suddenly assailed him.

But if anyone could put him at ease, it was Sam. His friend had a way of making others feel comfortable, no matter what the circumstance. Joseph would never forget that day, years ago, when thirteen-year-old Jacob returned to school after sustaining burns in a barn fire. Humiliation had been written all over the boy's face as he clearly avoided interaction with other kids. But at the first recess, Sam made a point to draw him into a game of kickball. From then on, it was as though everyone else seemed to know how to respond.

"It's good to be back," Sam replied, his voice sounding deeper than Joseph remembered.

"I heard that you arrived yesterday."

"I can believe that. Boulder's gossip mill seems to be in perfect working order."

He threw his head back and laughed, knowing full well that he'd been the brunt of informational tidbits lately. "Ha! That's an understatement. And to think we used to make sport out of feeding it, then watching it fly into high gear."

"We were shameless, you and me. I'm not sure how we both ended up riding the right side of the fence."

He grinned at the strand of memories that inched through his mind. "Glad I got it out of my system when I was young."

"I'm sorry about your accident. I heard about it when I got into town." Sam's voice sounded solemn but not pitying, and for that Joseph was thankful. "How are you getting along?"

Joseph pulled his shoulders back, not surprised at the way Sam cut a sure path right through formalities. "Ah... I'm great, just have to put up with this ridiculous costume for another day or two." He gestured to the bandage circling his head. "Should be good as new in a couple of days."

"I understand you're going to go see a doctor in Denver?"

"I leave tomorrow." Joseph nodded, shoving his hands into his pockets. "Are you planning on being in town for a while?"

"That's the plan." Sam gave a long exhale. "What do you say we get in some fishing while I'm here?"

"I wouldn't miss an opportunity to show you up with a pole again. You and I both know who always caught the biggest—"

"Well, well, well," Sam breathed, his voice thick with adoration. "There she is."

"Who?" Amused, Joseph couldn't help but grin.

"Only the most beautiful woman in Boulder. Wait— make that *this* side of the Rockies." In the long moment of silence that followed, Joseph could almost imagine his friend's adoring gaze fixed on the little lady as though she were a rare jewel. "I was smitten by her at first sight, Joseph. Smitten."

"That captivating, eh?" Curiosity nipped at him like a pack of unruly pups.

"Yep. That captivating," Sam agreed in a case-closed kind of tone.

"You never were one to miss a pretty lady. You've had a soft spot for them as long as I've known you."

"What about you?" Sam shot back with a nudge to Joseph's arm. "If my memory serves me right, I think we had our fair share of fights over girls throughout the years. We scrapped over the best of them, didn't we, Joseph?"

He winced. "Maybe we did."

"No maybes about it. That's probably why neither of us got married. In the end, we always deferred to one another."

On a low chuckle, he nodded his agreement. "So, who is she? I probably know her."

"I wouldn't be so sure. She said she's new to Boulder. I met her yesterday—right after I arrived on the afternoon stage. What a way to start off my stay here."

Was Sam referring to Julia? He always did seem drawn to brunettes. And if he kept himself as tailored as he did the last time Joseph had seen him, then Julia was sure to notice.

It had started irritating Joseph how Julia couldn't seem to help dropping hints about his attire. Apparently she preferred a fancy three-piece suit, and frankly, he'd wear nothing rather than be confined to a suffocating suit day in, day out.

"Come with me. I want you to meet her." Sam grasped Joseph's arm and started walking.

"Nah. Really, I don't need to meet her." He slowed to a stop. If it was Julia, there'd be awkwardness that he had every hope of avoiding.

"Are you sure?" Sam spoke low, leaning toward him. "I want to know what you think. You're a good judge of character."

Wanting to be good-natured about this, Joseph shoved down his unease—after all, it wasn't every day he got to do a favor for his friend. He conceded with a sigh.

"That's the spirit!" Sam maneuvered Joseph forward once again. "I just want to know what you think of her."

"Just don't say I never did anything for you."

"Good morning, ma'am." Sam's gallantry had the corner of Joseph's mouth quirking.

He sniffed the air around him, searching for Julia's strong perfume on the breeze. It'd be a dead giveaway this close, but surprisingly the air was free of the choking scent.

When Joseph felt Sam ease to a stop, he sidestepped out of his friend's grasp.

"I'd like to introduce you to a friend of mine." The timbre of Sam's voice was as smooth as a finely sanded heirloom. "This is Joseph Drake, we go way back. Joseph, this is—"

"Good morning, Joseph."

He snapped his focus down, furrowing his brow. "Katie?"

"You know each other?" Sam chuckled.

Gritting his teeth, Joseph tried not to show his shock, but confusion swirled around him. A stranger, he'd bargained on, seeing as how new people were moving into the area almost daily. And Julia, he wouldn't have been shocked by because she seemed to have a knack for spreading her presence around town.

But Katie? Sam had set his sights on Katie?

Joseph swallowed hard, the hair prickling at the back of his neck as the realization sank in. A herd of emotions raced through his mind, the front-runner being irritation. That Sam was referring to Katie had him thoroughly unsettled. Even though Joseph had laid no claim to her other than as his teacher, why did he feel sick knowing that Sam had taken notice?

Shrugging his shoulders, he jammed his hands into his

pockets. "Katie's my instructor. She's been working with me."

"You didn't tell me that you knew her." Sam chuckled.

"You didn't ask," Joseph responded wryly. "And I couldn't exactly see her, remember? I figured you'd stumbled across someone new in town that I hadn't met since I've been laid up."

"Well, what do you know?"

"Yeah," he agreed under his breath. His jaw muscles clenched tight. "What do you know?"

"How are you today, Joseph?" Katie asked, breaking his ire.

"Just fine." He tried to shove off his shock. "Yourself?"

"I'm well, thank you." She paused for a moment, then said, "You're probably really looking forward to your appointment?"

"That I am."

"You better believe I'll be thinking of you as you go, my friend," Sam said, giving Joseph's shoulder a firm squeeze. "I hate to cut out so soon here, but I'm being flagged down over by the wagons. I'll catch up with you later, all right?"

Joseph nodded. "Sounds good. You know where to find me."

"Miss Ellickson, it has been a pleasure seeing you once again." Sam's voice was low with sincerity, and Joseph could easily imagine him sweeping his hat off on a dramatic bow.

"Nice to see you, too," Katie responded with equal sincerity that had Joseph inwardly cringing.

When Sam strode away, Joseph couldn't help speculating what kind of eye contact had transpired between the two of them just then. He set his back teeth at the grim possibilities that were floating through his mind, but when Katie moved a step closer, that pleasing lily scent of hers distracted him.

"I hate to say it, but it looks like you've been left high and dry again," she said next to him.

"Yeah. It appears that way." He chuckled, sweeping his focus around as if confirming that fact. "Guess there's no sympathy for the wounded guy, huh? That's just fine by me, as long as I'm not left here all night, there's no harm done."

"Well, rest assured, Joseph, I won't let that happen."

"Thank you kindly, ma'am." He tipped his head toward her and smiled.

"So, how are you really feeling about your appointment Tuesday?"

Joseph raked a hand through his hair. "I'm anxious, nervous, excited…. How's that for emotions?"

Katie sliced the air through her teeth on an inhale. "That pretty much covers most of them."

"One minute I'm chomping at the bit to go and get it over with," he said, balling his fists tight. "So I can move on with my life—whatever it looks like. The next minute, I'm climbing the walls with excitement that I'll actually see again."

"Oh, I hope so, Joseph," she breathed, touching his arm for a brief second. "I really do. We'll definitely have to celebrate when you get home."

"We will. You'll still be here, won't you?" he asked, selfishly hoping that she wouldn't head back to Iowa—ever.

"I'll be here."

"When I can see again," he focused down at her, "I'll enjoy every sunrise, every sunset, every cloudy sky—" he cut himself off, shaking his head as doubts suddenly assailed him. "But then when I think about the possibility of being permanently blind…" he continued, jamming his hands into his pockets and grimacing. He swallowed hard. "If I can't see anything more than the gray shadows when Ben removed the bandages two weeks ago, I don't know what I'll do, Katie. I really don't."

"I'm sorry, Joseph, that must be very difficult." Her voice…her sweet understanding ways, gave him such comfort.

"I mean, I try not to even think about being blind because if I do, I get scared—and angry. Really angry. At myself for being careless, at the world for being sighted," he said, his mouth drawing into a tight line. "And at God if He doesn't answer my prayer for healing."

After a long, not uncomfortable moment of silence, Katie finally spoke. "I'm sorry you're going through this. I can't imagine how hard it must be to consider the possibility and what all of that would mean for you."

Angling his head down, he dug the toe of his boot into the hard ground. As good as it was to admit how he really felt to someone, he was determined to keep things light. "Yeah! I mean, what do you do with someone like me who's used to being self-sufficient?" He held his arms out as if offering himself. "If I can't see, I'd have to find some kind of employment, because I'm sure as anything not cut out for the ladies' quilting circle."

Katie gave a wistful sigh. "Yes, I don't imagine you'd be welcome there. After all, they do call it the *ladies'* quilting circle."

Jamming his hands on his hips, he cocked his head to the side. "Who knows, maybe they'll make an exception."

"Probably not," she retorted, her quiet laughter putting him so at ease.

"Well, I guess I'll have to ford that creek if I get to it. For now, however, I'm going to ask you for a lead home seeing as how Ben must've gotten caught up again."

"Absolutely. I'd be glad to."

"All of the worrying, excitement and outings are tiring." On a hearty exhale, he puffed out his cheeks as he reached for her arm. "Between this snappy little teacher that's been running me ragged and the—"

"Ha! That's not a very nice thing to say, Mr. Drake," she retorted, her voice filled with mock exasperation. "I might not be so willing if you keep that up."

"Nah…you'll walk with me because you feel sorry for me with these bandages on and all," he teased.

Her light laughter was the most wonderful music to his ears. "Not hardly, sir. I do, however, enjoy your company."

Chapter Eight

Joseph had been to Denver dozens of times. But none of his experiences had ever been like this. Every sound within earshot seemed amplified tenfold. The nickering horses—their hooves clomping on the barren ground, the carriages creaking across the rutted roads and the board-walk echoing with the click of boots.

Standing at the entrance to the stagecoach house, his nerves buzzed with all the sensations. His ears rang from countless unfamiliar voices coming from every direction.

He pulled back his shoulders and steadied himself against the rough-hewn clapboard at his back. His journey to Denver hadn't exactly started the way he'd planned. After Ben had shown up early this morning, announcing that he was unable to go along, frustration had hit hard and fast. Joseph had anticipated this day like his next breath. This appointment was his doorway to freedom from the suffocating confines of blindness. But when Ben went on to explain that he couldn't leave because Ellie's condition was shaky at best, Joseph didn't give the appointment a second thought.

That Ben had asked Katie and her Uncle Sven to accompany him instead set Joseph's thoughts on a completely different course, driving him into a dense thicket of emotions. He didn't know whether to be glad for another opportunity to be with her, to hear her sweet mellow voice, feel her warm gentle touch. Or be irritated at having to wrestle his rebellious emotions into submission again.

He definitely couldn't deny the feelings he had for Katie now. Especially since he'd run into Sam yesterday. He'd tossed and turned all night trying to reason it all out. Sam was his friend, a good friend. Joseph wouldn't let anything come between their long-standing friendship. But when he thought about Katie, he didn't know if he could just let her slip away.

His prayers for restored sight took on a whole new focus. Being able to see again wasn't just about having his life back—it was about being free to follow his heart to Katie. And if Sam was inclined to do the same, then at least the playing field would be fair.

Katie. She was a ray of sunshine on a cloudy day, a gentle rain soaking the thirsty ground. Side by side, they'd enjoyed the eight-hour journey with Sven, sometimes in comfortable conversation and other times in amicable silence. But upon arriving less than twenty minutes ago, the ease of the trip was quickly swallowed by the hectic pace of the booming city.

The tinny sound of the piano coming from the saloon just doors away, and the raucous laughter knifing through the warm evening air set the hair at the back of his neck on end. With the hour nearing dinner time, Denver's night life was probably just beginning. Joseph would be a heck of a lot more at ease when he had Katie checked safely into the nice hotel he'd stayed at not far from here. The restlessness he felt waiting for her to return from the washroom made him wish that he'd taken Sven up on his offer to see them to the hotel. But Joseph knew that Sven had a hearty list of things he needed to do while they were here. Running a busy lumber mill back home, supply ordering trips like these were meant for business only.

He pushed away from the building, tilting his head from side to side to remove the kinks in his neck from the long ride. As he slid his fingers over his buttons, he felt, more than heard, someone cross slowly in front of him, stopping as if to give him a thorough perusal.

For a fleeting moment he wondered if Katie had returned, but he knew she wouldn't sneak up on him unannounced. It could be that he was the object of rude scrutiny from some stranger, his bandage standing out like a white flag of surrender flying high in enemy territory.

He loathed feeling as if he was on display like some sideshow and would be so glad to be rid of the ridiculous getup.

Joseph drew himself to his full height, jamming his hands into his pockets. Catching the remnant of stale liquor hanging in front of him, he sniffed the air, scowling as he steadied himself against the prickly sensation working up his spine and neck, setting his hair on end.

Then he heard Katie's voice from around the corner. "Excuse me, sir. Please let me pass by."

He jerked his focus to the right, furrowing his brow and listening intently. The slight tremor he'd sensed in her voice set his pulse pounding.

"Katie, I'm over here." He turned to the right and

stepped cautiously, trailing his hand along the building as he tried to gauge the length of the wooden platform.

Fierce protectiveness rose within him like some dormant warrior—as did the reality that he couldn't see a thing. That she might be in trouble made every nerve snap to attention.

"Where you goin' in such a hurry, sweetheart?" a man's voice cut through the city noise, taunting flecked in careless chunks through the words. "I just wanna talk is all."

"Katie?" he called again, hearing a small scuffle.

"Well, whata we have here?" the man tossed in Joseph's direction, his sloppy drawl summoning an image in Joseph's mind that had him moving faster. He heard the man spit, the juicy wad plinking against something metal. "With all them bandages he's wearin', I'd say you must be his nurse, lil' lady. Ain't that somethin'?"

A throaty chuckle rumbled from the man. With a low whistle, he added, "Yep. Wouldn't mind havin' a perty nurse like you tend to my—"

"That'll be enough!" Joseph slapped the side of the building and stalked toward the direction of the man's voice. "You can step away from her now," he ground out, his jaw muscles tensing, a heated flush working up his neck and face. When his foot found the edge of the platform, he stopped.

He stretched out his hand. "Katie, come on, darlin'," he spoke, the endearment coming as easily as his next breath. "Let's get to the hotel."

"Well, now…what're ya gonna do iffin' I don' let 'er pass?" the man slurred on a contemptuous snicker. "Chase me?"

When laughter, thick and dark, erupted from the rogue,

anger shot through Joseph like a cannon blast, ripping through his calm reserve. He'd knock the scoundrel to kingdom come if only he could see him. But the lack of control he had over the situation and insufficiency he felt stared him in the face.

His neck tensed as tight as a pulled cord. He sucked air through his teeth and kept a hand on the side of the building as he lowered his foot, hoping to locate a step.

"Get away from her," Joseph warned, a foot connecting with the second step and then another with the hard ground.

He wanted to tear off the bandages, but what if he obliterated the wraps and found nothing had changed? No light to illumine his path, no clear image, no sight by which to make his way in life.

"It's all right, Joseph," Katie urged, her words far from convincing. He could hear her struggling to free herself.

When he pushed away from the building, aiming toward the sound of Katie's voice with his hands outstretched, all he could think about was getting her out of harm's way. And of how he could never watch over her if he couldn't see.

What kind of protector would he be? How could he ever ensure her safety?

The questions ricocheted through his mind mercilessly, but he shoved them down. He couldn't afford to think about those things now. Katie needed him.

"What's going on out here?" A man's voice pierced his silent nightmare as he came to stand beside him. "Is there a problem?"

"Nope. No problem as I can see," the drunk who'd stood near Katie answered, the sound of his heavy, unsteady footsteps quickly carrying him away from the stagecoach house.

"Everything is fine now, thank you," Katie answered, her voice still trembling.

"All righty, then," the man responded as he trudged up the steps and walked back inside the building.

Humiliation, cold and harsh, crumbled over Joseph like a wall of ice. He tried not to think about what would've happened had the man not appeared from inside the building.

"Katie?" he breathed.

When he felt her touch at his arm, relief nearly bowled him over. As did the sickening realization that without his sight, he was as useless as a bug on his back. She deserved more than having to look to others for her protection.

When she drew in a shuddering breath, he turned and wrapped his arms possessively around her, pulling her close to his chest. The quaking he felt coming from her shook him. Shook him to the very core, stirring up the insecurities he'd faced these past five weeks.

He just had to get his sight back.

When Joseph's appointment finally arrived, flagrant insecurities haunted him from the previous day. He was desperate to finally see again, and was beyond grateful that the day had finally arrived because he didn't ever want Katie to have to go through that again.

She'd tried dismissing the event as nothing, but Joseph knew it had affected her far more than she was letting on. He'd kept his arms around her for some time, and it was long moments before her shaking subsided and her breathing evened out.

After they'd checked into the hotel and met up with Sven for supper, they'd all parted ways until morning.

Sleep eluded him once again because he'd lain awake thinking of Katie. The horrible reality of his limitations if he didn't regain his sight was at the forefront of his mind.

In the early morning hours he'd finally pushed through the morbid thoughts and slept. He was going to see again. Surely God loved him enough to answer his desperate pleas. Surely the providence of Katie coming into his life wouldn't be dangled like some carrot just out of reach.

With a gentle grasp on Katie's arm, he steadied himself, anxious to finally get this day behind him and get on with his life. But as he crossed the threshold to the office he couldn't seem to shake the feeling that a thousand guns were aimed directly at him—their sights firmly set upon his vulnerability.

Shortly after arriving, they were ushered into an exam room where a lingering scent of antiseptic pervaded. While they sat waiting for the doctor, his mind and body buzzed with anxious energy. He dragged his fingers through his hair and shifted uncomfortably, unable to recall a time when he'd been so nervous. The anticipation of seeing again had his stomach bound in a tight knot.

Worse, the fear of not seeing again had his heart grinding to an agonizing halt.

"It'll work out, Joseph." Katie touched his shoulder, her fingers lightly, briefly stroking his tense muscles.

"Thanks." He turned to her, knowing that his attempt at a smile fell painfully short. "I'm sure it will, too."

He caught her fingers, pulling them down to cradle her hand. He rubbed his thumbs the length of each soft, slender finger and up to her dainty wrist, where he felt the wisp of lace edging her sleeve.

"Do you know what I want my first sight to be?" His voice grew tight with emotion as the door creaked open. "I want to see you," he whispered, releasing her hand and standing from his chair.

"Good afternoon. I'm Dr. Becker." The man's voice boomed confidence as his feet swept steadily across the wood floor like fine-grained sandpaper. "You must be Mr. Drake."

Joseph faced the doctor. "Good afternoon, Doctor." When he returned the man's handshake, he noticed how the doctor's hand felt considerably smaller in his own.

"And you must be Mrs. Drake?"

Joseph sat down next to Katie again. "Miss Ellickson is a teacher who's been working with me."

"Oh, I see. Well, it's nice to meet the two of you," the doctor said simply, exuding nothing but pure professionalism. "I hope we can help you today, Mr. Drake. Your doctor—and brother, I understand—informed me of your situation."

Joseph heard him shifting some papers and assumed he was probably skimming over Ben's notes that they'd left with the nurse. The muscles in his jaws worked overtime, and his forearms ached from the tight fists his hands formed.

"Uh-huh." A long silence followed. "Now, let's see. It's been over five weeks since the accident?"

After the doctor gathered firsthand details of the accident from Joseph, he gave a harsh cough. "I know you probably want to get this over with, so why don't we do just that."

Joseph's pulse picked up. His stomach churned.

"Let me tell you that I'm hopeful. Knowing that you

were able to see some dim shadows when the patches were originally removed is a very good sign. Very good, indeed. Hopefully we'll see even more improvement today."

"That's what I'm hoping for," Joseph said with a nod.

"Your brother did the right thing in ordering bed rest," the doctor confirmed. "Now, I'm going to remove these wrappings around your head first."

His nerve endings thrummed. His ears rang and his pulse pounded heavily as a heated flush worked up his chest, neck, head. Every noise suddenly annoyed him, especially the short-winded whistling sound as Dr. Becker breathed.

The doctor snipped at the bandage with cold metal scissors, then began unwinding. "I'll have you open your eyes slowly, so it won't be too bright. It can be over-whelming at first."

"I suppose," he responded with a forced chuckle. His heart slammed against his chest wall. "I'll take overwhelming."

A suspense-filled silence hung in the air, making it stifling. Joseph wanted to reach to Katie, but resisted the urge. The confidence he'd felt only a week ago, an hour ago, a moment ago, seemed like a mirage in a hot, dry desert.

Once the bandages were finally off, he sighed with relief. The air was cool, liberating against his skin.

"Now, I'm going to lift off these patches." Dr. Becker's voice was girded with caution. "Are you ready?"

Nodding, he gripped the arms of the chair and steadied himself, as if waiting for a stunning fireworks demonstration, full of light, color and form.

Or was he waiting for the knockout blow in a fight?

"Now, Joseph, be patient and let your eyes adjust to the light. I want you to slowly open your eyes."

He tightened his grip on the arms of the chair, every muscle tensed with anticipation as he leaned forward. He felt confident again, and hopeful as he determined to look Katie's way just as soon as the glorious light seeped into the offending darkness. Slowly easing his eyelids open, he blinked.

Was there something in his eyes?

He clutched the arms of the chair and blinked again. But he couldn't seem to find anything more than the dim shadows he'd seen before.

"I—I don't know. I can't tell," he said hesitantly.

Desperately wanting to believe that remnants of the bandages still remained on his eyes, he reached up, his hands trembling as he felt where the patches had been.

Nothing.

"It's all right," Dr. Becker offered. "We'll go over here by the window. The sun is bright this afternoon. Let's see if your eyes can register more light here."

Joseph struggled to his feet when he felt the doctor's hand beneath his arm. Once standing, his knees threatened to buckle. He closed his eyes as he was led across the room. When they stopped, the doctor placed Joseph's hand upon a wide wooden sill, smooth and polished under his fingertips.

"Do you see anything now?" The measure of hope in the doctor's voice gave encouragement.

Opening his eyes wide, he again searched for light-bathed images. He opened and shut his eyes several times. Sweat beaded his brow. His breath came in short pants. Desperate, he searched wildly.

Nothing.

Dr. Becker stood directly in front of him, appearing

like a vague, undefined image in a thick, unrelenting fog. Try as he might, Joseph couldn't make out color or even the most obvious detail.

He turned his head toward where Katie was sitting, straining to see her through the dense gray filling his vision. He saw nothing, but heard her whisper, "Joseph?"

The weight of the doctor's hand upon his shoulder was a faint contact point as he felt himself drifting farther away. The stark reality of his fate threatened to drive him to the darkest depths.

Turning back to the window, the warm, inviting sun bore down upon his face as if mocking him, but again he couldn't make out anything more than a murky shadow of light.

How could this be?

Slamming his eyes shut, he opened them with the fading hope of finding something more than formless shadows. Trembling, he plowed his fingers through his hair, then pulled a hand down over his face, his fingertips briefly resting upon eyes that couldn't see. Slowly he raised his chin, fighting not to fall prey to complete and total despair.

I'm blind. Oh, God, I'm blind.

The realization hit like a sudden blast, annihilating hope. Never had he felt more alone or forsaken.

Where are You, God? Don't You know I need my sight?

His silent plea, one he'd prayed hundreds of times, seemed to hang suspended in the dark unknown.

"There's no change," he finally admitted, his jaw tense, his stomach churning. "It's no better than before."

"I'm sorry, son. This must come as a surprise." Dr. Becker's tone was tight, forced. "Let's go back over here and sit down."

Every single step felt short and clumsy once again, as if all the progress he'd made with Katie had been a figment of his imagination.

After the doctor performed a couple of tests, he rested his hands upon Joseph's shoulders. "I'd hoped to have more encouraging news for you. I know this must be difficult."

He wanted to run far away. But he probably couldn't make it out of the room without attendance, let alone the building.

"You'll get through this, Joseph. I know you will." An undercurrent of shared discouragement and sadness was evident in Katie's voice as he felt her familiar, comforting touch upon his arm. "Give yourself time."

"This isn't an easy lot in life," the doctor added. "But in time you will grow accustomed to life without sight and your other senses will compensate for the lack in vision. There have been some significant advances made for the blind." The words were meant to lend hope, but nothing could mask the pity in the doctor's voice. "And it sounds like, with Miss Ellickson here, you're already on the right road."

Although he was thankful for what Katie had taught him over the last two weeks, he realized now that he'd been going through the motions, counting on things taking a favorable turn for him.

"Is there any chance that restoration could still take place?" He forced the tremble from his voice as he mined for some vein of hope. "I mean, could it be that maybe my eyes just need more time? Maybe you should wrap them again."

The doctor gave a measured sigh. "I don't make a habit of leaving my patients with false hope. I find that that can be counterproductive, so I'll be very honest with you."

The nervous cough coming from Dr. Becker had Joseph bracing himself for words he somehow knew would set his fate in stone. He wanted to cover his ears. Storm out of the room.

He'd never run from a challenge, though. Could he find it within himself to face this one head-on? The way he saw it, he didn't have much of a choice. God had ignored his pleas and left him high and dry.

"With this kind of head trauma and the amount of time that has gone by since the injury, I regret to say that we've likely seen as much restoration as we're going to get."

Joseph stared into the darkness while listening to the bleak prognosis. He set his face like the calm of a glassy sea. Inside, however, huge waves battered his soul.

"It's apparent the damage done was very serious and irreversible," the doctor continued. "If there was going to be a return of sight, we would've seen it by now."

Chapter Nine

The trip home was strained at best. For most of the journey Katie had sat squeezed between Uncle Sven and Joseph, and crammed to capacity into the stage along with the other six travelers. Joseph had leaned his head back, shutting his eyes tight beneath furrowed brows. The way he held his body so rigid and fists so tight, she would've thought they were careening down a mountainside. He surely felt that his life had just hit a steep, rocky slope.

The times she'd tried to make conversation, she'd feel him tense as though he couldn't bear her presence. Finally, she'd given up. She understood how devastated he must be.

What she couldn't understand was why he'd wall himself off from her. Hadn't she developed a trust with him? Hadn't he found comfort with her as much as she'd found with him?

Even Uncle Sven couldn't break Joseph's dark silence. When the stagecoach arrived back in Boulder after supper, Katie had quietly insisted on walking Joseph home, hoping that if he felt less crowded by others, she could get him to open up.

Peering over at him now as she led the way home, compassion again welled inside her. He'd banked on regaining his sight and had gotten no return. The anger creasing his brow and frustration clenching his jaw spoke volumes of his distress.

On a measured sigh, she turned her attention back to the path and gasped. Tripped down a step, her arm jerking free from his tentative grasp. "Whoa!" Katie cried. "Be careful—"

He followed a split second later. He reached in vain for something to steady himself as he dropped face-first to the packed dirt like felled timber.

"Oh no! I'm so sorry." She scrambled to kneel beside him.

"What in the—"

"It was my fault, Joseph." She placed a trembling hand on his back, inwardly scolding herself for being so distracted. "I wasn't paying attention."

"Apparently," he snarled over his shoulder. He lay sprawled out in the middle of the road for a moment, then shoving her hand away, quickly levered himself up. With his face set in a scowl, he slapped his hands together, sending a plume of dust into the evening air. "I don't need you to walk me home. I'll do it myself."

"I'm sorry, Joseph. Really I am." She stared up at him, confused. Up to now he'd been quiet, not explosive. "I should have been more attentive to where I was going."

"My house can't be far from here. What…another block?" He turned his head opposite his desired direction. Kneeling, he patted his hand along the ground, feeling for his bag that had flown from his hand, scattering the few things within.

"A little over two blocks, actually." Katie shook her head at his stubbornness. "Here, let me get that for you."

"No! I can do it myself," he ground out.

He stretched out his arms and swept them across the ground in broad movements. Scooting forward, he repeated the action, finally locating his bag and all but one item. When he'd stuffed them back inside, he stood, his chest rising and falling in rapid rhythm.

With trembling knees, she crossed to retrieve the shirt he'd missed. "You forgot something," she uttered, unable to resist the urge to breathe in Joseph's scent woven within the threads.

When she handed it to him, her heart squeezed as she watched the embarrassment tainting his features. Maybe his vision hadn't changed, but the Joseph she knew was not who stood before her now. He'd erected a wall the size of a mountain around himself, and he was intent on keeping her out.

She couldn't make herself look away as he focused directly on her, his sightless gaze bearing into hers.

"Please let me walk the rest of the way with you."

"I told you I'd do it myself," he retorted, stuffing the shirt in his bag.

She sighed. "Fine. Go right ahead."

Hugging her arms to her chest, she witnessed his brow crease and his fists clench as though he'd expected her to put up a fight. From her experience, she knew that it was best to just let him find out the hard way—as long as doing so didn't pose any danger. Had the streets been busy, she would've put up a fight and dragged him home regardless of his protests.

"Fine," he echoed. He shoved a hand in his pocket, but not before she noticed the tremble undermining his composure.

After a moment's pause, she slowly walked away, her heart constricting inside her chest, her gaze fixed on him. He stood at the side of the road, a study in stoicism with his shoulders drawn back, head held high and his chin set. At a quick glance, he didn't look as if he needed help. Maybe in a couple of weeks after more training, maybe in a month. But right now, at the very least, he'd need the aid of a cane.

After nearly a minute, he made a tentative move forward to cross the street, then another and another. Dragging his fingers through his hair, he came to an abrupt halt.

She stopped in her tracks. A soft moan escaped her lips as raw fear played across his features in the evening light. Bracing herself, she walked back to him, her heels lightly ticking across the boardwalk.

He turned his head in her direction, a look of irritation sweeping over his face.

Standing in front of him, she struggled with many different emotions. She was angry with him, frustrated by him, but mostly she felt so very sad for him.

He gave a loud, long exhale. "If you could just point me in the right direction, I can do the rest."

How did he think he was going to get home without help?

"I'm sure I can figure it out," Joseph added firmly, as if he'd read her thoughts.

"Why don't you stop being so *stubborn*," she urged,

unable to keep her irritation at bay. "It's all right to let someone help, you know."

"Easy for you to say," he ground out, his frustrated gaze set down the road.

Hugging her arms to her chest, she sighed. "You're right. It's a lot easier for me to say those things when I don't have to face this." She took a step closer, then gently grasped his hand, inwardly cringing when he jerked at her touch. "Please," she whispered. "Let me help you."

When he didn't pull away, she placed his hand at her elbow and led him home, acutely aware of the stiffness in his touch.

At the familiar sound of the front gate opening, he relaxed ever so slightly. And when they reached his porch, she turned to find his unseeing gaze fixed on her, his eyes—the most beautiful golden brown she'd ever seen. The first time she'd really caught a glimpse of his eyes this morning, she'd nearly lost her breath. Prominent cheekbones and perfectly shaped brows served as a masculine frame, enhancing his stunning eyes.

Surely they'd once sparked with life like his brother's. But right now, exhaustion, fear and anger weighed heavily on him as he lifted his chin a notch.

Hearing a rustling at the side of the house, she glanced over to see Boone lumbering into the evening shadows, his tail wagging lazily from side to side in greeting.

"Hello, Boone." She knelt to pet the dog.

"Hey, boy." Joseph hunkered down and reached out, his hand connecting with hers on Boone's back.

For a moment neither one of them moved. Comforting warmth spread through her when he swept the pad of his thumb over her hand in a light caress. Much as she'd tried to remain professional concerning Joseph, something had changed over the past two weeks. Her heartbeat quickened at his comforting presence. Stirred at his soothing voice. She found herself longing for his touch. Longing for his nearness to lend her hope and confidence. And to calm her deep fears.

Katie deserved a whole man. And whole, he was not.

Joseph swallowed hard, burrowing his fingers next to Katie's into Boone's fur as he thought about what he had to do. For her sake, he had to sever all feelings other than those of friendship. His blindness was a thorn in his flesh, and he sure wasn't going to inflict its sting upon a wife. Especially someone as sweet, as special, as Katie.

Had things turned out differently for him, he might've proposed marriage by now. There was really nothing keeping him from still doing that except that if she said "I do," he'd forever wonder if it was out of pity or some warped sense of obligation. Over the past two weeks they'd shared tender moments laden with unspoken promises that maybe she felt some misplaced duty to fulfill.

He couldn't live with himself if that was the case.

But he didn't know if he could live without her, either. Each day he looked forward to being with her, having her near, hearing her voice. And whenever he'd held her or when she'd given him encouragement by a simple, innocent touch, the connection had bolstered him with strength he needed to face this challenge.

Since his appointment this morning, he'd been as rigid and unyielding as the mountains surrounding this valley. And right now he was starving for comfort.

So maybe he could indulge himself just once more

before he let her go. He wanted to walk away with the memory of her warm and soft and caring touch.

After a long moment of silence, he slowly came to standing, pulling her along with him. Joseph focused down at where he cradled her hands in his. He traced a path with the pads of his thumbs. Heard and felt her quiet sigh.

He threaded his fingers with hers. And for a moment in time, he closed his eyes, imagining that he could see again. He'd hold her close. Look deep into her eyes. He'd protect her the way she deserved. Drive away her fears with his love.

Joseph dragged in a deep breath and with it the delicate scent of lilies. So simple, so natural and so Katie.

If he didn't go inside now, he might never let her go. And that set off warning bells that clanged loudly, slicing through his longing.

He couldn't allow himself to do that and then dismiss her like some discarded waste. She didn't deserve that.

He slowly slid his hands from hers, committing to memory this moment as he opened his eyes to the harsh darkness. "I'm sorry for my impatience, Katie. I'm just not very good company right now."

"No. Don't apologize," she whispered.

He stepped away from her and shook his head, slamming his eyes shut. He was sending her mixed signals, being so harsh just moments ago out on the street and then showing tenderness.

"Joseph, I—"

"I really should just get inside," he blurted.

"It's been a hard day, I know."

When he grasped the cool door handle, he shuttered away the warmth and affection he'd felt just a moment ago, steeling himself to do what needed to be done. It was for her sake.

"Katie, I think it's best that you not come over to-morrow." His voice sounded flat as he stared downward.

"Oh? So—so you want me here Thursday, then?"

He swallowed hard. "No. Not Thursday, either. I don't know when—or *if* I want you to come back."

Something felt innately right when she was by his side.

The moments when their hands touched or his leg brushed against hers in the stagecoach, or every single time she spoke his name or a word of encouragement, he felt something that was undeniable—a connection that seemed as though it'd been established even before their paths had crossed just two weeks ago.

But he could barely stand himself right now. He didn't need to subject her to his anger or his rampant emotions. His response when he'd fallen flat on his face had surely tested her patience with him. It was an accident—accidents happened. He was in for his fair share of them in the future.

Joseph shook his head, recognizing that until he could resign himself to his blindness, he wouldn't be good company for anyone. Especially not Katie. Even then, if he did decide to ask her to work with him again, there could never be anything more than friendship between them.

He would *not* strap Katie with the burden of living with a blind man for the rest of her life.

Stepping through the doorway after Boone, Joseph stumbled slightly, then steadied himself by grabbing the doorjamb. His balance wasn't too keen after being on the road for so long. In fact, his whole life seemed off balance now and he didn't know when he'd get his bearings again.

He dropped his bag at the door and shuffled forward, each uncertain step a reverberating reminder of his affliction. All day long he'd wanted to revolt against the imposing darkness. He'd wanted to scream, throw something, run, but instead he'd shut himself up tight like a tender young tree in a mature forest, crowded, dark and confined.

Alone now in the privacy of his own home, he could give in to the compulsion to release his anger, but he just didn't have the strength. What good would it do now, anyway?

He massaged the tight knots at the back of his neck, realizing just how weary he was. Every muscle in his body ached from the rigid stance he'd assumed all day.

With outstretched hands, he carefully counted his steps until he reached the bedroom at the back of the house. As usual, Boone found his place at the foot of the bed while Joseph crawled into bed, not even bothering to remove his clothes or boots.

He lowered his head to his pillow and closed his eyes, wishing that this horrible nightmare would finally come to an end. But opening them, the nightmare loomed as real as ever.

Boone laid his chin on Joseph's knee and Joseph smoothed his hand over the dog's soft fur. He could almost feel Katie's fingers there, beneath his again. It had almost been his undoing. He'd wanted to hold her.

And be held.

But he steeled himself against the deep need for reassurance. Like it or not, his well-ordered world had been overrun with an all-consuming darkness.

Why had God sentenced him to this sightless, black prison?

He'd silently railed against God on the long trip home,

demanding an answer. He'd received none, and questioned if he was fighting a war more for his soul than for his livelihood.

When Boone nuzzled his soft wet nose into Joseph's palm, Joseph gathered in a shaky breath.

"How could you allow this, God? What did I do to deserve this?" he whispered. It was an honest question void of the accusation that had filled his unspoken barrage earlier.

Opening his eyes to nothing once again, he clenched his fists and trembled.

That still, small voice Joseph had learned to recognize as God's came once again, beckoning for his trust.

Hungry for any response, he let it sink in. It wasn't the answer he was looking for, but it was a reply. And he wanted desperately to know that God hadn't forgotten him.

"I want to trust You, God. But I don't know how. I'm so used to taking care of things on my own. Who am I now?" The shop and deadline that loomed in the not-too-distant future swirled through his thoughts. "Everything I've worked so hard for in the past—it's just slipping away."

Even though he couldn't see God, he knew that He was here with him. An unexplainable peace he needed now more than ever seemed to blanket him.

Joseph was desperate to understand, desperate to hold on to that comfort. "Help me, God. Please," he whispered.

Lying with his eyes wide open, he stared into bold, unrelenting darkness. The peace he'd felt just moments ago was already slipping away as he searched in vain for a fragment of brightness in his dark world.

If there were a moon to light the sky or stars to illuminate the heavens, he'd never know.

* * *

"Oh, God! No!" Joseph woke with a jolt.

He sat up, panting. Grasped the edge of the mattress and held it as though it were a lifeline keeping him from falling into a deep chasm. Sweat drenched his body as he tried to force the nightmare from his mind, but the images lingered.

"Lord, please. I *need* to know You're here." His breathing was ragged.

Even in his dreams he was living out his present nightmare all over again. The scene replayed once more in his mind.

A woman stood off in the distance at the edge of the woods. She was calling to him. Begging him to come. He started toward her. Turning momentarily away from her, he saw an endless black hole. Its expanse stretched as far as the eye could see. It pulled at him. Dragged him backward. Into a place so bleak that he clawed at the ground to remain in the light. Hearing her faint cries, he strained to free himself. But it was wholly engulfing and he kept slipping farther…farther away into darkness.

He forced his mind away from the hopelessness. Wiping his brow, he struggled to still his turbulent emotions. Joseph slowly lowered himself to his pillow with a long, shuddered breath.

Darkness was his enemy now. Forever mocking him. Forever taunting him.

"Ellie lost the baby?" Katie whispered, echoing Ben's words.

She didn't think things could get much worse since Joseph had received such devastating news about his vision, then proceeded to close the door on his training, sending her away last night. But when she knocked on Ben's door just moments ago to inform him that she and Joseph had arrived home with Sven a day earlier than planned, she stood stunned, her eyes wide with disbelief.

"Late last night." Ben slid a hand over his unshaven face. Dark circles shadowed his eyes as he stared down at his hands. "I tried everything I knew to do, but it wasn't enough. The little guy just wouldn't come around."

Katie swallowed hard. A torrent of emotions and images swamped her as she slid trembling fingers up the tiny pearl buttons to her neckline, clasping the small brooch.

She remembered how Ellie would lovingly caress the baby she carried inside her. How Aaron would, without embarrassment, ease his large, work-worn hands around his wife's belly. They'd been so excited about the birth of their first child.

Katie couldn't imagine the overwhelming grief they must feel. She dabbed at tears pooling in her eyes, knowing that if she allowed herself to fall apart now, she might not be able to get herself back together.

"How is she doing?" she forced out, clearing her throat as she followed him to his buggy. "How is Aaron? I mean…is there anything I can do?"

His shoulders hanging low, Ben sighed with a nod. "Yes, there is. Right before I left there this morning, Ellie asked for you and Joseph. She wants to see you." He hauled his doctor's bag up to the black leather seat. "I think it would do both of them good to have the two of you there."

"Well, of course. Of course I'll go." She grabbed his offered hand and climbed into the seat. Glancing to the west where Aaron and Ellie lived in a cabin outside of town, an ominous shiver passed through her as she spotted the dark gray bank of clouds crawling over the horizon.

"It was a good thing you caught me when you did," Ben said, grabbing the reins. "I was coming after supplies, then going straight back out there. Aaron's trying to get a coffin made and tending Ellie, too. She's still not out of the woods."

"Will she be all right?" she braved.

His mouth formed a grim line. "I don't know. It wasn't an easy delivery. She lost a lot of blood."

"I'll do whatever needs to be done. Just let me know."

As the buggy lurched forward, rolling over the rutted ground, he glanced at her. "I saw Sven on the way here and he told me about the appointment. It must've been a difficult trip for all of you. I'm sure Joseph is very upset."

On the way to pick up Joseph, Katie proceeded to tell Ben about the day, from the way Joseph had courageously handled the discouraging news, to his silence and the unfortunate incident on the walk home. She was careful not to dishonor Joseph in any way, but she felt that Ben should know the extent of things.

He pulled in a deep breath, blowing it out in one big gust of air. "I really hoped things would turn out better than that. But I can't say I'm surprised." Furrowing his brow, he jammed his hat down on his head. "Did you get much out of him after the appointment?"

"I'm afraid not. I tried, but he wasn't in any mood to talk, and I don't blame him."

Thunder rolled in the distance, penetrating the silence. "This is one of the toughest things he's had to face." Slicing a glance her way, he added, "It's a good thing he has you."

Katie blinked back hot tears as she stared down the

street toward Joseph's house. "I'm not sure he sees it that way. And I doubt that he'll be too keen on my coming along today, either. He didn't want me coming back to work with him."

Ben gave her hand a brief, comforting squeeze. "He may be stubborn. But knowing Joseph, he'll put aside his trials if it means being there for Ellie and Aaron." With a jerk of the wrist, he slapped the reins, urging the horses to move a little faster. "When it comes to doing for others, he always looks past his own needs."

Chapter Ten

Joseph's heart clenched at the unmistakable sound of Aaron working a saw in the barn. Each pass of the sharp-toothed blade through the wood echoed like some mournful cry as Joseph approached the barn with Ben.

When Joseph had learned of the baby's death, he'd felt deep sorrow. It had multiplied as they'd arrived a few minutes ago and he'd sat by Ellie's bedside. Her voice sounded so small, so sad, so weak. And in spite of the warm August day, her hand had felt like ice in his. When she'd tried to comfort him about his own discouraging news, Joseph had fought hard to bat down the raw emotions that flapped like gaping wounds in his soul. It was just like her to encourage others in the midst of her own pain and loss. He'd tried to offer the same in return, but what could he say that would possibly bring any consolation?

That God was with them? That God had a plan in it all? That God would turn it all for good?

Having heard enough of that from well-meaning folk over the past few weeks, he was weary of assuaging answers like those. True as they may be, sometimes sentiments like those seemed trite. Sometimes just the quiet strength of another's presence was worth more than a whole book of words. Besides, wasn't God more than capable of showing Himself to be true, sovereign, loving? Did he really need folks to defend His honor or what He allowed in our lives?

Thunder rumbled through the valley and the saw blade groaned to a halt. A lump rose in Joseph's throat as he took a tentative step out of Ben's lead and into the barn.

"I'm sorry, Aaron," he expressed, as Ben headed back toward the house. "So very sorry for your loss."

Aaron's feet scuffed over the dirt floor and stopped in front of Joseph. After several seconds, Joseph reached out and found his brother's arm, pulling him into a strong embrace.

"I'm sorry, too, Joe-boy," Aaron rasped, his tall frame quaking in Joseph's arms. "Both about my baby…and your vision." Stepping out of the embrace, he added, "I can tell…it's not any better, is it? Your vision?"

Joseph slid his hands into his pockets. "No. But don't worry about me. And don't worry about things at the shop. Take all the time you need," he urged, knowing full well that time was ticking away and the deadline loomed closer. Right now, though, it didn't matter. Not when Aaron and Ellie had just lost their baby, and she was struggling for her own life. "Just get Ellie better. That's all you need to think about now."

Aaron drew in a fractured breath.

Joseph tried to focus his unseeing eyes on his brother. He'd always believed that eye contact, man-to-man, was important. But with the dim lighting inside the barn, murky shadows were barely visible through the gray haze. Outside in the daylight, he could at least make out the barn's faint, rough outline or a person's foggy silhouette.

"I'll be here for you, Aaron," he finally said. "Whatever you need. Just ask. I'll do my best."

Aaron grasped his arm and pulled him over to the small workbench in the barn. "I could use your help trying to get this built." He paused, clearing his throat. "So we can bury him...our little Jeremiah."

The lump in his throat grew larger just hearing his nephew's name. He wanted to help, but how could he build something when he couldn't see?

Moreover, how could he tell his brother no?

Then Katie's words came back to him. Her encouragement that he could be a carpenter even without sight. That his skill had as much to do with touch as anything else. Although she had no carpentry experience, she'd had students in the past who'd succeeded in the trade. She'd assured him that there were many things he could do if his vision wasn't what it had been.

Awkwardly, he raised his hands and felt the wood that Aaron had already cut. The pieces were so small. Just like little Jeremiah, whose lifeless body Ben had wrapped and placed in a handmade crib that should've cradled life, not death.

While he slid his hands over the individual sections of the crude box, he heard quickened footsteps approach the barn and turned his attention to the doorway.

"Aaron," Katie breathed. "Ellie's asking for you."

Without a word, Aaron squeezed Joseph's shoulder and ran back toward the house.

A wave of compassion rose within Joseph. Had he

ever married, he would've counted himself a blessed man to know love like Aaron and Ellie's. Aaron had found someone he cherished, and who treasured him.

Swallowing hard, he turned back to the wood pieces and began estimating the width and length. When Katie approached his side, he stilled his hands on the wood. "He wants me to help build a coffin."

Rain, steady and serene, made a pitter-patter sound on the barn roof as Katie stood silently beside him. The faintest aroma of fresh rain mixed with the lily scent she wore wafted to his senses, making him already miss her sweet presence.

"I don't think he's trying to push you too fast, Joseph. I just think he wants to know you're here for him."

"I know. I told him I'd help out and I intend to make good on my promise," he said with a nod. Turning, he leaned back against the workbench. "I'm probably not a good judge since I couldn't see her, but the way Ellie sounded in there...he needs to be with her. Doesn't he?"

Katie sniffed in front of him. Several moments passed in quiet and with each one he fought the urge to reach out and comfort her. But holding her was sure to weaken his resolve. Once she was in his arms he'd be overcome with the sense that she somehow belonged there.

But she was upset. Even though Katie had known Ellie for only a brief time, they'd become close friends. Just moments ago Ellie had urged him not to let Katie get away—an urging that Joseph had silently pushed aside. Now that he couldn't offer himself as a whole man, he had to let Katie go.

Sooner or later, he'd have to get used to having her around and not wanting her for his own. She'd told him once already that she had no intention of going back to Iowa. If she stayed, Sam would probably pursue her with more allure than a snake charmer. When Sam wanted something, he usually went after it with lightning speed and solid assurance.

Hearing her quietly sniff again, he shrugged off his silent deliberation and shoved away from the workbench. "Come here, Katie," he whispered, reaching out and pulling her to himself.

He drew his arms around her, spanning a hand at her small waist, and one at her back.

On a quiet sob, she curled her arms in front of her and relaxed against him. Like sunshine on snow, she seeped into him, melting his defenses. Closing his eyes, he took in her scent, her form, her sweet presence in his arms. For a full, magnificent moment, he held her as if they belonged together.

Pressing his lips to the top of her head, he knew that he could bring her comfort.

But when he opened his eyes to find the darkness again, he realized that that'd be about it. He couldn't protect her. He couldn't drive his own team of horses without her by his side. And he probably couldn't provide enough for a family to live on. What could he do if he couldn't be a carpenter?

The image of himself, begging on some street, a tin cup held out to those with pity, crawled through his mind.

Joseph cringed at the picture. No matter what happened, he'd never, *ever* be reduced to that. He had too much pride and resourcefulness. He might not make a nice, comfortable living again, but he'd never beg.

Katie deserved far more than he could give her. She

deserved the world—and more. He could only give her a small bit of comfort. But comfort couldn't put food on the table or see danger and circumvent it.

On a shudder, she finally spoke. "Ellie doesn't look good. Not at all." Her voice was so solemn that it made his heart hurt. "She's so pale and very weak. I'm really worried, Joseph."

He trailed his hands to her arms, cherishing this touch as he stepped back away from her. "Me, too. And I know that Ben is—I can hear it in his voice. He'll do all he can medically, and we can pray and do what we can here to help them."

Brushing against the wood pieces behind him, he slowly turned around to try to make sense of the pile. "I don't even know where to begin. I mean, I've made one of these before.... I just haven't ever done it without sight."

Katie sidled up next to him. "It looks like Aaron put the pieces in piles according to size."

That struck him as odd—Aaron was never so organized before. Joseph furrowed his brow and carefully slid his hands over the neat piles, remembering how Aaron's haphazard ways had always driven him mad.

Katie grasped his hand and set it on a pile. "These are the longer, narrow boards." Then she slid his hand to another pile. "And these, the wider, short boards."

"They must be the outside end pieces," he added, making mental notes as she continued showing him each pile.

After she'd placed a hammer, nails and the pieces he needed within his reach, he was about to give it his best try when Aaron came back inside the barn. He said that Ellie had finally fallen asleep, and Katie excused herself to return to the house and do some quiet chores while Ben kept tabs on Ellie.

"So, do you think you could help me with this?" Aaron's voice was ragged with emotion. "It's not a task a fella wants to do alone. You know?"

"Of course I'll help."

The pain and grief Aaron had to be feeling and the way he kept going regardless inched through Joseph's mind. When had Aaron gotten so mature? When had he grown up to become the man who worked beside him with patience, steadiness and precision?

Joseph pondered those things while they completed a job no father would ever wish to do. While they made the finishing touches on the small, modest coffin, Joseph didn't feel as if he'd offered much in the way of expertise. But he was sure that being there for his brother, walking through that heartbreaking task together, meant more than if he'd built the most splendid, elaborate coffin fit for a king…or a baby prince.

Dawn's first light barely cracked through the pouring rain, gray skies and cool temperatures. Katie quickly donned a pale green dress made of thin wool challis and over that, her cloak. With a covered basket heavy with food prepared by Aunt Marta, and a roofed buggy made ready by Uncle Sven, she picked up Joseph and they drove out to Aaron and Ellie's early.

With the baby's death and funeral all in the same day, and Ellie's unstable condition, Ben had dropped them off just before midnight. But at least there'd been a positive turn of events before they'd left the cabin, as it seemed that Ellie's bleeding was lessening some. Katie had lain awake and prayed all night for her friend, but something ate away at her, undermining any peace she had.

Morning hadn't come soon enough.

When they neared the cabin, she narrowed her gaze to see through the wind-whipped rain. Staring ahead at the large old pine tree that stood as a silent, settled guardian at the foot of the baby's grave, she caught sight of a dark form hunched over at the fresh mound of dirt.

"Is that—Aaron?" Alarm slithered through her.

"Where? Where is he?" Joseph leaned forward, clutching the seat.

Urgency overwhelmed her and she pushed the horses faster. "I can't tell. The rain...it's—" The breath whooshed from her lungs as the image came more clearly. Cupping a hand to her mouth, she held back her moan.

"What is it, Katie? What's wrong?" Joseph grasped her arm, his touch the only thing that kept her from crying out.

Disbelief knifed through her. Her heart twisted in pain. "It—It's Ellie. She's lying on the grave."

"What about Aaron? Is he there?"

She nodded, swiping at the tears pooling in her eyes. "Yes, he's there. He's holding her." Struggling to hold back the deep sob that threatened to release, she focused on driving the horses into the rain-soaked yard. "Oh, dear God, no," she whispered, a lump lodging in her throat at the unmistakable stain of red she saw covering Ellie's muslin nightgown.

Joseph catapulted down from the bench, reached up and found her hand. "Take me there. Please, Katie," he urged.

"Oh, Joseph, it's awful," she whispered. Thunder clapped, shaking the ground. "Something terrible must've happened."

When she and Joseph approached the grave, Aaron lifted his head, his boyish features contorted in anguish and his

tear-stained face streaked with dirt. "I've lost her, Joseph."
He nuzzled his face into Ellie's strawberry blond hair,
dripping wet and plastered to her ashen face by the rain.

Katie's insides balled tight at the wounded cry. She
breathed a desperate prayer for Aaron as thunder rumbled
over the valley floor.

Dropping to his knees in the mud, Joseph felt his way
to where his brother clutched Ellie's limp body. "What is
it, Aaron? What do you mean you've lost her?"

Katie's stomach churned. She was unable to move or
think beyond the horrific fact that Ellie was dead. How
could she be? Hadn't she taken a turn for the better? Her
bleeding had lessened. That's what Ben had said....

Quaking from head to toe, Katie peered through her
watery gaze at the bloodred stain, already being diluted
by rain. The sight of Aaron's broad shoulders shaking
with silent sobs twisted her heart. She slipped out of her
cloak, spreading the light wool over him and adjusting it
so it draped over Ellie, too. Stooping to kneel beside
Joseph, her breath caught and heart dropped at the sight
of the small booties Ellie had knit for the baby, clutched
in her lifeless, dusky hand.

"She didn't want to—to leave the baby," Aaron cried
as a blast of thunder shook the ground. His voice was so
forlorn that Katie thought her heart might break in two.
"After you left last night she begged to see Jeremiah's
grave. But she wasn't strong enough, Joseph. She wasn't
strong enough."

"I know, Aaron," Joseph soothed.

Katie bit back a sob when he grasped Aaron's shoulders, as though trying to lend him strength. "I know how
much she wanted to be here to lay the baby to rest."

Joseph's voice was thick with emotion. "But she was so weak from the blood she'd lost."

Closing her eyes to the sight of her friend's lifeless body, Katie recalled how frantic, how inconsolable Ellie had been when Katie had sat with her yesterday, during Jeremiah's funeral. She'd held Ellie until the grieving mother had cried herself to sleep.

Unwilling to believe that Ellie was really dead, Katie stretched her hand toward her friend. She touched Ellie's arm, which dangled stiffly from her husband's embrace. Her stomach churned at the hard, cold feel of Ellie's fair skin. The touch left no question as to whether death had left its distinctive, chilling mark.

Pulling her hand back, she blinked away hot tears stinging her eyes. For a moment, her vision narrowed to a black, cavernous tunnel and she thought she might pass out. Inhaling deeply, she glanced up to see Aaron's face crumple in agony.

He stared at Joseph, his desperate gaze begging for relief from his torment. "I told her I'd take her as soon as she got strong enough. I promised her I'd bring her out here to see where we laid our son to rest—under our favorite tree."

Smoothing back rain-soaked hair from her eyes, Katie slid her gaze up to the tree. She swallowed hard and took in the initials surrounded by a heart that had been carved into the thick trunk. Remembering when Ellie had told her about Aaron's first true and hopelessly romantic declaration of love.

"Ellie begged me to bring her out here, Joseph." Aaron settled a desperate kiss on his wife's forehead as though hoping that his love for her would be enough to bring her back to life. "I wanted to. But I didn't th—I didn't think she'd be strong enough. And the rain…"

"I know, Aaron. It's all right." With a compassion that gripped Katie's heart, Joseph tentatively reached up and wiped at the tears streaming down his brother's face. "You did the right thing. You're a good, loving husband."

His brother shook his head sharply. "No. No, I'm not," he moaned, rocking Ellie's limp body back and forth over the fresh grave. "I should've stayed awake all night watching over her. She was so upset. I couldn't have nodded off for long when—" His words broke on a loud sob.

Tears trickled down Joseph's face and mingled with the droplets of rain beading his face. Katie allowed her own tears to fall as he slid his hand down to find Ellie's face and then to her arm, as though feeling for himself, whether the cold, hard touch of death was really there.

Aaron pulled in a broken breath. He lifted Ellie's hand that held the little booties to his mouth, pressing his lips to each finger. "Somehow she made it out here by herself. I found her here at daybreak. Laying dead on Jeremiah's grave."

A quiet groan escaped Katie's lips. She squeezed her eyes against the tears, knowing that Aaron's pain must be almost more than he could bear. To see this man, so strong and capable, and so full of despair, made her weep for him.

"I'm so sorry." Joseph's low voice was barely audible over the pounding thunder and unyielding downpour.

Aaron rained kisses over his wife's serene, pale face, his whole body shuddering with quiet sobs. He stared into his Ellie's face for a long, agonizing moment as though memorizing her beautiful, delicate features. Then he pulled her even tighter to himself, rocking her back and forth again in some silent rhythm that perhaps only heaven knew.

Joseph grasped Katie's arm and leaned close. "We need to get him inside. Can you help me?"

She lightly squeezed his hand, blinking off the raindrops beading her lashes. "Yes. Just tell me what to do."

For the next few minutes Katie wavered between strength and weakness as Joseph coaxed Aaron step by heartbreaking step back to the cabin. Although Aaron was exhausted physically and emotionally, he refused to relinquish his wife's body to Joseph's strong arms. Witnessing the way Joseph took charge of the situation with the utmost compassion as he helped his brother back to the house made Katie's heart nearly break.

When they reached the door, she turned and peered through the heavy drizzle to stare at the fresh mound under the tree. Tears came hard as she saw where Ellie had lain, her lifeless body heaped on the grave, her blood soaking into the earth where Aaron had buried their firstborn son.

Chapter Eleven

The three days since Ellie's funeral had felt like a month. And the six days since Joseph's appointment in Denver, like a year. The hours had dragged by and his agitation had grown tenfold knowing that Aaron had resumed work on the furniture order at the crack of dawn this morning. Over the past couple of days Joseph had urged Aaron to take plenty of time off, insisting that a weekend full of family and friends visiting and offering condolences, food and help wasn't a sufficient amount of time.

And now here it was Monday morning and Aaron was back at work, pouring himself into things.

Joseph hadn't stepped foot in the shop since his accident. He'd banked on digging into things upon the return of his sight, and that hadn't happened. Since his return from Denver, there'd been one tragedy after another. But knowing that his brother was in the shop this very moment, working so hard to escape the pain of his loss, drove Joseph to try and find his way to the building at the back of his property, to help if he could.

In spite of the long list of trials, the order deadline hadn't been lengthened even a day. And even though the chance of completing it on time was slim to none, he had to at least try.

Standing on his back porch, he gave a sharp whistle and immediately heard the sound of Boone's large, heavy paws padding across the ground. The dog gently burrowed his head between Joseph's knees, a trait he'd recently adopted.

"Hey, boy. How are you doing?" Joseph bent to scratch him behind the ears. "Do you want to go to the shop with me?"

Boone lightly pressed his full body against Joseph's legs and Joseph slid his hands down the dog's back. He could feel the way Boone lobbed his tail from side to side, his back end moving almost independently of the rest of his body.

"I take it that's a yes." He chuckled.

Boone didn't get to go to the shop often because his hair wreaked havoc with the work. Like homing pigeons, the fine hairs inevitably landed on whatever had been freshly varnished.

"Do you think I could tag along? Unless Aaron's been snitching, I bet we could find some jerky for you in my stash." He stepped down from the porch and trailed the dog.

"Good job, Boone," Joseph encouraged as he opened the shop door and poked his head inside.

"Aaron? Are you here?" he called, his voice echoing in the large wood-filled room.

He was surprised when there was no reply, so he stepped inside with Boone scurrying in beside him, no doubt determined to cash in on the tasty incentive. Clos-

ing the door, Joseph reached down and ruffled the unruly
hair on Boone's head, then stood upright. He found the
can of jerky he kept by the door and gave a couple of
pieces to Boone.

"Aaron, you here?" he called again, wondering if
maybe he'd caught his brother at a bad time, when words
were hard to find. No matter how strong Aaron had
seemed over the weekend, Joseph knew very well that his
brother was devastated.

Aaron's pain was far worse than the sting of going
blind. That awareness had struck Joseph deep over the
past few days, bringing some needed clarity and perspective to his situation. Life without sight was difficult, but
maneuverable. But Aaron's heartache seemed cruel.

Swallowing hard, he inhaled the distinctive scents surrounding him. The fresh-cut wood, the varnish, the stain.
Even the old leather chair by his desk. He closed his
eyes and drank everything in, strangely invigorated by the
experience.

When Boone dropped to his place at the door, Joseph
stepped forward, the familiar, muffled crunch of sawdust
bits beneath his feet, like some kindhearted grandfather
drawing him out of hiding.

He reached out, his fingertips connecting with the large
workbench that sat like a massive centerpiece in the room.
Grasping the bench's thick edge, he ran his hands across
the surface, noticing how scarred, how well used it was.
After a long moment, he turned and moved over to the
wall, feeling for where the small hand tools were usually
hung. He carefully worked his fingers over the wall, surprised to find each tool suspended neatly in its place, as
though he'd never been gone.

A little farther and he reached his desk. Afraid he might find the surface littered with papers and tools, he tentatively set his hands on the desk. He patted the expanse of oak and furrowed his brows. There were no tools, no papers. Just one neat pile at the left-hand corner where he'd always set aside any paperwork related to ongoing jobs.

Aaron had not only kept the shop from complete disarray in Joseph's absence, but he'd managed to maintain a condition that was tidy. The shop was essentially just as he'd left it.

"You make me proud, Aaron," he whispered, determined to tell his brother that face-to-face.

He skimmed his hand over the old and slightly torn leather chair pushed into his desk, then moved on to find a row of unfinished furniture. A good number of the pieces were lined up in the back of the shop, their broad surfaces rough and awaiting the fine finish for which he'd gained a reputation.

A small tremor of satisfaction shook him from deep within. And a sense of belonging settled over him like a warm, life-giving breeze after a cold, harsh winter. This was a part of him. This shop and the work done here was not only a solid part of his past, but a promising part of his future.

Moving over to the workbench again, he used it as a guide as he slowly worked his way around the room, savoring the revelation. An overwhelming sense of contentment stole over him and he found himself eager to work with his hands again.

But when his fingertips came into contact with the large steel clamp bolted to the workbench, icy aversion sliced through him. He pulled back as though bitten.

Images of that day when he'd fallen from the ladder came hard and fast. Reaching to grab a board. Losing his balance. Falling backward. He'd tried to right himself. He'd groped for something to hang on to.

Trembling, he raised his hands to the cold, hard steel. Held his breath and slid his fingers over the unyielding shape. Bleak and dank to the touch, it seemed as though it mocked Joseph and his blindness. With a strong grip and an even stronger determination, he held the vise and outlined the shape, with its combination of sharp edges and rounded curves.

Standing here now, he knew that he couldn't go back and change things. Instead, he removed his hands from the vise, breaking free from all the what-ifs and lingering regret. For the first time since his accident, he didn't feel overwhelmed, or depressed, or even bitter…but resolved.

Although he could begin to embrace the idea that he could be a carpenter again, he would never let himself grow used to the idea of taking a wife.

Standing in the mercantile, his hands positioned nervously on the glass counter, Joseph jerked to attention at a familiar odor.

Julia. He'd know her cloying scent a mile away.

The sound of her footsteps lightly tapped across the scarred plank floor, her overwhelming perfume blocking out the various dry goods scents that wafted to his senses.

He clenched his hands into fists, steadying himself as he stood there waiting for Aaron to return from the storeroom with Mr. Heath. Almost a week had passed since Aaron had buried Ellie beside their baby boy. Aaron had spent every waking hour at the shop, working his hands raw, then sleeping on a cot near the stove in the shop. He'd submerged himself in his job, rather than seeking out others for comfort. Joseph had worked alongside him and considered it a small victory that today his brother had agreed to accompany him to the mercantile.

"Well, Joseph Drake! I didn't dream I'd run into you today," Julia announced, slipping up next to him.

He turned toward her, sure that by now she must know the outcome of his appointment. With Ellie's funeral, there'd been enough friends and townsfolk around that she'd have heard.

"Didn't plan on running into you either." He shifted uncertainly, pulling his shoulders back.

When she perched her hand on his arm, her touch stirred up unease. "I see you have those awful wraps off. Quite frankly, I can't imagine how you could stand them for so long. I'm absolutely certain I would've ripped them off, had it been me."

He forced a congenial look her way. "Can't say I miss them much."

Julia trailed her fingers up his arm to his shoulder. "So…is it true?" she uttered conspiratorially. She leaned toward him, her powdery perfume nearly gagging him. "You're…blind?"

He cringed when she whispered the last word as though it was socially impolite, offensive. He still had a hard time admitting the truth—that he was blind. In the presence of others, except his brothers, Sam and especially Katie, he sensed awkwardness. As though people didn't quite know what to say or do. Well-meaning though they may be, sometimes people would treat him as though he was deaf, mute *and* blind.

If Katie was around, she'd almost always come to his rescue, though never by making it look as though she had to—a small detail for which he was thankful. She had a very tactful way of diverting attention.

He hadn't asked for her to return to work with him again, though he surely felt the lack. Joseph was grateful for the two weeks he'd had with her, knowing that without them, he'd be fumbling around like a babe in nappies. He'd been trying to get by without help from his brothers, but some things he just couldn't manage on his own.

Maybe when he was certain he could be around Katie without feeling the intense draw he still experienced, he'd ask her to come back. And if Sam would just get the ball rolling and propose marriage, then she really would be off-limits. Sam had commented that they'd had several in-depth conversations on her aunt and uncle's front porch, and that he was just waiting for the "right" time to tell her of his intentions.

For now, Joseph had to fight his own desire for her.

Through the deaths of Ellie and the baby, Joseph had gotten a closer glimpse into Katie's character. Her compassion, her strength and her gentle caring ways. She was everything and more of what he wanted in a wife. He cared deeply for her. But she could never know. And Sam could never find out.

When he felt Julia's breath fan across his face, he jerked his attention back to her lingering question. "Yes. It's true. I'm blind," he answered, loud enough to make her uncomfortable.

Her tsk-tsk-tsk set the hairs of his neck on end. "That's what I'd heard, though not from numerous sources. Just one *very* reliable source." On a dramatic sigh, she patted his arm. "Of course, you can imagine my surprise. I scarcely believed it, since you were absolutely certain things would be fine. But now that I'm here, seeing with my very own eyes, I must concede that it is true."

"Yep. It's true," he echoed, waving a hand in front of his face for effect. "Can't see a thing. If you'll excuse me…"

Slipping away from her, he tried to picture the layout of the mercantile, wanting to move as far away from her as possible. But uncertainty assaulted him and instead he scooted down to the end of the counter. A heated flush worked up his neck and his pulse pounded in his ears. Drumming his fingers against the glass, he willed his brother back. Now!

Although he tried to look nonchalant and unaffected by her presence, doubts as to whether he'd buttoned his shirt correctly suddenly assailed him, undermining what little composure he had. He resisted the urge to check, knowing for certain that she was still standing there. He could smell her, for goodness's sake. And he was sure she was staring at him. He could easily imagine her curious gaze, taking his full measure as if he were a piece of meat that had spoiled.

He hated this!

Jamming his hands into his pockets, he pulled his shoulders back. He could loathe this kind of incident and let it get the best of him or get used to it, knowing that people would be curious whether he liked it or not.

And Julia was curious to a fault.

"So, did you want to ask anything else?" he began, drawing his mouth into a tight line as he raised his brows. "There must be some kind of burning question on your mind, like maybe if I've made a mess of a meal lately?"

After a stunned silence and imperious sniff, she muttered, "Uh…no."

A self-satisfied grin stole across Joseph's face. And even though Julia still stood there, no doubt glaring at him, he didn't even try to wipe it off. It felt too good.

The sun had begun a leisurely descent in the western sky, sinking low and dragging with it the minute bit of light Joseph treasured. He sat on the porch steps and stared into the sky, letting the waning light of day wash over him before night crept in and the dim shadows turned dark again.

He'd worked in the shop with Aaron from sunup until now, and was exhausted from the level of concentration he'd maintained all day—every day. He wondered if, given time, things would grow easier. Every task seemed twice as hard and took twice as long. Even though they'd made surprising headway on the order, finishing it on time was still a long shot.

But he wasn't about to go down without a fight and lose his shop because of some intimidating deadline. He'd do whatever it took to make sure the job was finished on time. And though Aaron probably didn't care one bit whether he received anything extra, Joseph was eager to reward his brother heftily for the hard, laborious work he'd given to complete the job.

The distant cadence of footsteps over the boardwalk generated a long, wistful sigh from Joseph. What he wouldn't give to walk to and from without relying on someone else. Since he'd joined Aaron in the shop over a week ago, his brother had picked him up in the morning or Joseph had coaxed Boone to let him tag along, bribing him with a handful of treats. If he kept that up, Boone would be so round that Katie's initial impression that the dog was a black bear wouldn't be so far off the mark.

The memory brought a low chuckle from Joseph. He didn't think he'd ever forget that day, when she'd squeezed behind him, afraid she was going to be bear lunch.

For an instant he'd felt useful, normal. But the bandages he'd had on his head had been a stark reminder that things had changed for him, he just hadn't known how much at that time.

In most every aspect of life he had made adaptations, from the way he prepared a meal, to something as small as making sure he'd pushed in a chair. Sooner rather than later, he'd have to start using the cane. That's why he sat holding it now, determined that today would be the day. Hadn't Katie said that it would make things easier for him? Affording him independence he was desperate to taste again? It had been almost two weeks since he'd returned from Denver, and though he'd come to some sort of resolution regarding his blindness, he still avoided the thing. It was as if using the cane as his guide would somehow solidify his fate.

He held the finely sanded object in his hands, feeling its length and narrow circumference. He tried to imagine himself with it, walking to the mercantile or to church or to the hotel restaurant. Humiliation rose hot and ready to sting.

Joseph ignored the caustic burn, forcing his focus to the cane. He set it on end at his feet and tapped the small tip on the hard ground again and again, determined to come to terms with this. He'd never imagined that a stick of wood, so insubstantial and harmless, could loom like some evil enemy.

"Good evening, Joseph." Katie's warm voice startled him.

He shot off the step, the cane dropping to the ground with a quiet thunk. "Hello."

"Sorry if I startled you," she called from the gate, the mellow lilt of her voice soothing something deep inside him.

He passed a hand through his hair, wondering if he looked as ruffled as he felt. "Don't worry. No harm done."

The gate opened and closed with a restful creak. "I just wanted to stop by and say hello. I hope you don't mind."

"No. Not at all. Come on up and have a seat." He gestured to the steps with a smile, then sat down beside her, recalling how he'd wanted to check in on her a couple hundred times.

She'd been so strong through Ellie's death. Joseph had been grateful to have Katie with him that morning. He'd worried plenty about her, but he couldn't very well check in on her when he couldn't make it to Sven and Marta's on his own. Besides, he didn't think he was ready to be in her quiet yet compelling presence without feeling so out of control of his own emotions. Even now his heart raced inside his chest.

Sam had told him just yesterday that he was encouraged by the interactions he'd had with Katie and hoped to make his intentions for her known by the time he left for the city in a week or two. If Sam didn't make a move soon, Joseph might just have to prod his friend some, even though doing so would be like ripping his own flesh.

"I hope you've been well," he finally said, turning to

face Katie. "What's it been? A week since I saw you last?" he asked, the irony of his own words hanging before him.

She gave his arm a brief squeeze and sighed. "I've been busy. Things have been so hectic for Uncle Sven at the lumber mill that I've been helping him with his ledgers."

Joseph furrowed his brows in surprise. "Do you like to do that sort of thing?"

"I don't mind it, really. I'm willing to try anything."

Regret prickled Joseph. He knew very well that she enjoyed her job as a trainer and teacher. She was good at it, too. If he could get over his feelings for her, he'd ask her back in a heartbeat. But with the order he and Aaron were trying to finish in the shop, he wasn't sure when he'd even have time to work with her. In the evenings he was usually so tired.

But being with her right now, it suddenly dawned on him how energized he felt.

"So, you looked like you were deep in thought," she probed.

He felt for the cane on the ground, then drew it up on end in front of him. "It's this thing."

"That *thing* again, huh?"

He sighed. "I know I need to get used to using it, but for the life of me, I can't seem to bring myself to do that."

"I understand. Just know that once you've gotten the hang of it, you'll wonder why you didn't take it up sooner."

He nodded. "Probably."

After a settling silence she cleared her throat. "Ben said that you've been working with Aaron. How's that been going?"

"Surprisingly well." Joseph turned toward Katie. "He has the patience of Job, and believe me…he's needed it working with me. I get so frustrated not being able to see what I'm doing," he ground out, tightening his grip on the cane. "But Aaron's been a great help, and between the two of us we've devised some pretty good systems."

"I'm so glad," she breathed, resting her hand on his arm.

Warmed by her touch, he chose to ignore the fact that he was nearing dangerous territory. "You were, too, you know."

"I was what?"

"A great help. I thought about what you'd said, that I could do carpentry work again, and that gave me hope."

"I'm glad, but really, your talent didn't diminish an ounce when you had your accident, Joseph. You just needed to discover that for yourself."

"I suppose," he finally admitted as he rolled the cane between his palms. "Listen, I'm new at this cane and I was wondering if maybe you'd give me some pointers."

"I'd be—"

"I know you're not officially working with me," he interrupted, half expecting she might turn him down. After all, he'd sent her packing when they'd returned from Denver. "I just wondered, as long as you're here…."

"Of course, I'll show you. I'd be glad to."

"I'll pay your wages for whatever time I use," he added.

"Don't be ridiculous!" She gave his arm a playful shove.

Standing, Joseph cocked his head down at her and smiled. "So, the lady has a feisty side…."

Katie stood, sighing. "I get that way when I have to."

He held the cane in front of him and readied himself as though facing a firing squad. "All right, then. Have at it."

Katie chuckled as she came to stand next to him. "Hold the cane this way." She lightly grasped his hand and adjusted his grip as he struggled to focus on her instruction, instead of on her touch. "Now move the cane back and forth like this."

As she demonstrated, standing behind him and threading her arm around his, he felt his resolve crumbling fast. "If there's something in your way or a step ahead of you, you'll know."

Doing what she'd instructed, he took a turn to his gate and back, counting steps and moving the cane the way she'd advised.

"Perfect," she commented as he stopped beside her.

He smiled. "Good instruction I guess, Sunshine." Tilting his head toward where she stood beside him, he pulled in a long breath, dragging a hand over the stubble on his chin. "I could use some practice, though. You wouldn't want to go on a walk with me, would you?"

"A walk sounds very nice." Katie's voice was light as the late-summer breeze filtering through his cotton shirt.

They took off down the street, and Joseph tried to remain fully concentrated on his technique.

"That's it," she encouraged as he slowed to a stop some distance from his home. "Just make sure you're keeping it far enough in front of you that if you come across an obstacle, you'll be able to stop in time."

He pulled his head around, searching for light. Finding none, he figured they must be beneath a tree. "If I'm correct, I'm standing outside the boarding house, right?"

Joseph wondered if Sam was there. He could hear the faint sound of voices floating through open windows, but he didn't pick up Sam's low timbre among them, which was probably for the best. If his friend walked out here now, Joseph didn't know how he'd react to Sam's tangible attraction for Katie.

He often wondered if Katie felt the same attraction to Sam. Why wouldn't she? Sam was a successful, good-hearted man.

A whole man.

"Yes, we're a little over four blocks from your home." She came to stand in front of him and grew quiet. "Can you see anything, Joseph?"

The tenderness in her voice melted his heart. It had from the moment she'd said one word to him. She was so caring. So considerate. So full of kindness.

Yes, he could see clearly that she was perfect for him—that's what he could see. But he wasn't perfect for her. And never would be.

Determined not to dwell on what could never be, he shoved the disappointment aside with a shake of his head. "With the sun going down and being under the tree here, I can't see much of anything. In daylight, though, I can see gray silhouettes. It's a far cry from vivid sight, but at least it's something."

While they stood in companionable silence, a wagon rolled by. Its wheels clacked and the horses' hooves clomped over the hard-packed ground. He pictured the wide street, the gracious boarding house, the wagon and horses. The expanse of skyline, sparse grass and the majestic mountains hemming in the valley.

But as Joseph focused down toward Katie, he wondered once again what she looked like. He'd heard enough from Sam and his brothers to know that she was beautiful. He'd love to see her for himself. Just once.

On a deep breath, he drew his sightless gaze from her. "Well, this was easier than I thought," he confessed.

"It'll certainly make things easier," she agreed, the sweep

of her hand rustling down her skirt. Katie paused and after several moments cleared her throat, her voice gone dreamy, as if she'd just awoke from a long, restful nap. "You're looking good, Joseph. I'm so glad to see you smiling."

Right now he wished that he hadn't become so astute to the emotions layered in a person's voice. Even though he'd like to pretend it wasn't there, he couldn't miss the deep affection, even longing in her sweet lilting voice.

Chapter Twelve

"Hello there, Miss Ellickson." The voice, low and pleasant, halted Katie on her perch. "Aren't you a fetching sight?"

Grasping the ladder for support, Katie twisted around from where she'd been hanging decorations for the Glory Days celebration to find Sam smiling up at her. Without a doubt, the man was dashingly handsome with his dark hair, stunning smile and trim build.

But seeing Sam didn't do to her insides what seeing Joseph did. Being with Joseph made her heart beat fast and hard, made her stomach quiver and made a smile form on her face that was hard to wipe off.

"Hello, yourself." She returned his smile.

Knowing she probably looked a sight, she brushed at the strands of hair that had fallen out of her loose chignon. When she began descending the ladder, she gasped as his hands circled her waist and gently hauled her to the ground.

"Thank you," she breathed.

"At your service, lovely lady." His playful bow made

her chuckle. "What are you doing climbing ladders anyway? Surely others can do that job." He glanced around the square.

"I'm fine. With two brothers, I spent many an afternoon climbing trees and haylofts." Katie laid her hammer and nails in the basket at her feet, then brushed her hands together.

"Oh?" He raised his perfectly shaped brows. "Climbing trees, huh? I know the best climbing tree around if you ever get the inclination. Joseph and I spent hours up in that tree."

A trickle of longing worked through her at the mention of Joseph's name. Wiping at the beads of sweat on her brow, she caught Sam grinning at her. "Sounds like you two had fun."

"That we did. Sometimes a little too much fun," he confessed, his mouth still set in a smile. He rested a hand at the small of her back, leading her into the shade of a tall oak, its branches draped outward like open arms of welcome. Folding his arms at his chest and leaning against the rough bark, he settled an intense gaze upon her.

"What?" she asked, furrowing her brows. She wiped her face with her sleeve and did a quick scan of her dress for signs of dirt. "Do I have a smudge of dirt somewhere?"

"You look perfect."

Embarrassment swept through her and she busily focused on smoothing out her robin's-egg-blue skirt, splashed liberally by a print of small white flowers.

"In fact, I don't believe I've ever seen a woman look so beautiful." His voice was thick with adoration. "I tell you, Katie, I'd be hard-pressed to find such elegance anywhere."

She raised her hands to her cheeks where a heated

blush embarrassed her further. Fighting to collect herself, she peeked up at him.

He dipped his head. Tenderly held her gaze.

Around Sam she felt as if she was the only other person walking the earth. He was a very kind man, generous with his compliments, though sincere. From all she'd heard, he was well-respected and loved in his hometown.

But there was Joseph.

She found herself thinking of him often. All the time, really. The way he'd held her, making her feel so protected and cared for, not evoking any of the fears she'd initially had with him. It hadn't taken long for her to realize he meant her no harm. Joseph Drake was a man she could trust with her life.

But could she trust him with her heart?

Clasping her hands in front of her, she scanned the city square where several people busily worked to complete the decorations in time for the celebration that started tomorrow.

"So what brings you out here?" She turned toward him. "Did you volunteer to help with the preparations, too?"

"I regret to say that I did not." He drew his mouth into a mock grimace, then settled a very direct, but warm gaze upon her. "I was hoping that perhaps I could whisk you off to dine with me on this beautiful afternoon. Does a picnic pique your interest?"

"A picnic?" Katie echoed in surprise.

She was sure he'd be a wonderful companion for a picnic. He'd been nothing but a gentleman each time she saw him, and he'd shown so much compassion in the aftermath of Ellie and the baby's death almost two weeks ago.

Katie's heart squeezed at the memory of her dear

friend. She sorely missed Ellie, their honest conversations and friendship. At times like these she wished for her friend's honest guidance.

"I'm sorry, Sam. I—I appreciate your offer, but there's still so much to do here," she faltered, wishing it was Joseph standing here asking her to go on a picnic.

There was something far more than just a passing fancy for Joseph resonating in her heart. His muscle-roped arms had made her knees weak, and the strength she'd found in his embrace gave her a security she'd never known. His hand at her back set her nerve endings humming, arousing sensations so innate she'd be hard-pressed to subdue them.

She'd relished the opportunity to help him out the other day when she'd given pointers on using his cane, but she had fading hopes that he'd ask for more than that. He was very busy and had made no effort to contact her about returning to work with him.

She hugged her arms to herself. Joseph had been pleasant enough the past two weeks. But since he'd found out his vision wasn't returning, he seemed set on suppressing the warmth and interest he'd shown her before, shutting himself off like a snowed-in mountain pass.

Turning, Katie sighed as she viewed all of the undecorated venues that stood like roughly clad women awaiting their transformation into finely dressed ladies. "I'm afraid I won't be able to slip away, even for a short time."

Sam stepped back, setting his hand to his heart. "You wound me, Katie. Here I was hoping to take you away to the perfect place."

"The perfect place?" She angled her head.

"Yes." He stepped forward, inches from her. "You see,

Katie, I'm not a man to make rash decisions. Nor am I a man to stand idly by while something so perfect is within my reach." He raised a long finger to touch the tip of her nose. "I have every intention of asking you to be my wife."

"But I—" She topped midstream.

Be his wife? Had she heard him correctly?

Surely he was just teasing her. He often did. He was always calling her "m'lady" or "lovely lady" or whatever else suited his fancy at the time.

She raised a hand to capture the laughter that erupted at his playfulness. Bringing her watery gaze to rest on his, her laugh piddled out to a weak chuckle when she witnessed the sincerity in Sam's expression.

Her cheeks flushed instantly hot.

"Can I look forward to seeing you tomorrow?" He captured her hand, lightly brushing her knuckles with his lips.

Mutely she nodded, staring blankly at him as she drew her hands together, fingering where his lips had just been. For a moment she wondered what it would be like to be married to Sam. Surely he'd cherish her. The depth of honesty in his eyes spoke volumes. His kindness and genuine concern would make any woman happy, she was sure.

Katie just knew she couldn't be that woman. Especially since she was soiled. If Joseph never opened his heart to her again, she didn't think Sam, or anyone for that matter, would want her the way she was.

With a finger crooked beneath her chin, he lifted her head. "I'm going to be looking for your decorated box at the box lunch auction. Then you will be mine for the afternoon."

* * *

Katie clutched the box lunch in her hands, half tempted to fling it under the wheels of a passing wagon and head back to her aunt and uncle's house. Instead, she trudged onward, the lovely little handbag Ellie had made for her swinging from her wrist as she made her way to the town's celebration.

Her heart was heavy, weighed down by loss. After talking briefly with Aaron last night and seeing his drawn features full of grief and pain, she'd settled on avoiding today's festive atmosphere altogether. But Aunt Marta and Uncle Sven had strongly suggested she attend, assuring her that nothing would be gained by staying home, alone in her sadness.

They were probably right. Isolation wouldn't help. Besides, Katie needed to knit herself into this community and make it home. She couldn't go back to Iowa—not as long as Frank Fowler was there. Attending today was as good a way as any to get to know her neighbors and fellow townspeople.

Seeing how charming the town square looked with wooden booths and townspeople alike dressed in their finest made her smile. Ellie had been so enthusiastic about this day, with its box lunch auction, lively barn dance and fireworks display.

Katie forced a smile on her face and returned a wave to a young woman across the way. Scanning the square, she noticed how the adorned booths flanking each side of the open area drew attention, like beautiful paintings hung in a prestigious gallery. A swell of pride rose within her knowing that she'd played a small part in the visual splendor.

Lifting her chin a bit, she stepped across the grass

sparsely peeking through the reddish soil, and tugged on the hem of her new silk taffeta bodice. She smoothed down her matching skirt, appreciative of the indulgence her aunt and uncle had insisted on purchasing for her. With no children of their own, they'd often sent gifts to Katie and her siblings.

Although Katie had several nice dresses, she'd never owned one that made her feel as elegant as this one did. The periwinkle-blue color was like that of the late-summer blooms dotting the countryside. The stylish scoop neckline her aunt had urged her toward was edged with a graceful white lace collar, and clasped by a delicate silver brooch. Her other dresses touted more traditional, full skirts with room for several petticoats. But this one was cut in a slimmer fashion—a design the dressmaker said was all the rage out east.

When Katie reached the long threshing table located on the flag-draped auction platform, she stared in amazement. Dozens of boxes lined the table, like twittering schoolgirls dressed for their first dance. Some were tied up with twine—plain as the dirt beneath her feet—and others were bedecked in such elaborate detail they teetered on the edge of being garish.

She'd been forewarned that being a young, single female in this community, some considered it her womanly responsibility to proffer a box for eligible bachelors to bid on. Wishing that she'd avoided this event, she tucked her decorated box lunch in among the others, glad that there was nothing spectacular to call attention to hers. That was just as she'd wanted it. Not too plain and not too overstated, the pale blue ribbon was tied neatly, without fuss or flourish around the box. Three small daisy blooms and a touch of greenery she'd picked from her aunt's garden garnished the top of the light maple box. Eyeing her offering one last time and hoping for a swift lunch with an agreeable companion, she gave a small sigh.

Her attention was suddenly grabbed by one box in particular, displayed prominently at the front of the table. Picking it up, she turned it over in her hands and studied it. The package was fixed with a sparkling green ribbon and festooned with overly large flowers, and had Katie wondering if the creation was Julia's handiwork. A distinctive aroma even lingered about the parcel…perhaps a remnant of the owner?

Setting the box down, Katie was unable to hide her slight grin. Julia was like a spoiled child insisting on being the center of attention.

If Joseph was present today, Julia might focus her overbearing, inconsiderate ways on him again. The very thought needled Katie. She could only hope that Julia would find some small amount of tact in her reservoir of social etiquette.

Coaxing her white gloves from her hands, Katie glanced around the square again when her gaze collided headlong with Sam's. He stood with Joseph just inside the grassy square.

Warmth stole up her cheeks remembering what he'd said yesterday about becoming his wife. Surely he didn't mean it—she'd done her best to convince herself of that all night long. Chided herself for thinking he could actually be interested in her. After all, why would he set his sights on her when he had a whole city of fine women to choose from?

Had he been sincere, she faced a hard decision. One she'd rather not think about. It seemed advantageous, if not cowardly, for her to steer clear of him altogether.

But Sam was so nice. So much fun to be around. She didn't have the heart to shun him or avoid him just because her heart still beat a steady rhythm for Joseph.

When she skimmed her attention their way again, he promptly removed his hat and bowed, his dark hair gleaming in the sunlight. Straightening, he gave her a ready smile and a long, slow look that had her heart swelling ever so slightly.

Twisting her gloves over in her hands, Katie smiled back, feeling like a cat in a room full of rockers. She could be perfectly congenial to him—he'd make that easy. If she could just act as if he'd not made his intentions so blatantly known yesterday, then things would be fine.

She glanced their way again. Both men looked exceedingly handsome today. Sam in his dark gray suit and matching bowler hat. And Joseph… Joseph in his bronze-colored vest, ecru shirt and brown breeches that hinted at his powerful legs.

Her cheeks flushed warm as she raised her gaze to the rebellious locks of wavy chestnut hair that fell across Joseph's forehead and then to the length that skimmed his neckline. Her gaze lingered on him and a shiver of longing passed through her. She sorely missed his companionship and the safe refuge he offered. The mere sight of him and the vivid memory of his strong, protective embrace called from within her a chorus of emotions and sensations that were irrevocably unsettling.

"Ah, Joe…" Sam breathed, his voice gone thick with adoration. "I don't remember the scenery being quite so beautiful around here."

"You really have been away too long," Joseph teased.

He clutched his cane as he walked beside Sam across the town square, struggling to keep his head above a wave of self-consciousness. Other than going to and from the shop he hadn't ventured out in the public with his cane, and right about now he felt like the Glory Days celebration sideshow.

With a great deal of lost time yet to be made up on the order, Joseph had been set to work with Aaron in the shop today. But his brother had all but pushed him out the door to attend the town's festivities with Sam.

Pulling his shoulders back, he tried to ignore the self-consciousness he felt now. He didn't want his insecurities to affect his time with Sam. "Has the valley changed that much since you left?" he asked.

He caught a fiddle's faint song lilting over the jumble of voices in the vicinity. Took in the different aromas that bombarded his senses—the home-cooked foods, late-summer blossoms, even the grass beneath his feet. In past years he'd really enjoyed himself at this annual celebration, but this year he doubted he'd have much to write home about.

"I don't mean *that* kind of scenery, my friend. I mean the any-way-you-look-at-her, gorgeous woman due north," Sam quipped, making Joseph squirm. "Katie is elegance and purity all wrapped into one beautiful package, just like that box lunch I just saw her set on the table."

"So you know which one is hers, huh?" Joseph asked, trying his best to sound interested. "Guess that's a good thing."

"Yep. It'll be easy enough to spot with that huge green ribbon and big flowers she tied around it." Sam gave a subdued whoop. "Yep. It's a beautiful day, indeed. But this mountain valley—luscious as it is on a day like today—doesn't hold a candle to m'lady, Katie."

Joseph swallowed hard, determined not to let Sam's words get to him. He might well spend each day with his heart aching and each night imagining her in Sam's arms, but he'd do it for Katie's sake. It'd be torture, plain and simple, but what choice did he have? His friend deserved a woman like Katie. A sweet woman with strength of character and kindness of heart—and as Sam had said—a woman with unequalled beauty.

Katie deserved a man who wasn't encumbered by blindness.

"Katie, it's good to see you," Sam greeted as he slowed to a stop. "Wonderful day for the celebration, isn't it?"

"Yes, it is," she responded, a hint of hesitance in her voice. "How are you gentlemen today?"

"Even better now that I've seen you." Sam took a step forward and a chill wriggled down Joseph's spine. "You look lovely today, Katie."

"Thank you." Her voice was quiet. "How are you, Joseph?"

He shoved a hand into his pocket. "Fine. And yourself?"

"I'm doing well." Melancholy burdened her sweet voice.

Joseph grew immediately concerned because he could almost always count on her sunny demeanor. "You sound a little down."

"Just missing Ellie today. She was so excited for this event."

He nodded, a reminiscent smile tipping his mouth. "She was like a little girl when it came to things like this. I'm sure Aaron won't be here at all today."

"Probably not," Katie agreed.

"He's going to need time and a lot of prayer," Sam added, followed by a long moment of silence. "I believe I saw you put a box lunch on the table, Katie."

She sighed. "I hear it's mandatory if you're single."

"According to Mrs. Duncan and her followers, yes," Sam agreed with a chuckle. "Every year, for as long as I've been around, that woman has hit the streets campaigning for the event. The way she goes at it, visiting every household in the valley, you'd think she was Herod himself, seeking out all firstborn males—or single females as the case may be."

The sound of Katie's quiet laughter seeped into Joseph, making him wish he was a little closer to her.

"I'll say this for her, she's very persuasive." Katie gave a big sigh. "If I didn't know better I'd think my entrance to heaven hinged on this alone."

"You can bet that she'll make sure everyone is involved, even if she has to hold a gun to their heads," Sam quipped.

Joseph reminded himself once again that he had no claim on her. She wasn't his. But she wasn't really Sam's either.

"I wonder, Katie, who will be the highest bidder on your box lunch?" Sam shifted his feet lightly over the ground.

"I'm sure that whomever I dine with will be just fine."

Joseph balled his fists, clenching his jaws tight as he envisioned Sam sweeping Katie off for a private lunch. Were he able to see, he'd pay whatever it took to secure a picnic with Katie, making sure he was the first and last to bid on her box.

"Joseph Drake! Well, I never in my wildest imagination thought that I'd see you here today." Julia's voice and overpowering powdery scent cut a brassy path through the pleasant atmosphere. "Miss Appleton," she clipped off, the greeting colder than an icehouse in January.

"Ellickson, Julia," Joseph corrected, shaking his head.

"And who is this man with you, Joseph? Is he yet *another* teacher?" Julia's voice was so loud that Joseph had to resist the urge to plug his ears.

"This is Sam Garnett, a friend of mine."

"Really," she oozed, making Joseph marvel at how she could make her voice rise and fall an entire octave in one word.

"And I'm blind, Julia." He tightened his grip on his cane, unable to miss how Katie cleared her throat. "Not deaf."

"A pity it is, too, Joseph." She perched her fingers on his forearm and sidled up next to him. "A pity."

He stepped out of her touch and closer to Katie.

"Knowing Joseph, he won't let his lack of sight get the best of him," Sam said, gently slapping Joseph on the back. "He's not one to shrink from difficulty."

Joseph didn't doubt that Sam was coming to his rescue, but for some reason he didn't feel as if he needed rescuing.

"Mr. *Garnett,* you say?" Julia's skirt swished and Joseph wondered if the gown she wore was the one he'd spilled grape juice on. "Would that be from the Boston Garnetts?"

"No. The Boulder Garnetts, Julia. Sam grew up here. His folks passed on a year ago."

"How dreadful," she simpered. Barely missing a beat, she continued. "Why have I not had the privilege of making your acquaintance, Mr. Garnett?"

"I'm not sure why." Sam sounded amused.

"I'm not sure, either," Joseph echoed, seeing as how Julia made Boulder's business her business. "He's been in town three weeks." He nudged Sam's arm. "This is Julia Cranston."

"It's a pleasure to meet you, Miss Cranston."

Joseph wanted to laugh at Sam's gallantry, but didn't dare. Sam was probably playing with Julia and no doubt enjoying her drama and outlandish personality. He'd always had patience for things like that, where Joseph had decided that he preferred things straightforward.

"Mr. Garnett," Julia said as though greeting a king.

Joseph could only imagine the coy look she was sure to give Sam. The slight tilt of her chin. The way she'd peer at him sideways with her big emerald eyes.

"Are you in town for a visit or have you plans to stay?"

"Just a visit. Though who knows, I may decide to stay if the fancy strikes me," Sam responded.

"Well, now, that is good to hear, Mr. Garnett," she gushed. "I presume you'll be participating in the box lunch auction? Though primitive compared to eastern entertainment, it promises to be quite a marvelous event."

Sam chuckled. "I wouldn't miss it."

"Joseph, do you plan on having someone do your bidding for you?" Julia asked, her tone almost motherly. "Since you are unable to see, that is?"

He pulled a forced smile. "No, Julia. I don't."

She tsk-tsked. "Oh…what a pity, I tell you. The auction will positively be the talk of the town."

Joseph held his cane between both hands and drew it against his chest when Julia gasped.

"Are you lame, Joseph?" she nearly shouted, stepping in front of him. "Did you hurt your leg?"

"*Why* would you ask that?"

Julia huffed, her stale breath fanning across his face. "Well, you're carrying a cane. What else is one to think?"

"You tell me," he shot back, enjoying her confusion.

He could hear her hands brush against her skirt, the material slipping under her touch. "Naturally I assumed that perhaps you'd fallen and hurt yourself. Given your condition, it would certainly be a strong possibility, you know."

He smiled, feeling a tangible sense of satisfaction. "No, Julia. My leg is fine."

"Oh, well, the cane is fetching with your outfit, Joseph," she dismissed with a verbal flourish. "I didn't take you as one to make a fashion statement, but then, wonders never cease."

"Thank you."

"Miss Appleby," she continued.

"Ellickson," Joseph and Sam spoke in unison.

"Have you a box lunch to offer today?" she asked, almost accusing in her tone.

"I do," Katie responded simply.

"Splendid. Don't you worry one bit. I'm quite certain that some young bachelor is bound to place a bid on it. The men around here, though they lack the class of those back east, seem polite enough."

Katie chuckled, apparently unruffled by Julia's barbs. And that made Joseph proud. "I'm not worried."

"Though, being new to town, mind you," Julia continued as though she was some authority on the matter. "I wouldn't expect for your box to draw an overwhelming amount of money. You do understand, don't you, dear?"

"Thank you for the warning, Miss Cranston. I'll be sure to prepare myself."

Chapter Thirteen

Joseph jammed a booted foot up on the lowest fence railing, amused as he listened to Mr. Heath—mercantile owner turned auctioneer for the day—ramble off the bidding. He tipped his head back to the afternoon sun's full brightness, enjoying the faint bit of light he could see. With his cane secured against the fence, he bent over and braced an arm on his knee.

Every single year he was caught off guard by Mr. Heath's surprising cadence as it filled the town square. Oohs, aahs and cheers erupted from the crowd when a box went for a whopping six dollars and fifty cents—no small change in these parts.

"Who bought that one?" Joseph leaned toward Sam. He could easily envision his friend, the relaxed way he'd hold his arms at his chest and the way he'd drape one foot lazily in front of the other, as he leaned back against the railing.

"I think it went to Jacob Watson. That banker has a payroll that could outfit three large ranches." A deep chuckle resonated from Sam. "Or maybe Julia's wardrobe."

Joseph grinned at his friend's assessment. "It might take more than a banker to keep her happy."

"She's something else, isn't she?"

"That's an understatement." Threading his fingers through his hair, Joseph dragged in a breath. "She means well. But sometimes…"

"You handled her well-meaning words with finesse, my friend. I was proud of you."

"Thanks."

"No, really, I mean it. You're acting more and more like yourself again, and I'm glad to see it." Sam clapped him on the arm. "You know, Julia really isn't all that bad. She's oblivious to how her words come off, but socialites can be like that. Until you tame them, that is."

"It's hard to hate her," Joseph agreed, sliding his hand across the fence to make sure his cane was still there. He'd had to use Sam's arm as a guide a few times so far today. But mostly he'd put into action what he'd learned from Katie.

"I took Julia on a few outings before my accident. Nothing serious, though. Not as far as I was concerned, anyway. My blindness has made her noticeably uncomfortable around me now."

Sam puffed out a sigh. "That has to be hard to take."

"Yeah…at times."

"I just met her, but from what I can tell, Julia's similar to women from more affluent circles," Sam explained. "Most likely she doesn't know what to do with you because she's never really had to deal with sickness or injury."

Joseph nodded. "You're probably right. But whether it's her or someone else, I'm going to have to get used to that sort of thing," he added with a conciliatory sigh. "I just know that I'll never get married, that's all."

He sensed Sam turning toward him. "What do you mean, that's all? You've been planning on marrying for as long as—well, for as long as you and I've been noticing girls."

Joseph raised his brows, hoping he came close to making eye contact. "You're one to talk, Mr. I'm-not-married-yet-either," he shot back with satisfaction. "And, for the record, I did have a lady who had captured my attention."

"Well, then? Where is she?" Sam pressed, his voice low.

"I gave her up."

"What did you do that for?"

"I had my reasons. Besides, without my sight I'm not exactly *prime* husband material."

Sam huffed, shifting his feet on the hard ground. "You're not getting sympathy from me with *that* attitude."

"I wasn't looking for sympathy," Joseph countered.

Sam might live in a world of honesty and directness, but he just didn't understand what it was like to feel so useless and unable to do what a man should. Joseph couldn't exactly fault him for that. "Listen, I have a lot to focus on with relearning things. I really don't need a woman in my life to distract me."

"*That,* Joseph Drake, is the most ridiculous thing I've heard in my life!" Sam jabbed a finger into Joseph's chest. "And believe me…being a lawyer, I've heard plenty of lame excuses."

Joseph pushed his friend's hand away. "Call it what you like. It doesn't change a thing."

After a long silence, Sam finally spoke. "Hey, they're holding up the box with the big green ribbon for auction. That's Katie's box."

Joseph sucked in a long, steadying breath, praying he could stay indifferent. "Well, then, you better pay close attention."

The bidding began at fifty cents, working up to two dollars, then three, three-fifty...

Joseph could almost feel the intensity coming from Sam. He knew the man was focused on one thing only. Securing Katie's box lunch for himself.

Five dollars, five-fifty, six dollars...

"I'm bidding against money bags over there," Sam whispered in a conspiratorial tone. "From the looks of him, he must be some wealthy rancher. Ah well, he doesn't know how competitive I can be, Joe."

He wanted to cheer his friend on, but felt as if he'd betray his own heart if he were to root for Sam. While sleep eluded him again last night, Joseph had decided that he'd do his best to congratulate Sam and Katie if they were to marry. But each step they took to the altar would twist the noose around his heart a little tighter.

Seven dollars, eight dollars, nine dollars.

For a split second, Joseph thought about raising his hand and getting in on the bid—all he had to do was make sure he was the last one called upon. But he couldn't do that to Sam. And he couldn't do that to Katie.

This is for Katie's sake.

Ten dollars, eleven dollars...thirteen dollars.

A hush came over the crowd as the auctioneer spoke. "Seems we have a high-priced lunch here, folks. The young lady who dolled up this box with all this frippery and what-not must be quite a catch. Do I hear fourteen dollars?"

"Fourteen dollars," Sam called out triumphantly, as though he'd just obtained the state of Colorado in some land auction.

"Do I hear fourteen-fifty?" the auctioneer queried, then paused. "Fourteen going once...going twice.... Sold! To Mr. Garnett for fourteen dollars!"

Sam let out a long, wistful sigh. "That, my friend, was money well spent," he said, his victorious grin glaringly apparent in his voice.

Joseph's heart tightened inside his chest. It didn't matter a coyote's hide what he wanted or that the mutual attraction to Katie was undeniable. What mattered was what was best for Katie.

He held out his right hand to Sam and forced a smile to his face. "Congratulations. You won," he said, feeling the full, painful brunt of those words. "I'm sure you didn't waste one cent of your money."

After an awkward silence, Sam moved his hand up to grasp Joseph's arm. "You feeling okay? You look a little pale."

"I'm fine," Joseph shot back as he jerked his foot down from the fence railing. He willed the irritation out of his voice. "Just not used to all this activity, I guess. I think maybe I'll go back home when the auction is over."

"You're welcome to join Katie and me for lunch."

"Now who's being ridiculous?" He reached toward the fence, carefully feeling for his cane. "You may be a great lawyer, Sam, but you're a lousy liar."

"All right, so you got me there," Sam retorted, placing the cane in Joseph's hand. "Are you sure you don't want to stick around? Ben and Zach are here. I could find them for you."

"I'd rather not." Hearing another round of bidding begin, Joseph grasped his cane between both hands, wondering if he could trust his sense of direction enough to make the seven blocks home, alone. "I think they had plans of their own."

"Apparently," Sam remarked with a low chuckle. "Zach's in on this round. Whew! That rancher he works for must be paying him good money."

"I don't think so. He probably just has a stash saved from his poker days."

Joseph pulled his head around and stared at the murky silhouettes of the buildings behind him, trying to decipher where, exactly, he was on the square. But everything appeared roughly the same height. Not one detail, large or small, could he make out through the dense haze.

"He must. The bid is already up to nine dollars."

Curious now, Joseph turned his attention back to the auction. "I wonder what young woman he's set his sights on."

Sam clucked his tongue quietly. "I don't know, but it looks like he's got some pretty stiff competition going with Ethan Hofmann."

Ten dollars, eleven, twelve...

"Neither one of them look like they're ready to drop out," Sam informed. "Ethan has those big meaty arms of his folded over his chest. I think he's trying to intimidate your little brother. If you ask me, he does look modestly imposing."

"Zach can take care of himself." Joseph chuckled, knowing that given Zach's respectable size and surprising agility, Ethan Hofmann didn't stand a chance. "Zach hasn't said a thing about being smitten by some lady. Do you know whose box it is?"

"No idea. I just paid attention to the one Katie set on the table. Sparkling green—"

"Ribbon. Big flowers. I know," Joseph cut in, irritated. Thirteen, fifteen, eighteen…

"What is Zach thinking spending money like that?" Joseph ground out under his breath. He nudged his friend's arm. "Does he look drunk? He vowed he hasn't been drinking, but if that boy's drunk, when I get done with him he'll wish he'd stayed out on the ranch mucking stalls."

There was a long pause as the bidding continued to escalate. "He doesn't appear unsteady on his feet. And he sure doesn't look like he just dragged himself out of a saloon. He looks sound to me, Joseph."

Twenty dollars, twenty-one.

"Folks, we must have ourselves some kind of royalty livin' here in Boulder, with the price this box is bringin'," the auctioneer bantered even as laughter rolled through the crowd. "Just look for the bright pink blush, fellas. You'll know who fixed up this perty little number with the blue frippery and—what are them—little daisies?"

Joseph braced a hand on the fence, genuinely amused at the expectancy swirling around the square. "Can you tell who's got the telltale blush?"

"Hard to tell who the box belongs to. Seems like all of the ladies have been pinching their cheeks today."

Twenty-two, twenty-three, twenty-three-fifty.

"What in the world is he thinking bidding more than half a month's wage?"

"I don't know. But he's looking over this way and has a smile a mile wide. Ethan, on the other hand," Sam added, in a sympathetic tone, "appears to be noticeably uncomfortable right about now. He's all red-faced. I can see the perspiration on his brow from clear over here.

Either his collar suddenly got tight or he's bidding out of his league."

Joseph threw his head back and laughed, and for a blessed moment in time, he felt normal again.

Twenty-five, twenty-seven, twenty-eight.

"Twenty-eight-fifty going once…going twice…sold!" Mr. Heath proclaimed as the crowd broke out into loud whoops and hollers. "Folks, that there is the *highest* price we've ever had a box go for. Zach, I ain't heard of you playin' the tables lately. What with money like that, it must be burnin' a hole in them britches you're wearin'."

A fresh round of laughter burst across the square, Joseph's and Sam's included. Joseph shook his head, trying hard to wipe the smile off his face. "Here we all thought he was starting to make good decisions. Be responsible. Guess he had a relapse."

Sam jabbed his arm. "Young love. Gets a man every time."

"Foolish love, maybe," he retorted. But Joseph couldn't deny that had he been bidding and that had been Katie's box, he would've done the same thing. He would've spent more if needed.

"He's coming this way," Sam whispered. "Try to go easy on him. I'd hate to see that look of pleasure he's flaunting like a prized mare turn sour."

Joseph slid a hand over his freshly shaven jaw. Shoving a hand on his hip, he pulled his shoulders back and tried for his best concerned, older brother look.

Zach came up beside him and grasped his arm. "You owe me twenty-eight-fifty, Joe-boy!"

"Twenty-eight-fifty?" he echoed, unable to wipe the

smile from his face. "You're a funny man, Zach. You know darn well I'm not paying your bill for some lady's—"

"You sure will, Joe-boy. And you'll do it gladly, too."

Joseph just laughed. Leave it to Zach to go to some wild extreme just for a laugh.

"Why, I would'a bid twice as high for Katie's box to put a smile back on your face."

It'd been four hours since the auction and Katie still felt the heat of embarrassment as she walked with Joseph to the barn where the dance was about to begin. She supposed she should be flattered, but the idea that someone would pay such an outrageous amount for anyone's box lunch, let alone hers, was awkward, to say the least. And that Zach would bid as if he owned the town and then gleefully dump the bill in Joseph's lap was downright mortifying.

At the time, she hadn't been sure whether to protest or just let things fall where they may. When she'd realized what Zach had intended all along, it had been painfully obvious that Joseph wasn't pleased. He was stiff with tension and looked as though he might snap his cane in two—his hands were fisted so tight. If he'd been a lesser man he probably would've flat-out refused to oblige Zach and his innocent, good-natured gesture.

Instead, Joseph had forced a half smile on his face and picked up the expensive box, then escorted Katie out to the mountain stream. It'd been awkward at first, but after they'd settled at the stream's bank, where the melodic trickle of water gurgled around bends and over rocks, and the sun's warmth peeked through the luscious pines and hearty aspens, Joseph seemed to relax. They'd slipped into the kind of easy conversation she treasured with him.

Katie cherished every single moment of the afternoon. She'd just spent four blessed hours with Joseph and she hoped she could be content with that.

"There you two are," Sam called jogging across the street toward them. "You were gone so long I almost rallied the Rangers and sent them out after you."

Katie peered up at Joseph to see his mouth suddenly pull into a taut line. The awkwardness she'd sensed from him earlier this afternoon multiplied tenfold.

"Guess I lost track of time." Joseph released his gentle hold on her arm. "That's easy to do out by the stream."

Sam glanced her way. "He showed you our old haunt, eh?"

A wistful feeling came from deep within as she stared up into Joseph's face. "Actually this is the second time. It's such a peaceful, serene place. So picturesque."

"How about you, Sam? How was your lunch?" Joseph asked.

"I'm glad to say that I had a nice time." There was a mischievous gleam in Sam's eyes as he narrowed his gaze on her. "But I could've sworn I was bidding on your box, Miss Katie Ellickson. I just know I saw you set a box with a big green ribbon and flowers on the table. I figured it had to be yours."

"Oh, I'm sorry for the confusion, Sam. Mine was the one with the pale blue ribbon... Well, you know that now, I guess. For some reason, that other box had caught my eye and I wanted to get a better look at it." With a certain amount of irony, she silently recalled holding the box. "Perhaps it was the flowers. They were just so...so large." She remembered Julia's potent, recognizable scent that had lingered like some caustic odor around the gaudy package. "You must've been glancing my way when I set it back on the table."

"Hmm." With a furrowed brow, Sam tapped his forefinger against his lips. "Apparently."

Joseph angled his head toward Sam. "So, what lucky lady was fortunate enough to go on a picnic with you?"

Sam paused. "None other than Miss Julia Cranston."

"Really?" Joseph's mouth twitched with a barely bridled grin. "I hope you had a nice lunch with her."

Feeling a giggle working its way up her throat, Katie set her hand to her mouth and coughed to ward it off. Honestly, she felt genuinely sorry for poor, unsuspecting Sam.

"I'll admit, I was disappointed that it wasn't you, Katie," he said, slicing his warm gaze to her. "Nevertheless, I did enjoy myself," Sam assured, giving her arm a tender squeeze before he clapped Joseph on the shoulder. "I must say, Joseph, I was taken aback when Zach handed over his…prize."

Joseph dragged in a breath. "So was I."

Sam passed a slow, studying gaze from Katie then back to Joseph. "Is there any reason in particular why he'd do that?"

"You'll have to talk with him about that."

Hugging her arms to her chest, Katie peered up at Joseph. "I hope that Zach won't really make you pay all that money."

"Don't worry about the money." He focused down at her, his eyes…those beautiful, dark amber-colored eyes radiant with instant warmth that seeped all the way to her toes. "Spending time with you would've been a bargain at ten times the price."

Katie silently drank in the moment, reveling in the unexpected show of affection from him.

"Well, kids, the fiddles are tuning up." Sam pulled her out of her small indulgence and nodded toward the large barn. "That means the barn dance is about to start. Do you enjoy dancing, Katie?"

"I love to dance," she breathed, then leaned toward Joseph and quietly spoke. "Do you want a guide into the barn?"

He lightly grasped her arm. "Sure. Thanks."

"And you, Sam, do you enjoy dancing, as well?" she asked.

"Love it!" He clapped his hands once, then rubbed them together as though warming himself over a fire.

"How about you, Joseph?" she asked, steering him around a large dip in the ground. "Do you dance?"

"*Does* Joseph dance? I'm surprised your reputation hasn't preceded you, my friend." Sam reached around Katie, needling Joseph with a friendly pat. "Joseph Drake may as well have been born-and-bred nobility, the way he dances. Come to think of it, all the Drake brothers can twirl a lady around the dance floor like they stepped out of some castle ballroom."

Sam leaned toward her and whispered conspiratorially. "The menfolk hate them for it, too. Makes us all look bad."

"This year they'll have two less Drakes to hate. Aaron's not here and you won't catch me out there doing any dancing."

"What harm could a waltz or two do?" Sam prodded.

When they stepped into the barn doorway, Joseph stopped beside Katie and pulled his head back as if adjusting to the change in lighting. "Without my sight, I'd be like a bull in a barn full of newborn chicks out on a dance floor."

"You never know, it might just make you feel more like yourself again," Sam urged.

"I'm feeling like myself without dancing, thank you." He dropped his hand from Katie's arm and held his head high. "If one of you'll point me in the right direction, I'll just find my way to where all the men with two left feet line up. You two go on ahead." With nonchalance, he gestured them away with small sweeping strokes of his hand. But his jaw muscles clenched, and his casual manner didn't quite reach his voice. "Enjoy yourselves. Dance all night."

Confusion tugged at Katie's heart, threatening to tear it in two. She just couldn't understand how Joseph could look visibly irritated when Sam showed her attention, yet seemed bent on shoving her straight into his friend's arms.

As good and as nice as Sam was, it wasn't his arms she dreamed of holding her. She yearned for Joseph's strong, muscled arms encircling her, making her feel tenderly cared for…and loved.

She swallowed hard. Joseph seemed set on shutting down his feelings for her. Even if he did want her, he very well might not feel the same way knowing the truth of her past.

But she could dream. No one could steal that from her.

Several moments of silence ensued. Sam continued to stare at Joseph as though seeing his friend for the first time, and then turned a hesitant, lingering gaze on Katie.

"Katie, if you wouldn't mind, I'd be honored if you'd grace me with a dance before the night's out," he uttered calmly, suddenly lacking the excitement he'd shown only moments ago.

She glanced at Joseph, then to Sam. "Well, I—"

"Yoo-hoo, Samuel!" Julia's shrill voice demanded attention.

The hair on the back of Katie's neck stood on end as she witnessed the woman whisk across the wide-planked floor with graceful elegance. Her dark silky hair was pulled back in a fashionable twist and her cobalt-blue dress glimmered in the barn's soft yellow glow. Julia's striking emerald eyes glinted hard as steel as she shot a look of warning at Katie, then slithered up next to Sam like a snake to sun.

"My dear Samuel, the music is about to begin," she cooed, trailing a finger down his arm. "You promised me the first dance. Remember?" she whispered, soft enough not to wake a baby. Loud enough for Katie to hear.

Sam peered at Joseph again, then with what seemed a deliberate, painstaking length of time, passed his gaze back to Katie. When her eyes met his, she found something strangely different there. Something that almost made her sad for Sam.

While he gave Katie a single measured nod, he responded to Julia. "I did promise you the first dance, Julia."

He peered down at where Julia possessively looped her arm through his and gave the woman a genuine but dim smile as he patted her hand. "If you'll excuse me, Joseph, Katie, I have a dance to enjoy."

Katie swallowed hard, watching Sam lead Julia out on the dance floor with gentlemanly grace and undivided attention. He was such a good man, so warmly attentive. She said a silent prayer for him, yet wondered if it was

Julia she really needed to pray for. Sam, perceptive and astute as he was, seemed to be able to see past all of the flash and flourish Julia acted out like some grand performance. She might not be prepared for the candid and guileless way with which Sam operated.

Chapter Fourteen

The night had just begun and Joseph already wished that it was over. Slowly inhaling the rich summer air, he listened as Sam ushered Julia toward the dance area, reminding himself that he'd vowed to go the distance tonight. If he was going to get on with as normal a life as possible, he wanted to start living it like he had in the past. Living like he had a future.

When he sensed Katie shifting beside him, he leaned toward her and asked, "Would you like something to drink? I'm pretty sure I caught a whiff of apple cider. If it's anything like in past years, I'm sure it's good."

"That sounds delicious. Thank you," she answered, her sweet voice raised a notch, compensating for the loud music and the dancer's stamping feet as the announcer called for the Virginia reel.

"Do you mind leading the way?" He reached up and grasped her arm. "I'm a little uncertain with all the people. Can't rely on shadows when it's so dark in here."

She briefly touched his hand at her elbow. "Not at all. It's just over here, to the left."

As she weaved through the crowd, Joseph returned several greetings sent his way, trying to appear as casual as possible. *Other than the fact that he was holding on to Katie's arm with one hand and the long cane in the other, no one would guess a thing was different about him,* he mused sarcastically.

He took in all the sounds around him...the voices, the music, the apple press grinding in the background. When the edge of his cane came into contact with a barrier, he reached out and touched the waist-high board that doubled as a beverage counter for these gatherings. He felt the nudging of people beside him and behind him, and was threatened with a moment of panic, but knowing Katie was there gave him confidence.

"I'm right behind you," she spoke low, edging closer.

"What'll it be, Joseph?" Mr. Heath's easy timbre was a welcome sound.

He smiled. "Two glasses of cider, please."

"Coming right up!"

"Joseph Drake, it does my heart good seeing you here today." Mrs. Duncan scooted next to him and barked out an order for cider.

"I'm glad I could make it," he answered, picturing the older woman's round, rosy-cheeked face.

"This event just wouldn't be the same without you." When she patted his arm as though she was burping a baby, a sliver of irritation wriggled down Joseph's spine. "I suppose you're bored stiff and just chomping at the bit for things to do now that you're blind."

Not wanting to appear rude, he endured her thick-handed touch and ungainly words. "Well, actually—"

"It's a shame about your eyesight and all, young man.

The whole town thinks so." Her stale breath fanned across his face and he could easily picture Mrs. Duncan's pinched features framed in wisps of carrot-orange hair. "A pure waste of a promising young man, that's what it is."

He set his back teeth. "I wouldn't consider—"

"You needn't feel ashamed of yourself," she half yelled as she pushed closer, bumping into him with her doughy-soft figure. "It's a cryin' shame you never married, seeing as how you'd probably be grateful for someone to take care of you now. But as handsome as you are, I'm sure you could find some young woman who'd be agreeable to marrying you in your condition."

Joseph threaded his fingers through his hair, striving to maintain his patience. After all, this was Mrs. Duncan, and it was no secret that she spoke her mind, the words flying from her mouth without a thought.

"Oh, really? Is that so?" he finally said, as though responding to news about the local logging industry.

"I don't usually do this sort of thing, but my niece, well, she may not be beautiful by some men's standards, but she's a good girl. Practical, nurturing and strong as an ox," she said, each quality emphasized by a sharp poke in his chest.

Joseph balled his fists around his cane and when Katie's hand came to rest at his back, he felt a sense of relief.

"She's from Longmont," Mrs. Duncan announced, her voice carrying through the barn as the music came to a snappy halt. "She'll be arriving before winter sets in. I'd be more than happy to introduce—"

"I appreciate the thoughtfulness," he interrupted, holding up his hand in hopes that she'd just drop the subject.

"I'm sure you'd find her pleasant-enough company. Why, she can read, cooks real good and is charitable just like me," she added as the music began again. "Mind you, it's not as if I've given this a lick of thought, but if the two of you married, you could just move in with Horace and me. We have plenty of room."

"Does she have all of her teeth?" came Katie's voice from behind him, the sharp but humorous bite in her words cracking a smile on Joseph's face.

Mrs. Duncan huffed and pressed in closer, making Joseph's level of irritation shoot upward. "As I was saying…the two of you could live with Horace and me."

He suddenly felt more compassion for Horace Duncan than he'd ever felt for another soul. "Mrs. Duncan, I—"

"That way Horace could tend to the *manly* things around the house." When she sidled even closer, it was almost his undoing. "Since you're not able-bodied, why, it'd be the perfect arrangement."

"Mrs. Duncan! Really, I'm *not* interested," he ground out, his voice raised a notch. Closing his eyes, he steadied his nerves, thankful again that Katie was behind him.

"Well!" The woman gasped. "I was *just* trying to help."

"I'll let you know if I need your help."

After Mr. Heath handed him the mugs of apple cider, he turned and gave Katie hers, then followed her lead back through the crowd.

"That was outrageous," Katie whispered.

"That's Mrs. Duncan for you," he clipped off, swallowing a mouthful of cider along with his pride.

When they reached the benches that were lined up around the barn's perimeter, Joseph secured his cane against the wall and sat down. He rested against the thick, sturdy walls as he tried to compose himself. His sour mood was in direct contrast to the light, playful music.

"I'm sorry that happened," Katie spoke next to him.

Hearing the quiver in Katie's voice, he knew he'd have to ignore his frustration or her evening would be lost on him. He didn't want that. She loved to dance and deserved to enjoy herself tonight, but if she stuck around feeling sorry for him, she might bow out of the frivolity, and Sam had yet to dance with her.

"Are you all right?" Her voice was tentative enough to broach a hibernating bear.

"I'm fine. Don't worry about me."

"But Mrs. Duncan...she was so thoughtless," she added.

"She's not known for her tact." He hoped his casual dismissal was convincing. "Go have fun now. I'm sure there are plenty of men waiting in line to dance with you."

When Ben chose to stop by at that very moment and pull Katie out on the floor for a lively number, Joseph tried to be grateful. He sat back on the bench, determined to enjoy the pleasant music, rhythmic stamping of feet and the satisfying sounds of laughter woven like a cheerful cord through the night. While the evening wore on, one dance after another, he remained resolute on staying to the end.

"Having fun over here?" Sam sounded winded as he sat down with an unceremonious plop next to Joseph.

"Sure. The music's good, as always. And I have a great view from here," Joseph retorted, smirking.

"So...the man has a sense of humor?"

Joseph gave his friend a disingenuous grin and stretched his legs out in front of him, hooking one ankle over the other.

"Where's Katie?" Sam asked on a deep exhale.

"I'm not sure. Last I knew she was out there with Zach."

After a pause, Sam said, "There she is, dancing with Mr. Heath—that sly, old dog."

A smile tipped the corner of Joseph's mouth. "Does she look like she's having fun?"

"She's glowing," Sam responded with a certain reverence. "Has been all night."

Hearing Sam say that, Joseph was very glad that he'd jerked himself out of his irritation earlier. Had he not, she might still been sitting beside him missing out on the evening.

"Katie sure is something, Joseph." Sam cleared his throat. "Listen, I came over here to let you know that Julia's come down with a headache and asked if I could see her home. You know, since I bought her box lunch…"

"Of course. Go ahead."

"I'll be back later to walk you home," Sam added.

"I'm sure I can get Ben or Zach to see to it. I might even be able to make it myself."

"You might as well get a lead. I know I would if I were you." Sam's voice suddenly grew serious. "There's something else…. I was wondering, since I haven't danced with Katie yet and there are probably a few waltzes left, I thought that maybe you could do the honor for me."

Joseph gave his head an adamant shake. "Sam, you're a good friend, but—"

"It's just a waltz. You could do it in your sleep."

"I'm flattered by your confidence in me," he shot back sarcastically. "But I'm *not* getting out on that dance floor."

"What will it hurt?" Sam prodded.

"If I talk with her again, I'll let her know that you had

to leave and were sorry you couldn't dance with her. I'm sure she'll understand."

Even as Joseph uttered the words, he wished he could take them back. Just one dance. Why couldn't he find it in himself to at least try one dance? One more chance to hold her, to touch her, to burn into his memory her scent, her soft skin, the sound of her sweet voice so near him.

"You know that I'd never leave without extending her my deepest regrets. I already did that." Sam paused a moment, the uncomfortable silence drowning out the fiddle music in the background. "There's no good reason why you can't dance *one* waltz with her."

Joseph stared straight ahead, wide-eyed. "Being blind isn't good enough reason for you?"

"Just try. Dance with Katie," Sam urged, his words sounding as though they'd passed through gritted teeth.

Joseph pushed himself up from the bench and drew his mouth into a tight, grim line. "Stop badgering me about this. Please."

"Let me put it this way," Sam ground out, coming to stand right in front of him. "I could continue to set my sights on Katie, falling over myself to win her affection, but it wouldn't do me a bit of good." When Sam moved closer, Joseph bridled to meet him, nose to nose. "I want you to listen, and listen good. There's a fall-off-your-horse gorgeous woman out there who takes my breath away. But believe me, it's been painfully obvious all night that she has eyes for only *one* person in this room," he said, jabbing a finger in Joseph's chest. "And it *ain't* me."

The words permeated every inch of Joseph, weighing down the protest that struggled to break free. He stared into darkness, confusion hanging over him as Sam walked away. A swirl of emotions rocked his mind and heart. Frustration at the helplessness that still snaked through him, challenging his sense of value. Dread that dare he follow his heart he'd find that he really did lack what it took to be a worthy husband.

And hope. Hope that *if* he dared to follow his heart, he'd find things to be far different than what he feared. He'd discover that Katie cared for him, not out of pity or loyalty, but because of who he was, blind or not.

Sensing his stubborn resolve slipping away like water through a sieve, he reminded himself again why he shouldn't be the one to pursue Katie. He wasn't a whole man—like Sam. He couldn't take care of her like a husband should. He couldn't love her like—

But he could love her. Maybe he already did love her.

All at once, the insecurities that had permeated his mind these past weeks now smelled more like pride than truth. And the gallant motivation that had held his focus captive seemed as unclear as the indistinct shadows in his world.

Turning to grab his cane, a tremble worked through him as he realized that Sam had just relinquished the object of his desire…Katie. He'd as much as pushed Joseph toward her, the last few words he'd said ricocheting through Joseph's mind like a bold flash of light jerking him from some strange, dark dream.

He was still reeling from the sentiment when he felt a light touch on his arm, and instinctively knew it was Katie.

"Joseph?"

He squeezed his eyes shut, trying to remind himself of why she deserved more. But he couldn't seem to grasp even the smallest bit of prior reasoning.

"Are you feeling under the weather?" she asked, her

touch working like a mesmerizing fire to calm his uncertainty, her light lily scent like an intoxicating draw. "Would you like to step out back for some air?"

"Sure," he heard himself saying.

He swallowed hard, fighting to sink his teeth into his resolve again. Each time he started to protest with some excuse as to why he couldn't go with her, he felt his tongue get thick, his mouth go dry with the unspoken words. When he grasped her arm and walked with her around the dance area, each step felt like a thousand mile's distance from his former rationale.

"Are you sure you're not feeling ill?" Katie asked as they walked into the cool night air. "You look a little flushed."

He shook his head, working his cane in front of him. "No, nothing like that."

His footsteps fell in perfect rhythm with Katie's across the hard ground as they neared the spot where a new fence line had been erected to flank the lot. Slowing to a stop next to her, he felt helpless to drag up even one argument.

As another melody ended from inside the barn, Joseph concentrated on the noises surrounding him. The crickets chirping their own playful song, pigeons cooing from their roost in the barn, the light wind whispering through the nearby pines.

When he thought he heard movement from the area of the trees, he turned, training an ear that way. Had someone run into the trees when they'd come out here? Perhaps some of the children who seemed to delight in spying on private moments? Listening closely, he knew for a fact that he didn't want an audience right now.

After he was satisfied that they were alone he pulled his attention back to the moment and heard her sniffing the air.

"Do you smell that?" she asked, sniffing again.

"Smell what?" he responded, wondering if maybe she'd caught the scent of fire in the distance. He dragged in a long breath, but the only distinct scent he caught was a faint whiff of some kind of tobacco smoke.

"Oh, I'm sure it's nothing," she dismissed on a shaky sigh.

"Are you sure?"

"Yes—I mean, I just thought I smelled cigar smoke out here. But I'm sure it's fine."

"I smell it, too. In these parts you could throw a rock and probably hit someone who smokes those things."

"I'm sure you're right." She sighed.

He tried to ease the tension cording his neck muscles, letting the music wash over him like some gentle waterfall. "It's a beautiful night," he uttered, awkwardly searching for something to say.

"Gorgeous." Katie gave a wistful sigh, making Joseph yearn to see the expression on her face. "Oh, Joseph. The sky is *so* beautiful tonight."

He swallowed hard. "What does it look like?"

"Hmm… Like a deep, dark blanket soaked with brilliant stars," she breathed, her carefully selected words painting a vivid, poignant picture. "And the moon—it's full. Like some perfect, priceless pearl hung over the barn just for this occasion."

Joseph's heart squeezed tight. Closing his eyes, he felt an irrepressible smile curl his lips. Although he'd never told her, she intuitively knew how important words were to him now, and had made such a touching, magnificent effort just for him.

Never once had he felt pity from her or been treated

with kid gloves. Never once had she responded to him as though he was incapable of handling a situation. She'd been a friend and a driving force in helping him find his way to normalcy.

She'd warmed to his show of concern, melted to his touch and given a part of herself he knew hadn't come easy for her. She'd given him her trust.

"Katie," he said, his voice low as he turned toward her. He clutched his cane between his hands, his knuckles tight. His heart thudded against his chest. "Would you dance with me?"

Throwing his cane to the side, he held his hand out to her.

When she slipped her hand in his, a connection traveled far beyond his fingers, flowing all the way to his heart.

The musicians began a familiar waltz and he closed his eyes, picturing the surroundings. The hard-packed ground, flat and free of obstacles. The barn with its doors swung wide, spilling a soft yellow glow of lantern light out into the dark night. The long, thick row of hearty pines, their boughs draped heavily with snug cones this time of year. The setting wasn't some grand ballroom or even a crude barn, but as far as Joseph was concerned it was the most perfect setting for a waltz.

With a slow intake of breath he set his hand at her back, pulling her a little closer, relishing the way she trembled ever so slightly at his touch. Before he lost his courage, he took the lead, stepping back, side, together, forward, side, together. Back, side, together...

He danced with Katie, drawing her nearer as he glided her across nature's ballroom with just the moon and the stars as his witness. He held this beautiful treasure, feeling something tug at his heart, then settle deep inside his soul.

After the song ended and another began, Joseph slowed to a stop, the space between them charged with some invisible, tangible force. He twined his fingers with hers, splayed his other hand at her waist. His heart drummed a steady, fast beat, and his breathing grew shallow.

Wanting to drink in this moment, he grasped both of her hands and drew them to his chest. He stared down at where he grazed her fingers with the pads of his thumbs. Felt her soft skin that belied her perseverance and hard work.

"Sam asked me to dance with you in his stead." He raised his sightless gaze. "But that dance—that was for me."

A small whimper came from her lips. "Oh, Joseph, you are so sweet."

He stared down at her, straining to see through the darkness. "I wish I could see you, Katie," he ground out, swallowing hard. "From the moment I first met you, I've wanted to see your face."

She drew his hands to her cheeks, holding them there for a long moment. "You can."

Awkward shyness crept over him at the idea of taking in her features with his fingertips. When he hesitated, she gave his hands a tender squeeze.

"It's all right," she whispered.

He swallowed hard, and then with a feather-light touch, moved his hands little by little over her smooth skin. Her warm, shallow breath fanned his palms, seeping into him like the welcoming spring sun thawing the frozen ground.

When she released her hold, he gently, hesitantly slid his fingertips to her forehead where a line of silken hair framed soft skin. Then to her brows, perfectly arched over closed eyes, her lids, satiny as rose petals. Her lashes, dense and long, fluttered like a butterfly's wings beneath his fingertips.

He smiled.

Then skimmed his fingertips down a little farther to high cheekbones that rimmed eyes he knew must sparkle with life and wonder. To her small nose, just the right size for her perfect oval-shaped face. He trailed his fingertips down to her mouth, where full, soft lips met his trembling touch. He moved the pads of his fingers slowly, reverently over her supple mouth, admiring the most perfect, flawless Cupid's bow. From these perfect lips came a constant flow of encouragement that had changed his life forever.

Cupping his hands around her face, he lowered his head, his lips settling on hers. He adored her with a soft, gentle kiss, the slight brush of his mouth against hers, awakening every emotion he'd tried so hard to bury.

Joseph pulled back and slid his fingertips down the line of her jaw to her silky smooth neck where her pulse, beating hard and fast, met his touch.

"You're so beautiful, Katie." His voice came as a harsh whisper. "So beautiful."

He wrapped his arms around her and held her tight, loving the way she snuggled into his chest as though hiding herself in him. She molded so flawlessly to him, her body the perfect mix of soft, rounded curves and long, steady lines.

Boldly, he smoothed trembling hands up to the nape of her neck, where petal-soft skin seared his sensitive fingertips. He breathed deep, resting his cheek against her head.

His heart skipped a beat and his pulse pounded faster, louder in his ears. In spite of the cool August night, he was suddenly warm. He released her, shuddering as an unexpected revelation hit him soundly. He'd never felt like this before, so moved, so taken by beauty he couldn't even see.

Chapter Fifteen

Katie could hardly believe the sensations and emotions that still rocked her as she made her way behind the barn again. Regretting every step away from Joseph's consuming presence and exhilarating touch, she'd left him waiting in front of the barn for Zach, remembering that she'd forgotten the treasured purse Ellie had given her out by the trees. She'd said she'd be right back because he'd insisted on walking her home, and she was now inching along the tree line peering into the deepening darkness to find the purse.

As she neared the place where they'd danced, she set a hand to her lips, recalling how she'd been hard-pressed to find her voice after Joseph had kissed her. She reveled in the way he'd held her, demonstrating to her what it means to be cherished.

The thick grove of pines whispered softly to her in the slight breeze. She stood, hugging her arms to her chest, relishing the memory of his embrace. Peering up at the stars, she swayed back and forth, made a slow lazy turn, compelled by the age-old love song Joseph had awakened in her heart.

He was the best thing, the most wonderful thing that had ever happened to her. God bless her Uncle Sven and Ben for asking her to come out here and work with Joseph.

A fading dread tried snatching her attention as she remembered how, after suffering through that first awful attack a year ago, her soul had been shattered. Then to have the same horrible man stalk and accost her again, leaving her with the lethal threat of a loved one's death and the wicked assurance of her ill repute, she'd given up hope of ever entrusting another man's touch to promise something other than pain.

But tonight she'd allowed herself to fully melt to Joseph's wonderful touch. His strong hands meant her no harm, only tender care, and his powerfully muscled body was like a shield of protection.

She swallowed hard, lifting her chin a notch.

Frank Fowler may have taken her innocence, but for the first time since he'd devastated her, she felt as if maybe, just maybe she could be free. Free from the clutches of his control. Free from the threat that promised she'd always belong to him. That no man would want her.

Doubt nipped like jealous demons at her newfound joy. Katie fluttered her eyes closed, knowing that she had to tell Joseph about her past, but not knowing how. She could only hope that he'd still find her desirable.

The uncertainty that perhaps he would reject her made her wonder if she'd ever be free from Frank's grip.

A chill worked up her spine, setting her hair on end. That scent, that bitter, musky cigar scent had been here by the pine trees when they'd stepped outside. For a brief second, her breath had caught in her throat and her blood had gone ice-cold. She'd remember that scent till her dying day. The way Frank Fowler's tainted cigar breath had fanned over her face, making her struggle for fresh air. For weeks after both attacks, the taste lingered on her tongue and she'd wondered if it was like some evil, sick mark. A lasting stain of contamination.

She caught a whiff of it again, and an icy chill blasted through her. She hugged her arms closer to her chest. Tried to ignore the familiar fear that had plagued her for so long.

She was being silly—plain and simple.

Like Joseph had said, many people smoked cigars. It was probably the pungent residue of someone else's crude vice. Besides, she was clear out here in Colorado, hundreds of miles from Frank Fowler. But even as she reminded herself of those things, fear coursed through her. She wanted to run and hide, but instead she slowly turned, determined to resist the urge to dart back inside—

A hand grabbed her hard and firm. Another wrapped around her waist, pulled her back against a solid wall of flesh.

She screamed. Struggled to break free from the hard, unrelenting grip. Kicked hard against the man's shins, her hair prickling on end.

"Help! Someone, help!" she got out before the man clamped a hand over her mouth.

She snapped her jaws shut, catching skin between her teeth.

"You little wench!" the man snarled, grinding his hand against her face.

That voice. Never in her life would she forget that voice.

Frank Fowler.

She fought to wrench her head around to see him, but he had a powerful grip on her. When he removed the hand from around her waist and reached for something, she broke free.

But he yanked her back, dragging her, kicking and fighting, away from the barn and farther into the trees. She thrashed about. Shrieked for help. But her screams died fast when he jammed an acrid-smelling wad of cloth into her mouth, and tightened his grip around her middle.

"Didn't think you'd see me here, did you?" he growled.

Her pulse pounded in her ears and her stomach churned with nausea as she strained to see in the darkness. The deeper into the trees he hauled her, the farther from help she was. And the lights from the barn were being doused one by one.

She tried again to scream, but it just came out as a muffled groan.

"Thought I'd pay you a little visit. But I'm disappointed, Katherine. I didn't expect to find you throwing yourself at some man." He dragged the backside of his hand down her cheek, his icy, rough touch sending a shiver of horror through her body.

She yanked her head away from his touch, sickened by the foulness of his words.

He gripped her chin and jerked her around to face him. "Here you are, off in some remote mountain town acting like a brazen woman." He heaved her hard against himself, his tight grip sending pain stabbing like hot irons through her. "How soon you forget that you belong to me."

She didn't move a muscle. Didn't make a sound. She wouldn't give him the satisfaction.

"I suppose with him being blind, you're as good as he's

going to get." He spun her around to face him and slowly pulled her up next to his unyielding body. "He'll have to find some other soiled dove because you won't be around to show him your kind of charity."

Her heart clenched tight. She forced his ruthless, cutting words away from her heart. If she didn't, she'd be right back where she started before she came out here to Boulder a few weeks ago. Before she started finding healing.

He dipped his head. Dug his fingers deeper into her flesh.

Refusing even a glance his way, she averted her gaze, trying to devise a way to get to safety. She could barely see in the darkness, but if she could just make her way back through the trees and run toward where she could still hear the faint sound of people's voices….

"Don't think you're going to escape from me now."

She swallowed the bile burning in her throat. Tears sprang to her eyes. She blinked them away, knowing that he'd love it all the more if she showed weakness, finding some sick satisfaction in seeing her vulnerability.

Joseph. She just wanted Joseph. To feel his arms wrapped around her, a refuge of warm protection.

"You're mine, Katherine," he taunted, his cigar-tainted breath fanning her face as he grabbed her bodice. "And I'm going to take what rightly belongs to me—again."

Her eyes grew wide as she stared at his black form, barely visible. When she saw his white teeth gleaming in a smile, she wrenched her arms, fighting to break free. Kicked at his legs. Bucked against his tightening grip.

He gave her a brutal shove, hurling her to the hard ground, where he pinned her firmly beneath him.

Her shoulder jammed into a protruding rock and she whimpered. Ignoring the searing pain in her shoulder, she

224 Rocky Mountain Match

scrambled to get out from underneath him, grunting with her effort. She couldn't bear this again. Not again.

For a brief moment, she felt herself drifting away, far away from the humiliation and agony of what seemed inevitable. But she had to fight back. She couldn't let it happen again.

Katie slid her hands over the ground, frantically searching for something she could use as a weapon. A rock, a branch, anything. When he snatched her wrists and slammed them above her head, she knew the possibility for escape was dwindling.

"Now, let's see if you can please me," he growled.

She felt the barrel of a gun, its cold, hard steel jammed into her ribs. As he thrust the gun deeper, she knew there was no way she'd escape now.

Katie squeezed her eyes tight and stifled a whimper as she held very still.

He laughed, an evil laugh that made her stomach churn. When Frank released her hands for a brief moment, she heard his belt give way.

Now. She had to make her move now!

Balling her fists, she jabbed them hard into his groin. Kicked and bucked to get him off her.

He yowled and drew back, leaning off balance. "You'll pay for that," he ground out.

Katie pushed hard against him.

He teetered.

She scrambled to get up. Felt a surge of hope as her feet gained ground.

He grabbed her leg. Held on with crushing force.

She kicked with all her might and as she grabbed for the cloth in her mouth, he gained his feet and caught her hand.

"You want it that way? Fine," he spat out, spittle spraying her face.

He jammed the cloth into her mouth again. Gripped her arms tight and slammed her into a tree.

Her whole body convulsed with sharp, stabbing sensations.

With an eerie calm, he held the gun at her heart, his breathing heavy and ragged. "You'll either stop your fighting and come with me," he growled, "or you'll die right here. Right now." He drove the barrel of the pistol deeper into her ribs. "What'll it be?"

She clenched her eyes shut. Forced her thoughts to rest on the sweet memory of Joseph, his protective strength, tender caressing touch and his warm, promise-filled kiss. She'd have to take that beautiful memory with her to her grave, because there was no way she'd go with Frank Fowler without a fight.

Joseph's blood ran cold as ice at the sound of a gun cocking not fifteen feet in front of him. His heart pounded loud as thunder.

He crouched low, advancing forward step by silent step, honing in on the repulsive noise of the man's ragged breath. And the heart-wrenching sound of Katie's whimper. He could only hope that the element of surprise would be enough to save her.

While he'd waited for Zach outside the front barn doors minutes ago, he'd heard a scream. Then another. The voice had sounded too much like Katie's. He'd charged toward the cry in spite of the taunting that crept through his mind, reminding him of his blindness. He'd called for Zach on the run, but there was no time to waste. He had to get to Katie.

His pulse pounded hard and fast now. Untapped power pumped through his veins at breakneck speed. He tightened his grip on the thick branch he'd found on the ground, hoping, praying it would be a solid weapon and not decayed on the inside.

He heard the man shift, his feet crunching against the dried bed of pine needles.

When Katie made another whimper, the hairs on the back of his neck prickled to ready attention. He'd kill the man—whoever he was—before he'd let him harm his sweet Katie. When he'd gotten within earshot and heard the man threaten Katie, Joseph had felt something snap inside him. It took every amount of self-control he possessed to move with stealthy silence in the cover of darkness, using his sharpened sense of hearing to his greatest advantage.

He clenched his jaw taut, drawing on the raw anger coursing through his veins. Narrowed his focus on the sound of her attacker's heavy breathing. He took a careful, measured step forward. Tried to determine the man's height and where he stood in proximity to Katie, each second praying she'd be all right.

Joseph's heart slammed against his chest. His pulse pounded in his ears. He inhaled quietly, steadying himself. Bolted forward, zeroing in on the man's heavy panting. Hauled the bulky branch over his shoulder. Aimed his focus and brought it down with full, concentrated force.

A gust of air whooshed from Joseph's lungs as the power-packed branch thudded heavily against the man.

With a grunt, the man's gun dropped to the ground with a solid clink of steel.

Katie whimpered.

The man gave an eerie howl, his breath forced through clenched teeth.

"Run, Katie! Run!" Joseph commanded.

Her skirts swished with sudden movement. Her feet shuffling slowly, laboriously over the bed of pine needles.

"Joseph! Where are you?" Zach's call came from near the barn, as Katie's assailant spat a vile string of curses.

"Over here. In the pines," Joseph yelled.

Joseph could hear the man struggling over the ground. He honed in on the sound. Brought the branch back. Focused every bit of power he had into his taut muscles. He let the swing loose. As the branch sliced through the air toward its point of focus, a gunshot sounded. The awful, unmistakable noise ricocheted through the dense grove of trees.

The branch slammed against the man, dropping him to the ground with a dull thud.

Joseph's stomach convulsed with horror as Katie whimpered not more than fifteen feet away. Fell hard to the ground.

"Noooo!" Joseph raged, aiming his raised branch at where the man lay, moaning.

"What are you going to do now, blind man?" the man jeered, his words forced between clenched teeth. "I'm going to kill you, too."

Joseph's emotions stormed between fierce wrath and enormous sorrow. All he wanted to do was get to Katie. Hold her in his arms. But when he heard the man's low, evil chuckle, he felt something untamed, something wholly violent, rise within him and he launched himself in the man's direction, landing hard on top of the attacker.

The man cocked the gun again.

Joseph zeroed in on the sound and grappled for the weapon. When his fingers connected with metal, he grasped hard, crushed the man's hand and flung the gun well out of the way.

Every muscle in his body bunched rock-solid. He balled his fists and pummeled Katie's attacker.

The man's fingers bit into Joseph's wrists, but Joseph jerked free. Then swung harder, faster, deeper. Slamming his fists into the man's face, one blow after another after another. Time stood still as he punished the man with every bit of force he could muster. So relentless that the form beneath him no longer tried to fight back, but was out stone-cold.

"Joseph, stop! He's not worth it." Zach grabbed Joseph's arms, pulling him back.

He wrenched from Zach's hold and sprang to his feet. "She fell somewhere over this way," he breathed, panting hard as he moved in the direction he'd last heard her. "Can you see her?"

"Who?" Zach asked.

"Zach, he shot her. He shot Katie."

"It doesn't look good." Ben's voice was low and grave, renewing the ominous sense of dread that darkened the night. "The bullet lodged just above Katie's heart and she's lost a lot of blood."

"What can you do? Is there anything?" Joseph pulled a painfully bruised and battered hand over his face as Zach grasped his shoulder.

Katie's Aunt Marta sniffed quietly. "Oh dear. My poor, poor Katie-did."

"Vhat else is der to do?" Sven echoed, his quivering voice belying his hulking size. "Der must be someting."

Ben's feet shifted heavily on the wood floor. "If she has any hope at all, I need to operate and remove the bullet—repair what I can. But as weak as she is right now, I'm afraid I'd lose her on the table."

Joseph trained an ear to the other room where Katie lay. "What are her chances otherwise?"

"Dis should not be," Marta whispered harshly. "Vhat kind of evil man vould do dis? Shoot our Katie like dis?"

"I don't know. I've tried asking her a few questions," Ben added in a hushed tone. "But I don't want to upset her."

"If'n Miss Ellickson 'members anything," Sheriff Goodwin offered, his gravely voice contrasting sharply with the hushed atmosphere, "it'd be a might helpful, seein' as how that varmint somehow slipped through our hands."

Joseph jammed his hands into his pockets, his jaw muscle tensing. He recalled how Zach had pried him off the man. Since Katie's attacker posed no threat being unconscious, they'd immediately tended to Katie. By the time the sheriff came along, the man had come to and had almost reached his gun. No doubt he would've used it.

But the sheriff put a bullet into him first.

Had the shot been as accurate as the one that took down Katie, the man would either be dead or in custody. Instead, the man had howled, but doggedly plowed on, managing to escape by stealing a tethered horse not far from the site.

"Seein's how she ain't in any condition to talk, I gotta git back to the jail. The deputy's gatherin' a party to track 'im down." The sheriff hacked loudly, then scuffed across the wood floor toward the front door. "Don' you worry none, folks. We'll git 'im."

When the door closed solidly behind the sheriff, Joseph felt the old familiar taunts snaking through his head…. He wasn't whole. Couldn't see danger if it stared him in the face. That he'd never be a protector. What if the man came back and tried to finish the job? Would Katie ever be safe?

"All I can say is…pray." Ben's admonition broke through the terrifying questions playing through Joseph's mind. "Pray like you've never prayed before."

While Sven began talking to God, his low Swedish timbre hanging in the room like some comforting blanket, Joseph felt his way back to the adjoining room. He stood next to Katie's bed and lowered his head, settling a kiss on her clammy brow.

"I'm going to die, aren't I?" she whispered, her weak, sweet voice barely audible.

"You can pull through this, Katie." Hunkering down, he trailed his fingers lightly down her right arm and found her delicate hand, grasping it in his. "You've got to."

"Did they catch—him?" Her voice caught with pain.

Joseph shook his head, wishing he'd finished off the guy when he'd had a chance. "Not yet. But they will."

Katie suddenly squeezed his hand tight and tensed in pain, making his heart ache for her. After a few moments she relaxed her grip, but his concern wouldn't be relieved.

"The whiskey should start working soon," came Ben's whisper next to Joseph's ear. "It'll help make her more comfortable."

Joseph nodded once in acknowledgment, then focused his sightless gaze on Katie. He smoothed a hand over hers, desperate to ease her suffering. "Just hang on, Katie. You're strong. You're going to make it."

"You're so good, Joseph." She slid her hand from his and set quivering fingers to his early morning shadow of a beard. "Such a good man."

He folded her hand in his and swallowed hard. "Not half the person you are."

"I hoped…I hoped that you and I—"

"That you and I what, Katie?" Joseph pulled her slender fingers to his lips and kissed them.

When he caught a whiff of the unmistakable metallic smell of blood, icy dread blew through him like a silent omen. He could almost feel the warmth of life slowly ebbing from her.

Sitting here feeling so helpless to change the course of things, he couldn't imagine how hard it had been for Aaron seeing Ellie struggle as she had. Finding her lifeless body, the warmth and cheer that Ellie emanated, gone.

Joseph may not have known Katie for long, but already he felt sick at the thought of not having her in his life.

Swallowing hard, he blinked back tears, determined to stay strong for her. He'd do anything to ease her pain. Anything to make her smile. Anything to make her last moments here on earth as meaningful as possible.

"Whatever you want, darlin', I'll do it for you," Joseph murmured softly, the endearment easy on his lips.

"I hoped that we'd—" She coughed suddenly, tensing again.

He eased her hand open and threaded his fingers through hers. Gave her hand a gentle squeeze, wishing he could somehow give her his strength. "Katie?"

Fear gripped hard. Trembling, he set his hand to her chest and felt the faint rise and fall there.

Joseph exhaled slowly, unspeakably grateful that she was still alive. And seething mad at the man who'd done this.

"The pain…it's not so bad now," she finally said. "It's that medicine." Her weak voice was almost childlike, and with the way he felt her relax, he figured the laudanum and whiskey was finally working. "What a good doctor. I like Ben."

"I like Ben, too," he agreed, his throat tight. "He's doing what he can to make you comfortable, darlin'." Closing his eyes, he hoped, prayed that she'd live through this. "What is it you hope for? Just ask me. Please."

She pulled in a shallow breath. "Mmm…it's nice having you here, Joseph. So handsome. So beautiful. I was smitten with you…from the moment I saw you." Her voice was wistful, dreamy. Her words slow on the tongue.

They stirred Joseph to the depths of his soul. She was smitten with him? Surely the whiskey and laudanum were having an effect on her.

"I dreamed of marrying you…." Her words trailed off like some long-forgotten love letter floating on the breeze.

Joseph's heart clenched tight inside his chest at the sentiment. His pulse thrummed loud in his ears. He lowered his forehead to her hand. Brushed it lightly over her fingers.

His throat constricted at the thought that Katie might not make it through the night. She had so much life yet to live, so much to give. She'd selflessly lavished her knowledge and patience on him these past few weeks— and he hadn't even begun to thank her. Until tonight when they'd danced, he'd fought off the growing feelings for her, but now he was certain he'd crossed over from deep fondness to love. So if marriage to him was her wish— very possibly her last wish—he'd do anything in his power to grant her that.

"Zach," he called over his shoulder.

Joseph pressed a gentle kiss into her palm, praying that she could hold on to his deep love. He leaned over and whispered next to her ear. "Katie, will you be my bride?" He swallowed hard. "Will you marry me?"

She gave a small gasp. "That's so sweet, Joseph." Her words were thick on the tongue. "Just what I wanted."

"What do you need?" Zach spoke low next to him.

"Go get Reverend Nichols." He smoothed a hand over hers. "If Katie wants a wedding, she's going to have one."

Chapter Sixteen

"I do," Katie whispered, blinking against the tears burning her eyes. She gazed up at Joseph, trying to focus on him, but she had a hard time fixing on anything for longer than a moment. "I do," she repeated.

This certainly wasn't what she'd dreamed of for her wedding day—lying in a doctor's office, her vision and mind fogged by remedies to help ease her pain, and a gunshot that had stopped her cold.

Katie didn't want to knock at death's door, even though she felt herself moving closer and closer toward that timeless passage. Even though she had an assurance that God was with her every step of the way, she wanted to live, but with each second that passed, she felt life slowly draining from her body.

It was peaceful, really. And Joseph was here. Her sweet Joseph. He'd been so kind to give her this last wish.

He was such a contrast to Frank Fowler. The thought of the evil man sent an icy chill through her and made her throat constrict with suffocating force. She couldn't think of him—she wouldn't think of him. This was her wedding day.

Joseph gently squeezed her hand, staring down at her with those beautiful, deep amber-colored eyes.

Willing her focus there, she tried to gather strength from him. She wanted to curl completely into the warm security of his embrace, lose herself in his tender strength. But weakness had swallowed her body and she couldn't lift her arm on her own.

Instead she eased her tongue across her dry lips, trying to remain fixed on Joseph. On staying alive.

"Reverend Nichols, please make this quick," came Ben's admonition from down by her feet. "I need to do surgery as soon as possible."

"Of course, of course," the reverend agreed. "So then, Joseph Drake, do you take Katherine Ellickson to be your lawfully wedded wife? To have and to hold—"

"I do. I do to all of those things." Joseph's voice was laced with urgency as he set a trembling hand to her forehead.

"Oh my, let's see now…where were we? For richer, poorer, sickness, health, 'til death—"

"I said, I do," Joseph spoke again, more forcefully.

"Oh my, my, my." Reverend Nichols leafed through his Bible. "Well, then, I—I pronounce you man and wife."

Joseph leaned over her and pressed his mouth, feather-light, on hers. He lingered there for several moments before he drew back slightly. "Hello, there, Mrs. Drake," he whispered.

His sweet words and warm breath whiffed softly over her face, sending a slow, invigorating tremor through her. She was heady with the aftermath of his kiss and the medicine that was fast taking over her ability to stay awake.

"All right, folks. The wedding's over." Ben sounded

unusually short-tempered. "I need to see to her now. You're going to have to leave."

Katie blinked several times, trying to focus on each person as they briefly stopped at her side. Her Aunt Marta's pinched features and Uncle Sven's red-rimmed eyes made her heart hurt.

"Love you," Katie murmured, struggling to form the two words as they each bent to place a kiss on her brow.

Sleepy. She was so sleepy. Her eyelids drooped. Weighed down by a force she could no longer deny, she shut her eyes, listening as Ben ushered the small gathering from the room.

"I'm not going anywhere, Katie," Joseph spoke close to her ear, his low, mellow voice lulling her further.

She tried to lift her hand to touch him, but her arm…it was so heavy.

"I don't usually allow others in here with me when I perform surgery, Joseph," came Ben's voice. "You know that."

"Yes, I know. But you're going to have to bend the rules this time, because I'm not leaving her side."

"Joseph, you should at least go in the back room and lay down for a while." Ben's voice sounded rough and weary from the grueling night. "Get some sleep if you can."

"No, thanks." He rolled his head from one side to another. Sitting up a little straighter in the wood chair, he smoothed his hand over Katie's. "I'll stay right here beside Katie."

Ben exhaled. "It's six-thirty in the morning and you've been here since midnight. I'm watching her closely. I promise I'll call for you if it looks like she—"

"I said I'm not going anywhere." He pulled his swollen, stiff hands over his face, the scruff of new growth meeting his touch. He tried to ignore the way his knuckles throbbed, painfully aware of how heavily he relied on touch now.

For a brief moment he thought about the shop and the unfinished order that was screaming for time and attention. But it'd have to wait. He wasn't about to leave Katie's side now.

"If you say so." Ben came around the bed to stand next to him. "At least let me take a look at your hands now that we have a quiet moment. They're a mess, Joseph."

He shook his head. "I'll be fine."

"Maybe. But it won't do you or Katie a bit of good if you're fighting an infection." He lightly grasped Joseph's right hand and turned it over, palm side then knuckle side up.

"Listen, I don't want you wasting time on me when Katie needs you. This can wait," he said, drawing his hand back.

"It won't take me but a few minutes to get those cuts cleaned, medicated and bandaged." Ben crossed over to the cupboard in the corner of the room and quietly rustled around, lifting metal lids that clanked softly against glass jars. "Someday, maybe, I'll hire an assistant to help out here—goodness knows I needed one last night. You could've done with a few stitches when you first came in, but it's too late now. Your hands should heal fine, it just might take a little longer and it won't look as pretty."

"That's fine by me. I won't be able to see them, anyway."

A deep sense of gratitude welled inside Joseph as his brother began smooth and efficient ministrations. This, after he'd performed a three-hour, tedious operation to remove the bullet and patch up Katie as best he could. Then a quiet vigil spent by her bedside, taking her pulse regularly and monitoring every little nuance.

"I'm glad Katie's in your care." Joseph swallowed hard.

"I hope I can help her," Ben said, his hands stilled against Joseph's. "I couldn't seem to help Ellie or the baby. That does something to a man who's supposed to bring healing."

"You're a good doctor, Ben," Joseph responded, knowing that often his brother carried a heavy weight of responsibility when a patient died. "Sometimes, it's just the way of things—and you're fighting against God as much as you are death."

"Yeah, well, I promise I'll do everything I can for Katie."

"Do you think she's going to pull through?" Joseph trained an ear and listened once again to the shallow, thin breathing coming from Katie—his wife.

His wife. The thought tumbled through his mind like a tender acorn looking for fertile soil to settle in and grow. He was a married man now. In spite of the vow he'd made after finding out he was blind, he'd jumped headlong into matrimony. And whether he was blessed to be Katie's husband for a few hours or days, he was going to do the best he could to love her.

"I wish I had an answer for you, but it's too early to tell." Ben began wrapping bandages around Joseph's knuckles. "Having almost lost her twice in the last two hours isn't a good sign. But both times she came around—which shows that she's still fighting for her life."

"Katie's strong," Joseph whispered, silently pleading with God to let her live.

He closed his eyes as different moments from the past

hours swirled through his mind like a cluster of dust devils in the summer. He didn't know if he'd ever forget her panicked scream that had stopped him cold or the heart-wrenching sound of her whimper when she was downed by the bullet. And he knew for certain he'd never forget the way she'd lovingly touched his cheek or the way she'd so innocently expressed her secret desire to be his bride. Each memory made him yearn to hold her tight and never let her go.

"It's a noble thing you did, marrying her." Ben spoke low, his voice sounding thick with emotion.

There was nothing heroic in what he'd done. He'd done what was right, and given Katie his life in hopes that she'd have joy for however long she might live—minutes, hours, maybe longer. She'd selflessly given hers these last weeks to offer him comfort and confidence for the rest of his life.

Joseph swallowed hard. "Nothing noble about it. I'm sure you'd do the same."

On a sigh, Ben wrapped the last of Joseph's battered knuckles. "Well, you didn't have to do that for her as a kind of last wish. But you did and it meant the world to her."

Joseph blinked back the tears burning his eyes. He raised a bandaged hand and sought out hers. "She deserves a lot more than that."

Ben's hand came to rest on Joseph's shoulder. "I may have been eager to move the ceremony along so I could tend to her gunshot, but honestly, I didn't want it to end. I believe I witnessed a beautiful act of love here last night."

Joseph wrapped his warm hand around hers, praying. Praying that it'd be enough to pull Katie through.

* * *

"Cain't say as we have any leads yet." Sheriff Goodwin's boots clomped loudly over the floor toward Joseph.

"How can that be?" Joseph furrowed his brow, unable to mask his aggravation.

"Wish I could tell ya."

Steadying his temper, Joseph slid his hand to Katie's shoulder. Deep concern for her weighed down every heartbeat and thought. She'd not regained consciousness, but seemed to be growing restless. Given her weakened condition, if infection had come calling, her slim chance for survival could diminish to nothing. Even though he'd been married to her for barely a day, he couldn't imagine life without her.

"What are your plans to catch him?" he finally asked.

"We been workin' on this since one o'clock this mornin'." The sheriff puffed a mouthful of stale coffee breath in Joseph's direction. "Got half'a Boulder scouring the countryside."

"And you don't have a single lead?"

"Well, this mornin', 'round nine, we thought we had ourselves a trail headin' west'a here, but the thing went cold on us." Goodwin hacked, sending an abrasive sound echoing through the room.

Clenching his jaw in irritation, Joseph moved down to the foot of her bed, hoping the sheriff would follow suit.

"Most'a the boys don' know what he looks like, but I told 'em he shouldn't be hard to spot with the way you laid into 'im. Not many men walkin' 'ound with their faces re-arranged. We're lookin' everywhere. He cain't git too far head'a us. I'd say by noon tomorrow we'll have 'im."

"I hope you're right."

He curled his fists tight around the footboard, ignoring the pain in his knuckles as he wrestled with the sense of helplessness assaulting him. If he could see, he'd ride out with the rest of the party. Push day and night. Because each minute that man remained out there untouched by the law, the more Joseph's apprehension grew regarding Katie's safety.

"I think that it'd be a good idea to have someone guarding this building round the clock—until you apprehend him."

"That ain't necessary," the sheriff said.

"It sure is necessary!" Joseph retorted in a harsh whisper. "The man could come back to finish the job."

"Hey, there, now. Simmer down." Sheriff Goodwin braced his hand against Joseph's chest. "All I was sayin' is…Aaron's out there doin' the job. That boy's been standin' guard since the search party formed. Ain't no one gonna git by him."

Joseph whipped his head around at Ben's familiar footsteps entering the room. "Aaron's out there?"

"I just found out myself." When Ben moved to Katie's bedside, Joseph felt a measure of relief that his brother was back tending to her once again. "We've been so busy watching Katie all night long that I hadn't stepped outside until just a few minutes ago."

Joseph raked his fingers through his hair, his knuckles bound with bandages. "I need to talk with him."

"Take your time," Ben responded.

"I won't be long." He felt as though he had to sever life and limb to leave the room. Stopping next to Ben, he said, "Her skin seems hot to the touch and she's been restless."

Ben groaned. "I'll check her over."

Emotion constricted Joseph's throat as he slid his hand

over the bed to Katie's head. He smoothed wisps of silky hair from her hot, damp forehead and placed a kiss there. "Don't give up, darlin'," he whispered. "You can make it."

Weariness creaked through his bones as he walked out of the room, feeling his way along the hallway toward the front door. He opened it and stepped out onto the porch, pulling in a slow breath of fresh air.

"How's Katie?" came Aaron's voice in front of him.

Joseph shook his head and took two more steps until he was standing beside his brother. "I don't know what to tell you. It's not good. She's not good."

Aaron cleared his throat. "Sorry I haven't been inside to see her, or you. I've thought about you both plenty and prayed a lot, but I just don't think I can see her like this yet." He coughed. "With Ellie and the baby passin' away, I just—"

"You don't have to explain." Joseph placed a hand on his brother's shoulder and felt a slight shudder. "I understand."

When a wagon rolled at a leisurely pace past the office, he could hear the faint sound of a conversation. People were probably well aware of what had transpired last night—the shooting, the operation, the wedding. Information like that just didn't stay concealed long in a town like Boulder.

"It's all too fresh in my mind, you know?" Aaron said. "But when I heard about Katie, I wanted to help."

"It means a lot that you're here. I know she'll be safe."

"I hope she pulls through, Joseph. I'm prayin' for her—for you. A person doesn't have to look long to see that you two are meant for each other. Ellie said so from the get-go."

Joseph gave a reminiscent smile. "She told me."

"And don't worry about the order in the shop. When I'm not here keepin' watch, I'll be workin' at it. Sven and some of the other men are helpin' out, too."

"I'll be back when I can, but right now—"

"Right now you need to be with Katie...your wife."

"My wife," he repeated. "That has a nice ring to it."

The door opened suddenly behind him. "Joseph, she's taking a turn for the worse. I don't think she has much time left."

Joseph held a cool, damp cloth to Katie's forehead, hoping for some kind of improvement, but nothing seemed to work. It had to be nearly midnight by now, and Ben had just left the room to see Sven and Marta out. The four of them had maintained a constant vigil at Katie's bedside for hours, praying for the violent fever to release its burning grip. Sam had stopped by, too, and joined in prayer with them for Katie.

Her skin blazed hot beneath Joseph's fingertips as she lay eerily still. The restlessness she'd shown earlier had passed.

"God, please don't let her die." He stared into the darkness, blinking against the moisture pooling in his eyes.

There'd been moments when God's abiding peace and comforting presence had rested like a warm glow in the room, and Joseph had been sure God had come to take her home. He didn't pretend to know God's plan for Katie, but if he had any say in the matter, she'd remain earthbound. Live to journey through a long life with him. Be his wife and lover, bear their children.

Apart from pausing for a brief moment to eat the plate of food Marta had threatened to shovel down his throat, he hadn't left Katie's side. Having been awake for almost two days straight, he was beyond tired. His head pounded and his hands throbbed with a dull ache, but he barely paid these things an ounce of attention.

Lifting the cloth from Katie's brow, he dipped it in a basin of cool water, squeezed it out, then set it on her brow once again. "It's all right. I'm here," he soothed.

He tenderly wiped the cool moisture over her brow, down both cheeks and to her mouth. Alarm shot through him at how quickly the heat radiating from her body permeated the cloth.

He drew a trembling thumb over her full lips, cringing at how they were already dry and cracked from fever. Dabbing the cloth to her mouth, he moistened her lips, trying everything Ben had shown him to do to keep her as comfortable as possible. After dipping the cloth in the basin yet again, he placed it on her brow.

Bone-weary, he sank to the chair, gathering her hand in his. "Please…please don't take her, God."

His heart twisted with the deep yearning to see her live.

Twisted even tighter at the thought of seeing her suffer.

Tears welled up in his eyes. Spilled over onto his cheeks as he realized that he had to be willing to let her go, though he'd really only held her as his for a day.

She was his. His teacher. His friend. His beloved bride. He loved Katie. Loved her with his life, his breath, his heart.

Leaning over the bed, he rested his arms against the feather mattress, and his head against the back of her hand. Joseph breathed deep, trying to catch her light, lily scent. But all he could smell was the metallic odor of blood, mixed with the perspiration beading her body.

He prayed for some movement from her, but all he felt

was the saltiness of the tears sliding down his cheeks. He brushed his mouth gently against the back of her hand, feeling the searing heat from her skin against his tear-dampened lips.

There were so many things he wished he'd said and now it might be too late. But if there was even a small part of her that could hear him, he had to tell her what was in his heart. If she died never knowing how much he really cared and how sorry he was, he wasn't sure he'd be able to live with himself.

Joseph drew in a steadying breath. "Katie, if you can hear me, darlin', I need you to listen carefully."

Burrowing his face into his shoulder, Joseph wiped his tears against the once-sturdy cotton fabric that now hung limp and wrinkled. Then he pressed his lips against her fingers, kissing each one, gently, slowly.

"If there was ever a time I wished I could go back and relive, it would be the last few weeks."

He held her hand, wishing for even the slightest response from her. But her hand hung limp in his.

"I've been a fool. A prideful fool who couldn't see the forest for the trees. I've been working so hard, tackling every task you set in front of me and diving into things back at the shop. I've been trying to make my life have meaning again." A steady trail of tears slid down his face as he lowered her hand to the mattress and laid his head next to her.

"When I found out that my vision wasn't going to get any better, I shut you out. I pushed away the one person who'd brought my life more meaning than anything else could've."

He grasped her fingers and drew them beneath his cheek, wanting to breathe her in for as long as he could.

"I don't have a good explanation for the way I've behaved." His throat ached with a pain he'd never known. Closing his eyes, he wished he could hear her voice, see her face. "You've been so strong. You've honored my wishes when they were nothing but pride. I'm so sorry I pushed you away when all I really wanted was to pull you close and never let you go."

Joseph pressed a kiss into her palm. "I love you, Katie. I thank God that He brought you into my life. And if the only way I could've come to know you was through my blindness—" his voice broke as the weighty, sobering realization hit him full force "—then it was worth it. I'd willingly go through it all again if it meant coming to know you and love you like I have."

A wave of profound emotion crumpled his face. He bit back a sob. "You see…that's why you have to get better."

Chapter Seventeen

Joseph peered off into the distance, the growing fog hampering his view. He caught sight of a woman, her golden hair tumbling down her shoulders in soft waves, the blue of her eyes piercing through the mist and gathering darkness.

Katie?

She beckoned him from the edge of the woods. Calling to him. Begging for him to come.

He started toward her, knowing that he had to help her.

But something from behind grabbed at him. Demanding his attention. Turning momentarily away from her, he saw an endless black hole. Its expanse stretched as far as the eye could see. It pulled at him. Daring him to focus on it, dragging him into a place he knew was so bleak that he clawed at the ground to remain in the light.

Hearing her faint cries, he strained to free himself from its engulfing grip, but kept slipping farther...farther away into utter darkness.

Until finally he forced his attention ahead of him, toward where Katie had stood. Wrenching away from the murky curse that lay behind him. He bolted toward the woman whose cries had gone silent, a memory carried on the night breeze.

Cut through the fast-growing shadows to the timber-line, scanning the area, searching for her. Darting forward into the darkness, his heart clenched tight with the horrific thought that he might've lost her.

He called to Katie. Then again, more frantic, once, twice.

Katie blinked once, twice.

Her name…someone had called her name.

She eased her eyes open to see light, brilliant and warm, shining around her in golden streams of glory. She fluttered her lids against the brightness, wondering if she'd died and gone to heaven. Comforting peace enveloped her in downy softness. A bird's lilting melody drifted to her ears. Opening her eyes again, she tried to get her bearings about her.

Where she was? Why did she feel so completely exhausted?

And what in the world was tickling her hand?

Gathering her strength, she lifted her head slightly and angled her gaze downward.

Joseph.

Katie's heart squeezed. Her beloved Joseph, asleep and as handsome as ever, had laid his head near her hand, the loose waves of his hair spilling over, dangling feather-light against her skin. A smile worked itself from deep down and spread across her face, warming her with more contentment than she'd ever felt. This wasn't heaven, but it was close.

Laying her head against the pillow, patchy memories floated through her mind of the past hours—days maybe?

The attack and the terrible dread it provoked in her. The gunshot…

Her pulse pounded inside her head as a huge wave of fear threatened to overtake her. She slowed her rapid breaths and resisted the taunting evil, determined to commit her thoughts to hopeful things.

Like her wedding…

Her throat swelled thick with emotion, her stomach quivered with excitement. Staring up through tears at the ceiling, she tried to make sense of it all. She recalled saying, "I do." She just didn't imagine she'd be facing her fanciful dream-come-true today. Instead, she thought she'd be strolling with her Creator through an endless field of radiant flowers or maybe basking in the consuming resonance of an angelic choir. As she'd spoken her vows, Katie was certain she'd been set on an eternal quest to know God's unfathomable riches and love. She would've gladly gone, too.

But something had called her back. Someone.

Joseph. Her beautiful Joseph.

His words—his passionate declaration of love and heart-wrenching plea for her to live—had called to her. They'd broken through her pain, her fever and fear, blanketing her in a love she never imagined feeling on this side of heaven.

When he'd poured out his heart to her, she'd tried to tear away from the fever's fiery grip enough to respond. Squeeze his hand…anything. But it was all she could do to focus on living through each minute, drawing another breath into her weakening body. And although, at times, she felt alone in her pain, she knew she wasn't. God had been there comforting her and carrying her through the night.

And Joseph was there, too. Wiping her brow, praying for her, trying to soothe her pain.

Joseph.

Remembering how she'd shared her secret thoughts with him, she felt a heated blush warm her cheeks. What had gotten into her? Facing death must've stripped away any amount of comportment and good judgment she embraced. Or maybe it just put things into the right perspective. Maybe God wanted to show her a glimpse of His goodness and love right here on earth.

Katie raised her hand from the mattress and worked her fingertips into Joseph's hair, loving the way the thick waves wrapped around her fingers. She slid her tongue over her dry, cracked lips.

"Joseph," she whispered in a raspy, weak voice. Swallowing, she tried again. "Joseph…"

Joseph slowly blinked his eyes open to the dull gray that met his gaze every morning. The nightmare he'd had last night came pouring back through his thoughts. The call for help. The woman standing at the edge of the timberline. The evil darkness. He'd dreamed the same thing several times since his accident. Had always dismissed it as just another reminder of his blindness and the sense of helplessness that plagued him.

Only this time, he saw it differently. The dream wasn't as much about his blindness but about Katie. And instead of being dragged by the darkness, he'd broken from its grip and gone toward the woman—toward Katie. Calling to her.

"Joseph," came the faintest of voices lifting him from the swirling of thoughts.

He raised his head from the mattress, felt the light brush of delicate fingers against his face.

His heart lurched to a sudden halt. "Katie?" His breath caught in his throat. Trembling, he reached to touch her. "Is it really you?"

"Hello, there, sleepyhead." She spoke weakly, the sweet sound of her voice making his eyes burn with ready tears.

When she settled her hand in his, disbelief swept through him. Was she really alive? Or was this just a dream?

Joseph couldn't control the quivering of his hand as he slid it up her slender arm to her face, where her eyelashes fluttered feather-light beneath his fingertips. Her perfectly shaped lips curved into a sweet, warm smile.

Closing his eyes, he released a pent-up sigh. "I thought I'd lost you," he choked out.

His horror, grief and sorrow faded fast. And fear—fear that he'd never have more than just a memory of Katie.

Joy flooded through him with exhilarating force. He'd never experienced anything so intense. So profound.

Leaning closer to Katie, he closed a hand around hers, relishing the way her skin no longer radiated with fiery heat. He swallowed hard against the emotion constricting his throat.

Katie nuzzled into his palm, and a warm, moist tear slid down her satiny cheek onto his hand. "I couldn't go. Not when you were calling me back."

He wiped her tear away. "Oh, God, thank You," he breathed, pressing a lingering kiss to her brow. "Thank You, God."

Trailing his fingertips lightly over each of her beautiful features, he felt the soft kiss she brushed against his hand and knew he could never get enough of her.

"Oh, Katie, I'm so glad you're back. I don't think I'll ever be able to let you out of my sight again." He gave a slow shake of his head and grinned. "What I mean is…I'm not sure I'll ever want to be away from you."

He settled the pads of his thumbs at her mouth, grinning at the way she melted to his touch.

She gave a contented sigh, the corners of her mouth tipping to a smile. "You won't get any argument from me."

"Good." He kissed each of her fingertips.

"You're hurt. What happened to your hands?"

"It's nothing. Just a few bruises."

"Are you all right?" she asked, concern cloaking her voice.

"I'm fine. The question is, are you in pain?"

When she shifted slightly, he felt her stiffen and grew immediately concerned. "Don't try to move. Just lay still and let me help."

"I guess I'm a little worse off than I thought." She pulled a breath through clenched teeth. "And tired. So tired."

"I'm sure you are." While he adjusted the pillow behind her and pulled the quilt up to her chin, a lingering fear prickled the hair on his neck. The horror of her scream and pitiful sound of her muffled moans filtered through his thoughts. Lowering himself to the chair, he pulled his hands down his face, wishing he had some kind of assurance about the future.

The familiar taunting voices ricocheted through his mind, vomiting the same vile curses he'd entertained for too long.

But he had been here from the beginning, providing comfort and prayer and love. He'd protected. And he'd circumvented danger in spite of his blindness. He hadn't given his abilities more than a moment of thought when he'd followed the cries. Had used his honed sense of hearing to his advantage, while working the cover of darkness to the assailant's disadvantage.

He held her hand, brushing his lips against her fingers. "I'm so sorry about what happened to you. I came as fast as I could, darlin'."

"And you got there just in the knick of time." She squeezed his hand.

"When I was close enough to hear the things he was saying to you—the things he wanted to do to you—I got so enraged I almost lost my advantage, Katie. I could've gotten you killed."

"Don't think about that," she pleaded. "You saved me, Joseph. You saved me."

He lowered his head, pulling in her scent and the sound of her strong, even breaths. "I don't know who he is or why he attacked you…but I'm so glad he didn't take your innocence."

Katie blinked back the tears crowding her eyes as Joseph left in search of Ben. His measured, quiet steps, and the way he held his shoulders back and head high, belied the fatigue that must weigh on him.

Alone now, she gazed up at the embossed-tin ceiling, trying to ignore the sick rush of nausea that coursed through her. Not from her injury, or medicine, or the fever.

But from the words that her beloved husband had spoken….

I'm so glad he didn't take your innocence.

She pulled in a shuddering breath, trying not to crumple beneath the overwhelming misery that stalked her like some rabid dog, threatening to poison her happiness.

Katie swiped at a single tear that trickled down her face, feeling afresh the deep cutting edge of those words. The pain they evoked, far worse than the gunshot or raging fever. It had taken everything she possessed to shut down the instant reaction she'd had—the small gasp and groan. She'd been quick to blame it on a sudden stabbing pain which thankfully propelled Joseph out of the room to find Ben. Giving her a few blessed moments to gather herself before her emotions wholeheartedly betrayed her.

Had Joseph been able to see, he would've known that something was amiss. She could try to hide the truth from him awhile longer. Except for the small fact that they were now married. Husband and wife. Destined to consecrate the union.

When Joseph discovered that she was used—irrevocably dirty—would he even want her? He'd said himself that he was glad her innocence hadn't been taken. And Frank had promised that no man would ever want her. She and Joseph had said their vows, but maybe, given the fact that he'd committed to the marriage thinking he was giving her a last, dying wish, it wouldn't really count. After all, she did remember the reverend being rushed through the ceremony.

The rapid clap of footsteps approaching from down the hall set her heart racing. She faced the warm sunlight pouring through the lace-curtained window and closed her eyes, forcing herself to relax as she tried to feign sleep. Even though her secret was still safe for now, she just couldn't face anyone. Not Ben. And definitely not Joseph.

"Katie," Ben spoke, his voice low as he neared her bed. "Katie, are you awake?"

When she felt his hand against her forehead, and Joseph's tantalizingly familiar grasp around her fingers, she stayed as still as a mouse in a field full of hungry cats. She focused on taking long, even breaths, on trying to keep her eyes from moving beneath her closed lids.

"Is she all right?" The level of worry laced through Joseph's whispered words seized her heart.

And the painful realization that he deserved more than he thought he was getting was almost her undoing. She braced herself against the emotions that blasted away at her shallow wall of strength.

"She must've worn herself out from talking," Ben murmured as he placed his thumb and two fingers around her wrist to take her pulse. "Her fever's nearly gone and she's fast asleep again. But her pulse…it's a little rapid. We'll have to continue to keep a close eye on her."

Guilt weighed so heavy over Katie. Each time Joseph offered a kindness or did some sweet deed, the knife twisted deeper into her heart.

"Are you comfortable, darlin'?" Joseph asked again, hunkering down next to where she sat in the rocking chair.

His words heaped burning coals on Katie's conscience and had her wishing she could just tell him the truth of her past.

Glancing around the bedroom—their shared bedroom—she felt her head swirl with sudden dizziness.

It had been four days since she'd been shot, and though she was feeling so much better physically, emotionally she felt as if she'd been riddled with bullets. It was the least of her concerns that Frank hadn't been found—dead or alive. But that her secret might somehow be exposed before she had the chance to tell her husband, worked overtime to unravel her peace and security. Her stomach lurched every time she thought of how she'd allowed Joseph to think he'd married a spotless bride.

She'd looked for opportunities to tell him, but something always snatched away her courage at the last moment.

Joseph had been very open about his feelings for her. How glad he was that she was his wife. How he looked forward to the day when they would have children.

Katie slammed her eyes shut, her head pounding with a sudden onslaught of painful thoughts. "I'm fine," she finally responded when concern creased Joseph's brow.

The lie was a bitter draught on her tongue as she glanced out the window to see the noonday sun shining with full force.

When she heard a tap at the door, she glanced over to see Uncle Sven poke his head into the room. His blue eyes shone through the crinkle of a wink, bolstering her heart a little. "I bring da trunks in und set dem by da door, Joseph. Mind dat you don't trip on dem, jah?"

She forced a smile at her uncle as Joseph moved toward the doorway.

"Thanks, Sven. I'll bring them in here when I get the chance." He turned back to her for a moment, the glint of joy in his deep amber eyes making her heart skip a beat. "I'll go get you a glass of water."

Katie slid her fingers along the wood buttons trailing down the bodice of her golden wheat-colored dress as she eased herself out of the chair.

"Jah, vell…I should go den, too, Katie-did. Da day is not half over und I haf plenty of vork to do yet." He moved toward her, sweeping off his wood-shaving dusted hat. Staring at her for a long moment, his gaze filled with worry.

The gentleness and fatherly wisdom shimmering in his eyes made her heart lurch.

"I love you like you are my own child," he said, smoothing wisps of hair back from her face. "Und I know dat you haf many tings to tink about over dis past days. But der is someting dat is heavy on your heart, jah?"

"Yes, I do have something on my mind," she admitted, threading her arms at her waist.

He gave her arm a gentle squeeze. "Can I help?"

Easing her hand over Uncle Sven's, she felt the weathered touch of age and hard work. "Just pray."

He peered at her for a moment longer when Joseph walked back in the room. "I vill pray," he whispered as he leaned over and planted a quick kiss on her cheek. "Marta...she brings by dinner tonight."

"Please tell her that we appreciate that." Joseph nodded and shook her uncle's hand. "By the way, thank you for everything you've done in the shop. Aaron says we're almost on schedule now with all the help we've had. I'm not sure how I'll ever be able to repay you."

Uncle Sven's mouth pulled tight, his chin quivering ever so slightly, forcing Katie to look away for fear that she'd cry. "Just take goot care of my Katie-did."

Joseph cleared his throat. "That I can do, sir."

After Uncle Sven left, Joseph stood in front of her and threaded his fingers around hers. "Welcome home, darlin'."

"Thank you, Joseph." Her heart pulled tight inside her chest as she stared down at where he held her hand. "Thank you for everything."

He leaned in closer to her, moving his fingers up to touch her face...her mouth. Then placed a kiss, warm and gentle, against her lips. Her cheeks. Her chin.

Katie closed her eyes, her breath caught. Stomach clenched. Her pulse thrummed at the base of her throat as he slid trembling fingertips almost reverently down her face.

His name was on her lips when he pressed another kiss to her mouth.

His touch…his tender, loving ways, left her feeling protected, treasured and loved.

When she finally opened her eyes, she found him inches away, staring at her with a steadfast gaze that belied his blindness. It was as if he was looking somewhere deep inside of her.

"Katie?" He dipped to place a chaste kiss on her lips.

She swallowed hard and drew a wad of her skirt in her grip. What would happen when he found out that she was coming to the marriage bed tainted by another man?

"Katie?" he said a second time.

"What?" she squeaked.

"I know that maybe you're worried about, well, us sleeping in the same bed now that we're married. I want you to know that until you're well, we won't do anything but sleep. All right?"

She shook her head, speechless.

"I would never do anything you weren't ready for. Do you understand?"

"I understand," she agreed, a yawn coming over her and insisting on her full attention.

He smoothed her freshly washed hair—a luxury she owed to her aunt—from her face. "You're tired, darlin'."

She was exhausted. "Well, maybe a little."

His mouth lifted in one of those sideways grins that sent a quiver all the way down to her toes. "Why don't you rest, then?"

Once she'd settled on the bed, she breathed deep, drawing comfort from Joseph's lingering scent on the pillow as he stared down at her.

Would he look at her like this after she told him? The fear of seeing his visible disappointment had Katie's insides knotted tight. Scraping together whatever courage she could find within herself, she knew that no matter what the outcome, she must tell him…tonight.

When he pulled a quilt over her from the foot of the bed, she felt herself drifting away, the agony of things left unsaid ushering her into fretful slumber.

Chapter Eighteen

"We ain't got no leads, but we're still lookin'."

It wasn't what Joseph had wanted to hear. He'd hoped that the sheriff had come over to tell him that they'd found the rogue dead. Unable to bring Katie any more harm.

The sheriff scuffed loudly across the front porch, making Joseph thankful the bedroom was located at the back of the house where Katie wouldn't be awakened.

"I know I got 'im. Sure as shootin'." He stomped a foot, sending Boone scurrying off the porch. "If'n he's laid up somewhere without some kind'a medical attention, he'll be festerin' so bad the wolves'll turn their noses up at 'im."

Joseph's jaw ticked. "Suppose he stopped at someone's home? Got help along the way?"

"He could'a, but we been checkin' with every livin' soul within thirty miles a this place."

Pulling his hands over his face, Joseph leaned back against the clapboard siding. "Ben said that someone found the Donaldsons' horse grazing near their home just last night."

"Yep." Sheriff Goodwin hacked, then spat, the wad plunking against the ground. "Don' look none worse for the wear neither. That means the scoundrel's either dead somewhere or he's on foot. Either way, we're bound to run across 'im, and with everyone on the alert 'round here, he'd be a fool to try and come back. Got wanted posters all over and sent a rider to the neighborin' towns to alert the law there."

"Sounds like you're doing everything you can."

"Miss Katie ain't been here long, but the whole town wanted to pitch in one way or t'other. She must be some special lady." The sheriff clucked his tongue, probably sporting that self-satisfied look he'd get.

"She's very special," Joseph agreed.

"If'n I was to guess…" When the sheriff sucked in a long breath, Joseph imagined Goodwin hooking his thumb inside his holster the way he always did when he was about to make some kind of proclamation. "I'd say the man's gone and died in some old shack somewhere. And Lady Luck just ain't been on our side enough to find his sorry be-hind yet."

Joseph tamped down his ire. "Let me know when you do."

"You'll be the first to know."

"I appreciate it."

"Well, time's a'wastin'," the sheriff announced, slapping his hat against his leg. "I got myself a town meetin' this evenin', but I'll be over to guard the place late tonight, if'n that's all right by you?"

Without sight, Joseph might not do the best job standing guard, but he could be prepared. He'd loaded his guns and made sure the locks on the two doors were secure. He'd even added a lock from inside the root cellar, in case

Katie needed to hide. And he could care for his wife, tend to her needs, love her the best way he knew how.

Joseph shoved his hands in his pockets. "That'll be good."

After the sheriff rode off toward the heart of town, Joseph strode back inside, Boone at his heals. "You and me, Boone, we're pretty lucky, aren't we?" he asked, bending to stroke the dog's long thick back as he locked the door behind him.

The aroma from the food Marta had brought over not long ago drifted through the kitchen to his senses, and his stomach growled with hunger.

"You liked Katie from the beginning, didn't you, buddy? You warmed right up to her, and she took a liking to you, too," he said, easily moving to the front room where he opened the mantel clock and felt the position of the hands to find that it was past six o'clock.

He walked back to the kitchen with Boone meandering along beside him, his furry feet buffing the floor and his toenails ticking quietly. Kneeling, he wrapped his arms around Boone's furry neck. "Just between you and me, I'd say I'm the luckiest man alive to have married such a beautiful lady. And you're lucky she likes dogs— not that you're like other dogs—but she obviously doesn't mind sharing a house with you. In fact, I think she really likes having you around."

When Joseph stood up again, he turned his focus to the bedroom down the hall. "Now we've got to get her to feel the same about me, because ever since she came to after the fever, she doesn't seem to want me around."

After a painfully quiet dinner where conversation came hard and moments passed with a guardedness that blared brightly, Joseph walked Katie into the front room to sit on the sofa for a while. He wished that she'd allow him to help carry whatever it was that seemed to be burdening her.

Resting his elbows on his knees, he was unable to deny the way her voice had lacked the sparkle of life that was Katie.

She gave a shaky sigh, then inhaled as though she were about to say something. When she stopped short, Joseph could feel the heavy, tension-charged air. But what could his sweet, innocent Katie possibly have to tell him that would be so bad?

He set his hand on her arm, wishing that he could see her faint shadow, but the dim mist of day had dispelled and a black curtain had lowered once again.

Could it be that she was nervous about sharing a bed starting tonight? He'd tried to allay any fears she'd had earlier. If there was one thing he didn't want, it was a bride who came to his bed out of some kind of obligation.

He wanted her heart, first and foremost.

"It's a little chilly tonight," he commented, turning toward her on the sofa.

"A little."

He reached for the blanket he kept on the back of the sofa, then wrapped it around her shoulders, taking care not to bump the wound that was heavily bandaged beneath her dress.

Joseph eased a little closer to her. "Katie, I know that this is all sudden—the marriage and all, but I want you to know that I'm so glad you came into my life."

She sniffled again, something he'd heard her do a dozen times over the last half hour. "That's sweet. So sweet."

"I just wish I could've given you a real wedding. In a church. With flowers and a ring and...and that kind of stuff."

"It was perfect. Really."

"It worked under the circumstances, but I want to make it up to you somehow. Maybe we can have a reception of some kind. Do you think your family could travel out here for that?"

She paused. "Perhaps."

"We'll plan that if that's what you want, darlin'. Just as soon as you feel up to it."

"You're very good to me, Joseph."

"Not good enough."

She made a small groaning sound in the back of her throat and his attention was pulled up short. "Darlin', what's wrong?"

She pulled her hand away from his. Took a slow, measured breath. "Everything. Everything's wrong."

Joseph dragged a hand over his face as he wondered if she was in the throes of regret. Maybe she felt trapped by her whimsical, passing fancy that she'd been so free to share, thinking she was dying.

But what could they do about it now? They were married. Joseph wasn't about to give her up. He loved her—so much that it hurt. He'd spend the rest of his life showing her, too.

"Katie, if you're having second thoughts, I understand. But we can work through them."

"No. It's not that at all." Her voice was strained with emotion.

"I want you to feel at home here. I know that it'll take a while with everything you've been through and the adjustments I'm still making. But I'll do whatever I can to make this as easy as possible for you. This is your home now."

"And it's a beautiful home," she offered, her voice breaking. She sniffed. "I love it."

"When you're feeling up to it, I want you to make any changes you want." He gave a broad gesture around the room. "I've been a bachelor for too long and I'm sure you'll probably want to add some nice feminine touches."

Her muffled cries broke his heart. "I wouldn't change a thing, Joseph. Not one thing."

He found her hand and grasped it in his. "Well, what's wrong, darlin'?"

Silence filled the air, and so did the faintest sound of something falling behind the house followed by a low curse. He shot his focus toward the noise, every single nerve ending springing to the alert. A warning knell, sure and strong, rang through him with deafening clarity.

"Joseph, I—I have to t-tell you something," Katie ground out. "Something awful."

He instinctively knew that each word came with a high cost.

"You don't know what you got yourself into marrying me." Katie pulled in a fractured breath at the same moment he heard another rustle.

"Katie, I need you to do something for me," he interrupted, wishing for all the world that he could've taken the time to bring her comfort. But there was no time for that now.

He levered himself off the sofa and grabbed a loaded gun from above the door. Angled his head toward another sound as he helped her stand, pulling her toward the kitchen.

"What is it? What's wrong?" she asked, sniffling.

"I need you to take this gun down into the root cellar

and lock the door behind you," he said as he held out an oil lamp for her. "Can you do that?"

"Why?" she whispered, her voice quivering. "What is it?"

"Just promise me you won't open the door for anyone else but me. Do you understand?"

He felt her tremble beneath his touch as he held the trap door open for her. "Everything's going to be all right."

"But Joseph, I—"

He lowered his head and settled a kiss to her brow, breathing in Katie. He loved her beyond words and hoped he'd get to show her for years to come.

"Go now, darlin'."

When he lowered the door and heard her lock it, he strode through the house to the back entrance. Prayed that God would help him. Pleaded that Katie would be safe as he grabbed another gun he'd loaded.

God, where's the sheriff? He prayed silently, suddenly remembering that the sheriff wasn't going to be here to guard until late. *I need help here.*

There was always Boone. Except that Boone usually took his nightly stroll through town about now, picking up a furry friend or two along the way. The dogs had taken to using their large brown, expressive eyes to win a scrap of meat here or a slice of bread there.

Quietly unlatching the back door, he passed through and stepped with stealthy precision around his house.

Listened. Honed in on the small grunt coming from near the side of the porch. And the heavy breaths that sliced through clenched teeth. The dry grass crunched and scratched as if the person was limping.

Joseph crept forward. Caught the fading scent of a

cigar. The same aroma that had lingered in the area where Katie had been attacked.

His pulse pounded harder, ricocheting through his head, arms, legs.

Thoughts of Katie lying soaked in fevered sweat, fighting for her life, splashed into his mind and his blood instantly boiled hot with rage. His muscles bunched, pulling taught, ready for use.

Riveting his focus on the man's ragged breaths, uneven steps and the direction they were aimed, Joseph breathed a prayer of thanks that he still had the advantage. Apparently too engrossed in his sick quest or the pain that was hampering his movements, the man seemed unaware that Joseph was close at his heels.

Joseph was less than ten feet away now and could hear Katie's name hissed through clenched teeth. Could smell the rank scent of infection coming from the man. He tightened his grip on the gun and narrowed in on his target.

If the man had scared up a weapon somewhere, Joseph had to be ready. He listened for the sound of clanking steel. Heard nothing and prayed to God the man wasn't armed.

Raising the gun, he took another step forward. Another. Then another. Zeroed in on the sounds of the man's labored breathing. The raking of his foot across the ground. The putrid scent of raw, infected flesh.

Joseph aimed the gun and fired.

He heard a *thwap* followed by an animal-like yowl.

Joseph dived forward and grabbed the man.

A vicious string of curses filled the air as the attacker tried to wrench free from Joseph's grip.

He could feel the sharp bite of a knife pierce his thigh. Ignored the searing pain and squeezed harder.

"Drop the knife, now!" he ground out. With one quick movement, he hooked an arm underneath the man's right bicep and jerked it up behind the man's neck.

The villain drove the blade deeper into Joseph's thigh.

He clenched his teeth, trying to disregard the pain as he locked an unyielding grip on the attacker's neck.

When he heard the front door unlatch, his heart sank. "Katie, get back inside!" he yelled, jamming a fist deep into the man's gut. "Go back in there and lock the doors!"

"Joseph, no. No!" she cried, her feet sweeping over the porch and down the steps.

"Ah, just who I wanted to see," the man hissed on a cough.

Followed by a low, steady growl.

Boone!

Joseph could hear the dog advancing from the side, his growl deepening. When the man jerked back and let out another howl, Joseph tried to maintain his hold.

"Call your dog off!" the man spat, trying to wrench his arm free from the dog's strong jaws.

But Boone must've sunk his teeth deeper, because the man suddenly released the knife and roared in pain.

When Katie moved closer, Joseph's sense of alarm heightened. "Get inside and lock the doors!"

"No, I won't." She was close enough that he could hear her breath now. "I got the knife, Joseph. I got the knife."

"Good, honey, good." Joseph grunted as he hooked a leg in front of the man's shins. "Now, get back, Katie! Go back inside!"

Tripping the man's legs out from underneath him, Joseph maintained his hold as they both fell forward to the ground. He could feel warm sticky blood seeping from the attacker's side as he wrenched the man's other arm up behind his neck and pulled up harder and tighter, until the man cried out in pain.

Boone didn't miss a beat but regained his hold behind Joseph, this time sinking his teeth into the man's calf. The scream that followed boomed like the hordes of hell.

"Hold him, Boone!" Joseph encouraged through gritted teeth.

"What in the world?" came the sheriff's voice into the yard. "Joseph, is that you?"

"Over here, sheriff." Katie's voice quavered close by.

The sheriff's booted feet clumped over the ground hard and fast. "You got 'im, Joseph. You got 'im."

Before he released him over to the sheriff, he wrenched the man's arms up even tighter and dipped his head down to the villain's ear. "You will never—" he warned through a clenched jaw, grinding the attacker's face down into the dirt, "—come near my wife again."

Katie's attacker struggled to jerk his head back. "You must like your women soiled, blind man," he hissed into the dirt, his voice low and barely audible. "'Cause that's all she is."

Joseph wanted to jam his fist down the rogue's mouth and rip his tongue out for saying such a vile thing about Katie. He ground the attacker's face into the dirt and held him there for a long moment. He gave one last power-packed push and propelled himself to standing, thankful the filthy words weren't loud enough for Katie to hear.

When the sheriff approached from the side and Joseph backed away, he heard a small scuffle, a single gunshot and an evil curse as the man collapsed to the ground.

"Stupid move." Goodwin spoke as if he was inspecting a piece of meat. "This time we stopped 'im fer good."

A shudder of relief reverberated through Joseph while the man lay silent on the ground. And Boone sniffed around the body, as if ensuring that the job was done.

"Wish my bullet had'a done the job the first time," the sheriff apologized, grunting as though he was hoisting the body. "Your husband, he done the right thing, Miss Kate. This dirt-poor excuse for a man won't be hurtin' you no more."

"Thank you." Her whispered words tore at Joseph's heart.

He stepped toward Katie as Goodwin dragged the body away.

"I'll just get his sorry be-hind out'a the way for ya."

Joseph nodded, letting loose a pent-up sigh. "Thanks. By the way, could you maybe send Ben over with his bag?"

Although he wished he could just ignore the wound and escape into the security of his house with his wife, the warm, moist feel of blood dripping down his leg made him think twice.

"Sure 'nough."

Joseph moved toward Katie, Boone at his side. He held out his hand to find her. "Darlin', are you all right?"

She stepped into his arms and melted into his embrace. "I'm fine. But Joseph—your leg—you're bleeding."

"Nothing that a stitch or two won't fix." Joseph nestled his face into her hair and dragged in her light lily scent. "You had me so worried. He could've hurt you. You should've stayed inside."

"I knew you wouldn't let him hurt me. And I couldn't let him hurt you."

He cupped her face. "Thanks for your help, darlin'."

Clenching his jaw, he closed his eyes as her words cycled through his mind. Not long ago the idea that he'd needed help would've pricked his dignity, infecting him with stubborn pride. But tonight, for the first time, he saw that the measure of his strength and ability to protect didn't necessarily lie in his hands alone.

But in God's.

And in those around him who loved enough to sacrifice.

Feeling Boone's weight leaning heavily against his leg, Joseph knelt down next to the dog. Drove his fingers through Boone's long, thick fur. "Thank you, my friend."

Chapter Nineteen

"You're all patched up, Joseph. Good as new." Ben snapped his bag shut and walked into the kitchen. "And you, Katie, are looking very well considering the night you've had."

Walking beside his brother, Joseph felt the tight pull of the dozen or so stitches Ben had sewn in the privacy of the bedroom while he'd cleaned up and changed. "Thanks, Ben. I appreciate you coming out so late."

"What are brothers for?" He braced a hand on Joseph's shoulder. "But the next time I dismiss the idea of getting an assistant, remind me of this moment, would you? It has been a whirlwind day—a whirlwind week—and I'm tuckered out."

With a chuckle, Joseph nudged his brother. "Get out of here, then. Go home and get some rest."

"Can I send some of Marta's cooking along with you?" Katie asked, stepping up beside them.

Ben blew out a full breath of air. "Much as I love her food, I'm so tired I don't think I could eat. I just want a bed," he said, opening the front door. "And a pillow. And a blanket."

"Go." Joseph laughed and gave his brother a playful push out the door.

"I'll check in on you two tomorrow. But not too early."

Joseph hooked one arm over the top of the door. "Fine by me. Thanks."

"Good night, Ben," Katie called, dipping her head beneath Joseph's arm and nestling into his side.

After Joseph closed the door, he turned and wrapped his arm around Katie, ushering her to the front room where he'd built a fire. He sat next to her on the sofa, breathing deep, taking in the room's comforting atmosphere. The crackling of the fire and radiating warmth. The popping sounds as flames licked up the dry wood, and mellow, earthy scent as it burned in the hearth.

And the wonderful feel of his wife here beside him, safe.

"Joseph, I have to tell you something," Katie whispered.

He reached for her hand. "I'm sorry, darlin'. You'd started to say something earlier and I—"

"I know. You heard the sounds. I understand you were protecting me." Katie threaded her fingers through his. "But really, this time I have to just say it."

Joseph hooked his other arm around the back of the sofa, setting his focus completely on her. "I'm listening."

"I—I knew him, Joseph. I know who he is."

When he heard the faintest, muffled whimper come from his bride, his stomach knotted. Blood slammed through his veins. He remembered the vile words the man had spoken—that he must like his women soiled—and his heartbeat ground to a staggering halt.

Had her attacker really violated her like that?

She dragged in a long breath. "Remember after I woke from the fever and you said that you were—that you were glad that man didn't take my innocence?"

God, no…. No. It couldn't be.

He couldn't have….

"Well, he did. He took my innocence." She jerked her hand away from him. "He was a deacon in my church back home. I thought I could trust him. I had no idea. No idea," Katie muttered the words over and over as if she'd unlocked an ancient door, the foul secret finally spilling out into the light.

He wrestled to control the rage that instantly rose within him as he reached out and pulled her into his arms. She shuddered uncontrollably against him, and thoughts of his beautiful, sweet wife being used like that coursed through his mind, feeding the fierce anger boiling within him. How could someone do that to her?

"You're safe now," he whispered. He smoothed a hand down her hair, his throat gone raw with emotion. His eyes burning with unshed tears. "Shh…. It's all right."

Katie stiffened and pushed away from his embrace, sniffling. "No, it's not all right." Bravery and courage as he'd never seen girded her voice, making his eyes pool with tears.

She scooted away from him, the distance feeling like some wide chasm. "You thought you were marrying a spotless bride. But I'm not. I never will be." Katie sniffed again. "Nothing can ever, ever, *ever* give me back what I lost to him."

Joseph reached across the sofa, to find her hand. "Everything's going to be all right, Katie."

"Don't you understand?" she pleaded, her voice rising

in volume as she backed farther away from him. "He attacked me more than once. I fought him, but it didn't do me any good. I was desperate to tell someone, but he said he'd kill me or my family. I didn't know where to turn, what to do. And he was always there in church, staring—"

The sofa shook with her violent trembling, and his heart weighted with sorrow. To think that she'd carried this devastating secret alone sent stabbing pain straight through him.

And righteous anger coursing through his veins.

That her attacker lay dead was of little value or comfort.

"I shouldn't have let him do that to me," she whimpered, her voice so small, so innocent that he wanted to hold her and never let her go. "I could've somehow stopped it."

Joseph slowly edged next to her, then scooped her up and settled her onto his lap, being careful to avoid his freshly stitched wound. He wrapped trembling arms around her. Gently pulled her head to rest against his shoulder. "Katie, sweetie, it's not your fault. None of it is your fault."

"But it is," she whispered, as though it was her duty to convince him. She was all tense and quaking like a harmless rabbit cornered by a hungry wolf. "He said that it was—all my fault. He said that I was the one who brought it on myself." She drew her arms into a tight ball at her chest and wrestled in a shaky breath. "That I had flau-flaunted myself in front of him. But I don't see how. I—I didn't think I did that."

Joseph cupped her chin and raised her gaze to his. "He was wrong, Katie. He was a sick man and he was wrong."

"But, Joseph!" Katie grasped his hand at her chin and held tight. "He took away the one thing I could've given to you and you alone."

Closing his eyes, Joseph shook his head at the lies—the filthy, sick lies that man had planted into her sweet, innocent head. "No, he didn't."

Her grip grew tighter. "How can you say that?" she cried in a voice so full of agony that it broke his heart.

A tear slid down his cheek. "Because, darlin', he didn't take your heart."

Katie had never felt more invigorated or alive as she stood before Joseph in their bedroom.

After she'd poured out her heart to him two days ago, disclosing her well-guarded secret about the attacks, she was emotionally spent. She knew he'd be compassionate, but had fully expected to see some kind of underlying regret evident in his eyes, or his voice, or his touch. And wouldn't have blamed him for it.

She was sure she'd never forget the way she'd felt when he'd held her so tenderly, responding in the gentle, caring way he had. He'd shown compassion, support and love. Pure, unconditional love that gave her hope.

And for the first time in a year she took the smallest glimpse at freedom from the haunting darkness of her past.

Glancing at the welcoming glow of shadows that danced and flickered across the wall from the fire Joseph had banked in the small bedroom hearth, she knew she was home. Right where she belonged.

Her body quaked. No longer with the painful uncovering of her secret, but with the anticipation of Joseph's touch.

"You're beautiful, Katie," he breathed, his voice husky as he reached up and stroked her hair. "So beautiful."

Apprehension rose within her at what was sure to happen tonight. They'd spent the past two days and nights recuperating, but she knew that tonight… Could she let her guard down so completely as to find joy in something that for a year had meant sorrow? She wanted to, for Joseph, but he'd told her that if she wasn't ready, he'd wait. As long as she needed.

And although a part of her felt horribly self-conscious and utterly unworthy, another part of her yearned for the nearness with Joseph.

She peered up at him, captivated by the warmth and sensitivity she found in his gaze and the serenity she found in his expression. Compelled by the absolute gentleness with which he treated her, as though she was a priceless, treasured jewel.

She swallowed hard, fighting to ignore the residue of lies that had made a deep rut in her heart. The thick groove was there and she had no earthly idea how it could ever be removed.

The kiss he settled against her lips made her tremble all the way down to her toes. "I couldn't have asked for a more perfect bride."

Tears stung her eyes as his words washed over her like a gentle, cleansing rain. Her head swirled with intoxicating emotion and her breath caught.

"So lovely," he whispered, contentment tipping his lips.

Her inhibitions began to crumble.

"So sweet." Joseph pressed a kiss to her neck, his warm breath fanning over her in a wash of liquid heat.

He made slow work of the next kiss he placed on her lips.

"So very innocent." He deliberately measured out the words as if he was marking her with a new name, etching it on her heart. Her soul. Her mind.

He skimmed his hands whisper-soft over her shoulders, then moved his hands to her waist, and Katie shivered at his magnificently tender touch.

He pulled her close to his warmth and strength. Every caring touch of his hands bringing her another measure of healing.

Joseph's eyes were closed as he trailed his fingertips, feather-light, down her neck, shoulders and arms.

He cupped her face in his hands then and stared down at her, the depth in his gaze drawing her, beckoning her. "Katie, I love you," he ground out. "Do you hear me? I love you."

Her shame fell away then, shattering into a million pieces.

She stared through joyous tears up at Joseph, her heart soaring to heights she'd never known.

When he settled his arms gently around her and pulled her close, she felt completely encompassed by a love that gave her wings to fly. To explore the beautiful, wondrous, God-given design of intimacy.

"Joseph, I feel so safe when I'm in your arms," she whispered, wrapping her arms around his chest and splaying quivering fingers against his back.

Joseph wasn't sure if he'd ever be able to express to her how much those words meant. With them she restored a foundation that had crumbled eight weeks ago when he'd lost his vision.

When she rested her cheek at his heart, his throat tightened with instant emotion. He nuzzled his face into her hair, loving the way she felt in his arms.

Her heart belonged to him and him alone.

He gloried in the revelation, unable to keep the smile from washing over his face. He'd seen beauty around him all his life. The mountains. The streams. The innocence of a child.

But to be entrusted with a heart so giving, and pure, and beautiful brought more joy than he'd ever known.

"You are so beautiful, Joseph. So perfect for me. I love you." Katie's sweet voice was laced with a strong sense of relief—as though she'd finally found what she was looking for.

He dipped his head to settle his mouth on hers, his lips brushing hers with a promise. The way she melted to his touch made his heart squeeze and allowed him another glimpse of God's abiding love and power to restore.

* * * * *

Dear Reader,

I hope you enjoyed Joseph and Katie's story and were touched, in some way, by the message of redemption. The characters I write and the internal issues they struggle with are often a reflection of my own fears and inner workings. However, when I started writing this story several years ago, I never imagined I would be closely affected by the kind of trauma Katie faces.

By nature, I'm a "fixer"—I want to give those who are hurting an antidote to make them feel better. That works for the physical, but most of the time it just doesn't cut it for the emotional or spiritual. Quick fixes and just-get-over-it attitudes often circumvent the total healing God can do. There is no substitute for His presence, His word and His love.

It is my hope that, like Joseph and Katie, you find yourself wrapped securely in His love.

Thank you so much for taking the time to read *Rocky Mountain Match*. Please watch for the next book in the Drake Brothers series. I'd love to hear from you.

With love,

Pamela Nissen

QUESTIONS FOR DISCUSSION

1. Joseph is afraid of what his future holds, and responds out of his fear. When you have been afraid, how did you respond?

2. Why does Joseph so adamantly refuse help? Do you think that is a good or bad attitude?

3. If you were Katie and your new "student" was curt and unfriendly, like Joseph, how would you respond?

4. Julia is a thorn in Joseph's flesh. Do you have someone like that in your life, and if so, how do you deal with those situations?

5. Did Julia's reaction to Joseph's blindness seem cruel to you? How would you have responded if a friend suddenly was injured as Joseph was?

6. Joseph's brothers are also his closest friends. How do they show that they care?

7. When Joseph learns his blindness is permanent, how does that affect the way he lives his life? Have you ever put your life on hold for something, and if so, was it beneficial?

8. Katie left Iowa because of an incident that happened to her. Was she right to have left and made a fresh start in another town? What would you have done?

9. Katie's flashbacks to her attack cause Joseph great concern. Do you feel as if he responds appropriately or should he have pushed her to talk sooner? How would you handle this situation?

10. Katie's near-death situation causes Joseph to face his worst fears. Have you ever faced your fears and found freedom on the other side?

11. Fearing that Joseph will not want her once he finds out she is "used," Katie is tormented by her secret. Have you ever revealed something that was once hidden, and if so, how did that make you feel?

Love Inspired.
HISTORICAL

TITLES AVAILABLE NEXT MONTH

Available July 13, 2010

REQUEST YOUR FREE BOOKS!

2 FREE INSPIRATIONAL NOVELS
PLUS 2
FREE
MYSTERY GIFTS

Love Inspired
HISTORICAL
INSPIRATIONAL HISTORICAL ROMANCE

LIH-10R

HARLEQUIN®

A Romance

FOR EVERY MOOD™

Spotlight on
Heart & Home

Heartwarming romances
where love can happen
right when you least expect it.

See the next page to enjoy a sneak peek
from Silhouette Special Edition®,
a Heart and Home series.

*Introducing McFARLANE'S PERFECT BRIDE
by USA TODAY bestselling author Christine Rimmer,
from Silhouette Special Edition®.*

Entranced. Captivated. Enchanted.

Connor sat across the table from Tori Jones and couldn't help thinking that those words exactly described what effect the small-town schoolteacher had on him. He might as well stop trying to tell himself he wasn't interested. He was powerfully drawn to her.

Clearly, he should have dated more when he was younger.

There had been a couple of other women since Jennifer had walked out on him. But he had never been entranced. Or captivated. Or enchanted.

Until now.

He wanted her—*her,* Tori Jones, in particular. Not just someone suitably attractive and well-bred, as Jennifer had been. Not just someone sophisticated, sexually exciting and discreet, which pretty much described the two women he'd dated after his marriage crashed and burned.

It came to him that he…he *liked* this woman. And that was new to him. He liked her quick wit, her wisdom and her big heart. He liked the passion in her voice when she talked about things she believed in.

He liked *her.* And suddenly it mattered all out of proportion that she might like him, too.

Was he losing it? He couldn't help but wonder. Was he cracking under the strain—of the soured economy, the McFarlane House setbacks, his divorce, the scary changes in his son? Of the changes he'd decided he needed to make in his life and himself?

Strangely, right then, on his first date with Tori Jones, he didn't care if he just might be going over the edge. He was having a great time—having *fun,* of all things—and he didn't want it to end.

Is Connor finally able to admit his feelings to Tori,
and are they reciprocated?
Find out in McFARLANE'S PERFECT BRIDE
by USA TODAY bestselling author Christine Rimmer.
Available July 2010,
only from Silhouette Special Edition®.